SCIENCE FICTION GEMS

Volume 3

C. M. KORNBLUTH
and others

Edited by
GREGORY LUCE and LEANNE WRAY

I0532653

ARMCHAIR FICTION
PO Box 4369, Medford, Oregon 97504

PONDER THE FUTURE

You hold in your hand another terrific collection of science fiction gems from the past. You'll read great stories by some of the genre's very best writers, who will give you food for thought about amazing future possibilities.

"A Gift from Earth" and "The Isolationists" are vivid accounts of what Man's pandemic venture into Universal trade may indeed look like. And of course we can never underestimate the tenacity of a woman. "Finders Keepers," "Venus is a Man's World" and "She Who Laughs" will teach any man to keep a sharp eye! In "Zeritsky's Law" and "With These Hands" you may find that technology isn't always the kind of fantastic advancement that Mankind is looking for.

So go ahead, stray from the everyday linear path of the mundane and embark on a bold adventure into the future!

TABLE OF CONTENTS

DANGER DIMENSION 5
By Stanley Mullen

ZERITSKY'S LAW 36
By Ann Griffith

WITH THESE HANDS 43
By C. M. Kornbluth

THE TROUBLE WITH ANTS 64
By Clifford D. Simak

THE ISOLATIONISTS 87
By Robert Silverberg

VENUS IS A MAN'S WORLD 97
By William Tenn

A GIFT FROM EARTH 118
By Manly Banister

JUDAS RAM 134
By Sam Merwin, Jr.

FINDERS KEEPERS 153
By Milton Lesser

THE RAG AND BONE MEN 166
By Algis Budrys

ONE LEG IS ENOUGH 174
By Kris Neville

SHE WHO LAUGHS 184
By Peter Phillips

Danger Dimension

By STANLEY MULLEN

Through the black portal they went—the advance guard of Earth's last chaos—into a universe that did not exist, filled with the spawning shadow life of a dimension gone mad—which slithered ceaselessly, ever closer—to the world of men!

CHAPTER ONE
Haunted Cyclotron

THE emergency faculty meeting was already in progress. One hand on the doorknob, John Storm hesitated, dreading to go inside and face the battery of coldly alien and unfriendly eyes. Eyes that would be wary, suspicious, and full of that uneasy resentment which age and experience feels for youth. It was hard for Storm to realize that he was a full-fledged faculty member, and not an erring student called before the hoary tribunal for judgment.

There would be questions inside, and Storm had given his fill of unsatisfactory answers in the last three days. He could offer no easy solution to the mystery, and some questions would suggest complicity in—or at least a subtle foreknowledge of—that event which first set all tongues wagging, then clamped frosty censorship on all concerned. The campus had become a madhouse the past three days since Morlake had disappeared; and Storm was the last person known to have seen and talked with him.

Storm hesitated, shuddering. Before, he had evaded questions, but now there would be no further dodging. Questions would be asked and must be answered. Trustees and faculty were gathered in grim thirst for the kill; the pack was in full cry; they wanted blood and anybody's—especially Storm's—would do. He opened the door and plunged into the sea of eyes. Blurred murmur of voices swirled about him; he was aware of pallid faces dancing like masks dangled on strings, of turbulent movement as if soberly clad bodies

5

rose and fell in waves. The voices thrust shrill questions at him and eyes hemmed Storm in like a frieze of naked rapiers.

Not immediately conscious of what was said, Storm knew already what the general trend would be. One voice, snarling and fretful, emerged from general tumult and became a symbol of it.

"...Last person to talk with him. Surely you must know something."

It was Old Frudey, the dean, who could have posed for a bust of Schopenhauer. There was a foxlike something about him, with his thin features, shrewd eyes, the ruff of untidy gray fur that curled over a dirty collar, even the quick, darting, vulpine movement of his balding head upon its scrawny neck. Fox, he was, and a mangy, ill-tempered one. Nobody liked Old Frudey—no one could—and for the first time, Storm realized the tragedy of being a Frudey— the ultimate tragedy of being so nasty-minded, bitter, proud and envious—of being so personally repulsive and being unaware of it.

Storm found himself talking, wearily repeating things said before. "I've told you everything I know. Simon Morlake came to my classroom after the faculty meeting three days ago. We talked, but about nothing in particular. I haven't seen him since."

Frudey's voice darted in again, a series of short, sharp barks.

President Arnold hushed him with a gesture. Arnold cleared his throat pompously; with him, every speech was an oration.

"And, apparently, no one has seen him since. No one has come forward with any information. Are you certain you have nothing to add to what has been said, Storm? Surely—"

"Nothing. Nothing important. He has said the same things many times before. To the rest of you, as well as to me. His ideas and speculations were always the core of his conversation. It was not new, nothing in any way different from his usual wild jumping-about, his mental gymnastics, deriving fantastic conclusions from distorted facts. You heard it longer than I have. I'm new—"

Storm's angry flash burned itself out.

Arnold shrugged and continued. "I won't hide the facts. The situation is serious. This is our last chance for discussion. If it fails to disclose any new facts about this...mysterious disappearance, I will have no choice but to call in the police."

If threat was implied, it backfired. Storm glared at the University president, at the assemblage. "That should have been done at once," he said savagely.

President Arnold wavered, made aimless, unnecessary gestures. "Let's not be hasty about this. I'm sure we have the good of the college at heart..."

"And your fat jobs," Storm finished. "I know I'm going to get the axe when the term's finished. If you want my opinion, Morlake was tired of faculty meetings. He was tired of your small-town minds, small-town interference. None of you liked him. Nor me, either. He clung to me because I listened. If I thought he was crazy, I had better manners than to say so. If the police ask me, I'll tell them plenty."

FRUDEY snapped at the opening. "Then he was unhappy here? If so, he may simply have locked his door and left. He was very strange in his behavior lately. I think he disliked us and the college. It would be like him to lock his door and—"

"Yes," Storm sneered. "Lock it and bolt it on the inside. The window, too. He liked mystery, so he created one for you. I remember now something he said Friday. He talked of ghosts and Modern Art, something about Frank Lloyd Wright not providing any space for ghosts, and said that a modern ghost would look like a semi-geometric figure from a painting by Picasso."

Frudey nodded sagely, as if something in his thoughts gave exquisite pleasure. Next, he would be tapping his temple in the universal symbol indicating insanity.

Storm raced on angrily: "He said that if he were designing a castle suitable for old-fashioned haunting and wanted a chamber of horrors for it, he'd pick Frudey above Frankenstein's monster anytime. I said that he was giving the building a bad name with his ghost hunting—that's what he called parapsychology—and he laughed about it. He said if Frudey did not approve, Frudey could crawl back in the woodwork. But he agreed that parapsychology was childish, a bunch of kids heightening themselves by climbing a dark stairway to experiment with their own sensations. He said he was through with parapsychology, because he had outgrown it, had exhausted its possibilities. It was a blind alley."

President Arnold's head jerked through a series of motions suggestive of a doll's head, rocking to the swing of a concealed pendulum. "That's very interesting," he said gravely, "but it does not help much. There was nothing in your discussion to indicate that Morlake was planning to leave Northside?"

"Not a thing," Storm stated definitely. "Quite the contrary. I know he would not have considered leaving at this time. He was finishing a paper to be published at his own expense. There were five notebooks of figures, and a desktop covered with loose sheaves of notes, the last time I was in his room. He had Dr. Adrian's permission to use the cyclotron during Adrian's absence; so his experiments probably had more to do I with practical physics than with psychology. He was very excited about the latest experiments and tied them in with his own advanced speculations, leaving his usual wide gaps in logic. But he said true science was always intuition, later supported by observed facts. He was about to go into details on the theories in his new paper—which he said, would blast the reactionary deadheads off their collective chairs—when he noticed the time. He jumped up and left. But I know from things he said that he could never consider leaving until he had observed first-hand your reactions to his latest brainchild."

Stephen Blount, one of the trustees, broke in with comment.

"I was always dubious about Simon Morlake's being appointed to our chair of psychology. He seemed too excitable. Has anyone looked over those papers to see if they will throw any light on his...disappearance?"

"I was about to suggest that Dr. Storm—" began President Arnold. A voice shouted him down. Frudey's.

"Not Storm. He's a troublemaker, too."

The meeting slid out of focus. Blount's voice was but one element of confusion. It overwhelmed the others by sheer weight.

"It would be folly to delay any longer in calling the police. I agree with Dr. Storm—it should have been done before. There is no reason to suspect foul play, but something must be done. It will look worse for the school if any cover-up is attempted. The man is missing, may be dead. Police investigation is the only answer."

Storm faced the imposing bulk of President Arnold, ignoring the frantic attempts of Frudey to waylay him. "If you don't call the authorities, I will," he said deliberately.

Then he was outside, in the echoing hallway. Descending the stairs, he felt odd hollowness, remembering that he had done the same thing before, with Si Morlake at his side. It was like a trick of double memory. Time seemed to have telescoped, which was a thought that would have interested Morlake. It was incredible that only three days had elapsed since he had last spoken to Simon Morlake...

MORLAKE had stopped by, at Storm's request. It was on his way, anyhow, since the psychology rooms occupied the second floor, while the mathematics department occupied the ground floor, with chemical labs in the basement, along with heavy experimental equipment like the giant cyclotron—the school's pride and joy. Dr. Adrian, nominal head of the departments housed in the Physics building, was out of town, taking his dead wife's body east.

Absently, Storm had gotten a whiskey bottle and two glasses from his desk.

"Here's to school spirit," Morlake had grunted, raising the glass to peer through the amber liquor. "Don't know why I drink the stuff. Don't like it. Like Frudey, the first taste is not too bad, sharp, a little bitter. It goes down and your stomach heaves to meet it. Reminds me of a faculty meeting with Frudey in the saddle. You've something on your mind. What is it?"

Storm swallowed his whiskey, made a grimace of distaste to hide sudden embarrassment. "You're right. Something on my mind. Not school spirit, not even the alcoholic variety. The Physics Building is haunted. Especially the basement labs and the room with the cyclotron. You've been hanging around the cyclotron a lot, mulling over your weird theories. I wondered if you'd noticed anything."

"Haunted?" Morlake glanced around at the glittering, well-equipped classroom. His gesture took in all parts of a building as modern as the day after tomorrow. It was not the kind of structure to house a ghost. "You're joking, of course?"

"It's no joke," Storm went on seriously. He hesitated. "It's haunted, all right. If not by ghosts, by something else…"

Perhaps Storm had imagined the shadow crossing Morlake's face. The psychologist had tried a laugh, which did not come off. "It's the ghosts of dead ideas," he suggested cynically. "Northside should he full of them, but why here only? It won't do, Storm. It won't do at all. No self-respecting ghost would take up residence in a dump like this. It wouldn't be comfortable—all glass and chromium, raw stone and stainless steel, weird angles and flat roofs, furniture that looks like plumbing, functional simplicity. Ghosts know better. They demand sprawling old mansions, Gothic, Tudor, Jacobean, sliding panels and smoking fireplaces, no plumbing at all, horsehair sofas, dusty wall-tapestries that hands can reach out of to light a cigarette for you. No nonsense. They want comfort."

Storm was stubborn. "You should know more about such things than I do. Spooks are in your line, not mine. This is the real thing—"

Morlake laughed. "That does it," he countered. "Ghosts are in the mind. They don't exist anywhere else. As you say, it's in my department. Psychology. You can stop worrying. When you get a real ghost, it stops being a ghost. Take a pill. Are you really serious about this?"

"Dead serious. It's not just me. The students are talking—it's becoming a campus scandal. I ridiculed the rumor when I first heard of it. Suggested to a couple of them that they transfer to your classes in parapsychology and study psychic phenomena. I thought then that a session of your card tricks would cure them. But I hadn't seen it myself then. Carl Redfield is a camera-bug; he got permission to stay late one night and work. I was impressed by his zeal for study until I found out he was taking pictures and developing them in the chem-sinks downstairs. He'd got some dillies by using infrared light and sensitive film. I wouldn't like to say what he'd aimed the camera at. Not then. Last night was Thursday, so I stayed late myself sweating over exam papers. I was too tired to go home by the time I finished, so decided to bunk in the supply room. Turned off the lights downstairs and was groping blind to the cot there. *Wham! I saw something!*"

Morlake glanced crookedly at Storm. "Bears out my theory," he murmured. "Eyestrain, fatigue, afterimage—the three musketeers of ghostland. Add general chuckle-headedness, careless observation, emotional hysteria. You probably bumped your head on something in the dark and saw stars." He stopped, squinted at Storm's pale face, and grew suddenly concerned. "Well, let's have it. What did you imagine you saw?"

Storm's forehead wrinkled with concentration. "It can't be described. It was dark, remember. The thing was faintly luminous, as if it fluoresced at some barely visible wavelength, just inside or outside the range of human vision. There was outline, enclosing a dark something. Not solid, exactly. Curiously geometric, like an arrangement of interlocking puzzle boxes. You got the feeling that it was not an object you saw, but a kind of three-dimensional shadow, vaguely luminous. What could cast such a weird shadow?"

Morlake was sober now, pale. "Language is a feeble thing to describe the inhabitants of the mental borderlands. You say Redfield took a picture?"

"I confiscated it." Storm extended a 5" x 7" enlargement, and Morlake studied the glossy print with growing interest.

"It looks just like those optical illusion diagrams," he remarked in a strained voice. "The kind of thing which reverses as you stare at it; first off, it looks like a solid seen from the outside, then like a hollow, reverse-block of the same shape. Your ghost has got himself in a box, Storm. I'm laughing at him, not you. He's in a blind alley. I think I can rout him out for you. But not now. I have to finish a couple of experiments first. And I want to put my notes in order for that paper. There's someone waiting for me. I'll see you tomorrow and explain your ghost for you..."

Morlake had gone then, with a few cryptic comments on the nature of his coming paper, the lateness of the hour, and the futility of studies in parapsychology. For the life of him, Storm could not remember an exact word said. There was a caustic hint that Frudey might be a mere figment of somebody's unpleasant imagination.

Half an hour later, when the watchman knocked at the door of the physics laboratory because the lights were on, there had been no answer. The classroom should have been empty, although

Morlake had been working there sometime until near dawn. A strange sound inside alarmed the watchman. The door was bolted on the inside and the passkey seemed no longer to fit the lock. Help was summoned when repeated knocks brought no answer, and the door was chopped down with a fire axe.

There was the cyclotron; like a fat metallic monster. There was the empty room, the benches, shelves, sinks. The table with the spectrograph, and a battery of powerful microscopes. There were the closets of laboratory glassware, and a small electric furnace, with retorts and shapeless blobs of metal. There were the racks of specimens gathered by geology students. There was a moth-eaten felt banner with the legend "Northside." The door to the target chamber of the cyclotron hung open.

Inside was a bottle of whiskey and a pack of cards.

There was no sign of Dr. Simon Morlake, and no one had seen him since. Prolonged search proved fruitless, and the incident of the bolted door made explanation difficult...

CHAPTER TWO
World of the Unreal

THE AIR was charged, oppressive, and behind piled cloudbanks of sinister purple flickered invisible lightning. The building showed a cliff-face of glass and aluminum, catching and reflecting the ugly flare of sunset. Tense, uneasy, troubled, Storm headed for the Physics building. He was not certain what he would do when he reached the place, but instinct urged him toward the basement workshops. Perhaps contact with the apparatus with which Morlake had been working might stimulate thought, or memory.

If only he could recall something significant that Morlake had said that last afternoon. Memory nagged at him...

Two bulky figures fell into step beside him. Irritably, he was aware of Frazier and Redfield. Storm would have avoided the meeting had choice been given him; he was in no mood for undergrad chitchat.

"Grapevine has it that you're investigating for the faculty. Investigating Morlake's disappearance. Right, Prof?"

"No," Storm answered. Frazier had the gift for causing annoyance to the younger faculty members, by calling attention to their lack of pedagogical dignity. "I'm not. Not that it makes any difference. There's nothing, to investigate."

"Not supposed to talk, huh?" guessed Redfield. "That's silly. Everybody knows he did a bunk. Old Frudey finally got his goat."

Frazier grunted. "I don't believe that. Any leads, Prof?"

Storm stopped and confronted the pair. Frazier and Redfield were two of nature's noblest extroverts; no hint would penetrate their rhino-hide protective shells, or have any effect on their juvenile sensibilities. Direct action was indicated.

"For your information, I'm not investigating anything. If Dr. Morlake has disappeared, there is probably a good reason for it. I don't know anything about it. I teach mathematics. Not amateur detection. Haven't you anything better to do than hang around and dig up possible gossip?"

"Not a thing better, at the moment," Redfield responded with amiable blankness. "If you're not investigating, you won't mind if we come along with you. I'd like to pick up those pix of mine you went south with. Mind?"

Storm minded definitely. But it was useless to argue. He shrunk away from any further jousting with the inevitable. The faculty and Frudey had been enough for one day.

Frazier's shuck of strawlike hair stood up, glinting in the sunlight, like some impossible crested helmet. "Be a sport, Prof. Maybe if we nose around, we might get some ideas. Si Morlake was a good guy. I was working with him, assisting. I might know more than most people. I do know what he was doing, or trying to do."

Storm shrugged; the presence of Frazier and Redfield would be no aid to concentration, but he resigned himself. In silence, they ascended the geometric, semicircular steps to the building's main floor. Through angled doors they entered a corridor tiled in red-marbled, soundless rubber. A flight of curving stairs railed in a swooping unfinished curve of aluminum led downward. In a soft flush of concealed lighting, the basement hallway split the lower floor in half.

The fourth doorway on the left gave entrance to a modern chamber of horrors. It was the room housing the cyclotron, the micro-spectrograph, directional Geiger counters, a cloud chamber, a battery of ordinary high-power microscopes, and a fabulous electron microscope. For a small college, Northside was unusually well endowed, especially in curious Twentieth Century instruments for delving into the Unknowable.

Still blocking the entrance, its blank face of polished mahogany split and shattered, was the door, which had been bolted on the inside. Wrenched awry, it hung crookedly on tortured hinges.

Stratified silence hung in the basement corridor like layers of invisible smoke. Storm tugged at the door. It moved, lower edge squealing viciously on the tiling. They entered.

Nothing in the room had been touched, nothing moved, in case later developments would prove need for fingerprints. In the open chamber of the cyclotron were still the bottle of whiskey and the pack of cards.

"Don't tell me Morlake was trying to activate good Bourbon!" said Redfield in mock horror.

"No, that wasn't it," explained Frazier aimlessly. "He had a lot of things he was trying out. I worked with him at first, but I was getting behind in other studies. Frudey put the heat on and I had to give up wacky non-essentials...like atoms and ESP—you know, extra-sensory perception. Morlake was bugs about it and said I was an ideal subject for him. Two reasons. The dice, first, I could shoot ten sevens in a row. He was as excited as a puppy over that, and as eager to believe as a kid asking about Superman or Santa Claus. I hadn't the heart to enlighten him. The dice were mine—loaded. He'd have seen it in a fluoroscope, but it didn't occur to him to check. The other reason was. I'm a blond."

Storm's interest picked up, but he was relieved of asking the obvious question by Redfield's suddenly coy nonsense: "He liked blondes?"

Blushing, Frazier stammered. "Not that at all. Blondes have funny vision. A blonde's eyes are sometimes sensitive to ultraviolet light in wavelengths invisible to other people. I was. Morlake said the range of my vision into ultraviolet was extraordinary. Si Morlake had a lot of wacky ideas, but some were interesting. I got involved in ESP, because I was wondering about applying telekinesis to football. What I could do with a ball that would come when I whistled, even if it were already ill flight..."

Frazier's words ran out, his eyes glazed, grew distant, as the possibility of using teleportation or telepathy in sport; lured his thoughts out of continuity.

"You say you knew what he was trying to do?" Storm broke in sharply. "Surely it was not...football?"

Frazier grinned. "No, hardly that. Something about co-existing atoms. I didn't get all of it, naturally. He was trying things out on me, like trying them on a dog. Called me by a Latin name, a dog's name, I think—*Fidus Achates*. But he didn't expect me to respond or pay any more attention than a dog would, if you talked to it. He talked as if the world were a tangle of extended dimensions, a kind of interlocking puzzle box, with other planes of space and matter co-existing with ours, kind of parallel. Not a new idea in theory. Morlake's approach was different. Original and ingenious. Nothing like analogy or pure speculative mathematics. He wanted to see and feel these other worlds. Said it was quite possible."

"Go on," urged Storm, intrigued.

"IT WAS Dr. Adrian's experiments with the cyclotron that put Morlake on the track of what he wanted. Morlake was helping when Adrian bombarded carbon with three hundred-eighty-million-volt particles of helium, trying to produce mesons, the secondary cosmic ray particles. It was not the experiment, itself, that interested Morlake, but some unexpected side results. There was talk that the use of the cyclotron was affecting people's vision in the region. If you'll remember, there were a lot of complaints. Arnold got upset, you know Prexy, and worried for fear public opinion might force the college to suspend operating the cyclotron. It didn't. Whatever effect the experiments had was short-lived, and furor died down. Prexy forgot about it, and when Adrian got a lot of publicity for his photographed results, Prexy was there as usual to elbow his way in and grab the bows.

"Everybody forgot about the complaints, everybody—except Morlake. He seemed as fascinated about 'em as he was about my dice throwing sevens in a row. He went and talked to people, by pretending he was a reporter or adjuster for the insurance people. There had been talk of lawsuits, remember. The people were eager to talk. Said their eyes blurred, half-seeing things that weren't there. "Well, that was it. Morlake claimed that the cyclotron had affected vision, temporarily. He said our cyclotron was a freak, a one in a thousand chance. That it extended the range of vision both ways, into the ultraviolet and the infrared, and that people could see things, which weren't normally visible. That the things they thought they saw *were* there all the time, but invisible to normal eyesight. Then Morlake thought that other senses might be affected equally. Vision first since it was more sensitive, and something you'd notice quicker. Hearing, smell, touch—then he said a crazy thing. He wondered what our first taste of the New World would be like. He called the invisible worlds around us his New World, the final frontier of mystery. He said someday we'd see and hear and smell and feel it, may be even taste it. Forbidden fruit, he said, might be bitter to the taste. After Adrian left, Morlake kept toying with the cyclotron, to see if he could enhance its effects on people in range. That's all I know."

Darkness grew swiftly in the basement room. Outside, the threatening storm broke. There was wind, with rain and hail in it; wind that shrieked and howled and drummed phantom fingers on the slanted windowpanes. Near trees and bushes, visible above the window wells, threshed wildly as if angry monsters rent a way through them.

Storm was thoughtful as he moved toward the light switch. When the time came, Frazier would have to repeat his story to the police. In the meantime, Storm tried to organize his thoughts. Absently, he flipped the switch. Fluorescents blinked, flickered and flared blindingly, then exploded. Burst tubes fell in jingling shower to the floor. In the darkness, Storm groped to a bench and sat down. He swore briefly.

A shadow moved against the lighter shadow-pool of fragmentary glass. Redfield was stooping over.

"Don't touch it," Storm warned. "You can get a nasty poisoning from the tube coating if you cut yourself." He came to a sudden decision. "Redfield, you go call the police. I'll take responsibility. Tell them to send a couple of detectives, intelligent ones if they have any. Too much time has gone by now. Someone should have called in the authorities before this. The police won't like it, but there has to be an investigation. The sooner the better. We'll wait for you here. On your way back, stop by the supply room and bring in replacement tubes for the lights. Get going."

Astonished, Redfield grunted, but he complied without comment. The sound of his departure diminished with distance.

In the darkness, with the froth of wind outside, and the restless seething toss of branches making an uproar of confused sound, Storm felt growing uneasiness. It increased by leaps and bounds.

Storm spoke to Frazier, raising his voice to battle the cry of turbulent elements. "You say Morlake chose you to assist him...because your vision extended into the ultraviolet ranges. Did you ever *see* anything?"

The reply was an embarrassed chuckle. "Did I? I think I was to blame for the rumor this place is haunted. I mentioned it to Redfield. He hung around one night, to take pictures. You know what he got—"

"I saw them," Storm corrected grimly. "I don't know what they were. Morlake seemed to know. I showed the prints to him..."

There was a burst of sound. The hall door moved suddenly on its wrenched hinges. Moved as if a blast of compressed air struck it, hurling the door shut with extreme violence. Probably an outer door had been opened, causing a draft. Outside, wind raved and moaned.

Storm thought it might be Redfield returning. He strode to the door, tried the knob. The slamming had jammed it tightly, the frame creaked under pressure, but the door resisted movement. Storm braced himself, got a shoulder against the wood, and shoved with all his strength.

"Give me a hand," Storm called to Frazier. There was an odd, sharp, gasping cry in the darkness. It sounded as if someone were strangling. The cry came again, muffled.

Storm turned. Something was happening to the room. It should have been dark, illuminated sharply at irregular intervals by the flash of lightning. Instead, it glowed.

It glowed in patterns, geometric patterns which shifted and swirled as if objects melted and flowed like the figures in a Dali painting, becoming something quite different from whatever they at first seemed. Curious movement pulsed through the arrangement of forms, as if numerous panes of transparent glass bore luminous designs, and the panes were shifted in a regular order of motion. Shadowy relationships constantly.

While Storm's brain tried to adjust itself to this illusion, his body continued its effort to force open the door to the hall. Something yielded with a sensation that the world was breaking apart. The door gave way.

His body careened through the opening. He tripped and fell, flinging his arms forward to break the fall.

As if from a tremendous distance, he heard voices. Frazier and Redfield...

His ears clung to the sound, as one clings desperately to the symbols of familiar things in a dream world.

Gray darkness swallowed him. For immeasurable intervals of time, he floated, bodiless, with no sensation of falling, or of being supported. Then, without warning, he sprawled headlong.

OUTFLUNG hands encountered an unfamiliar, jagged surface. He struck hard, rolling. Dazed, he sat up, conscious of bruised and abraded skin. Clothing felt damp, sticky, clinging. He raised one injured hand to evaluate its damage.

The hand was part of nightmare. It was a hideous thing of jumbled angles and curving planes. Its color was wrong dreadfully wrong. His brain refused to translate the vibrations into familiar color ideas.

He was in a strange place, part of a dream world, but not a pleasant part. It was someone else's dream world, not his. Storm scrambled to his feet and looked about. Vision was limited. The glaring light poured from unseen sources, illuminating little and distorting what it revealed. He stood on a bare, rocky slope and the surface about him was textured with minute pitting effects. A swirl of luminous fog drifted everywhere and seemed to cling loosely to the nearer shadows.

There was no other way to describe the bulky forms obscured by the mist. Even those close at hand resembled nothing previously known. Outlines wavered, one could not be sure of solidity.

Storm dared not look too closely at his own body. Patches of it, which thrust into his line of vision, were utterly wrong; disturbingly wrong. Storm tried to concentrate, and found that even thought was difficult, distorted. He must have struck his head in falling. That was a possible solution, but too easy. Unconvincing. This was unreal. He should pinch himself and wake up. But he was not sleeping. Moments ago—

But was he sure of that? Time seemed to have telescoped, as it sometimes does in dreams. Recent events were blurred, confused, unreal. Sometime, in another world, something had happened. Storm was no longer sure what had even happened, when, or where. He was here. The surroundings were new, strange, different.

He heard voices. Familiar voices. One was calling his name, repeating the sound over and over. Storm had difficulty recognizing the alien syllables as a symbol pertaining to him.

Two shadows detached themselves from the indefinite background. They moved toward him in an odd drifting motion, completely unlike walking. They glided in a series of jerks and swoops. After an interval, they were close. But everything about them was strange. The form was human, but blurred, shadowy, and there were ugly hints of luminous geometric outlines of something else. What he saw seemed only a shadow cast into solids. Two shadows.

It was like that *thing* he had seen before in the Physics Building and mentioned to Morlake. Everything came rushing back upon him. Memory and identity fused into a whole. He was John Storm. He remembered the school and Morlake, the faculty and the students, sudden flashing details about himself. The rush of memory should have changed the world back into familiar pattern, but it remained as before.

He staggered and felt ill, weak, more confused by the recalled knowledge than he had been before.

Again the voices. They sounded like Redfield's and Frazier's. But they seemed hardly voices at all. He could *see* them. Like waves expanding in a pool from a dropped stone, the voices were shimmering, expanding globes of transparent luminosity. He was aware of direction in the effect, as if the globes distorted in his direction, bent and converged toward him.

"It is always like this at first," said Frazier. "Don't strain too hard. You will adjust to it. I've come so far before..."

What did it mean? Had Morlake opened a gateway in the Known and stumbled into the nightmare world of the Unknown?

CHAPTER THREE
The Shadow Beings

STORM stared at the shadows. His eyes screamed with pain; glaring light probed his eyeballs, got inside his skull, twisting his brain. Waves of nausea paralyzed all perception of distance, of relation, of reality...

He spoke, the words reaching out like undulating ribbons of light. "You—have—been—here—before?"

Again, spheres of rippling color expanded. Ears and brain tingled.

"Not exactly. A glimpse or two. Morlake was afraid to expose me to unknown danger. I said he was a good guy. He took the risk himself. He came exploring twice. Told me about it. This time he did not return. Something must have happened."

Resentment and anger made Storm momentarily speechless. It was cruel and unfair. He had been trapped by a stupid plot. But was it intentional? Had Frazier known, or suspected, what might happen? What had happened?

Anger burned itself out suddenly. What had happened? He put the question in words, amazed by the visible phenomena that accompanied sound.

The reply was ironic, bitterly humorous. "Nothing—really. You just think so."

Storm started a savage protest.

Frazier went calmly on. "The door gave way before you, and you fell into the hall. If you hadn't turned around to see what was happening, you would still be there. But you were convinced that you were somewhere else. So you are. The mind creates some force, which translates even your physical body to a different plane. You haven't gone anywhere, in terms of time and space. These other, unknown worlds co-exist with ours, parallel, perhaps on a different vibration level. I don't pretend to understand all of it. I'm just guessing. Morlake rarely explained; he dropped a few hints, and I'm trying to make sense of them.

"He said our eyes catch a lot of things that our brains don't believe. The brain is a strainer, filtering out the parts of any sensations relayed to it, which are not pertinent to our accepted existence. Lots of people see these related worlds. Some of them are very close, really visible to us. People see ghosts only if they are 'in tune'—which means tired, or in a trance-like state with conscious judgment set aside for the moment. The ghosts are always there to see, if our minds let us see them.

"The cyclotron has a leak somewhere. It's a freak, Morlake says. Some energy form released or generated by it can be stored in the air or 'the ether'—and, given certain conditions, will heighten normal perceptions. It may affect the organs of sight, smell and taste directly, or the nerves relaying perception, or even the brain itself. Touch and hearing are not so easily hurt or stimulated. Maybe they function according to a different vibration pattern, coarser; or maybe the brain has to be convinced first, and will then translate sensations of touch and hearing into new terms. I don't know. But *something* would happen to anyone if he were around that particular cyclotron for any length of time.

"Whatever the energy is, it diminishes in time, but gradually. It functions chiefly in the dark. Ordinary octaves of visible light seem to cancel out its effect. You know how some odors will blanket ultraviolet light. There is a clash—I know because the fluorescents burst like that several times while Dr. Adrian was operating the cyclotron. Probably it works like sounding a note in music that is exactly tuned to the critical vibration level of a glass or mirror. It shatters."

Storm saw an objection, made it. "But Dr. Adrian was working with the cyclotron more than anyone else. He saw nothing."

Frazier laughed harshly. "Do you *know* that? His wife died very suddenly. But did he have to take her body east? I think he was scared, running away. Probably thought his mind was cracking."

A thought occurred to Storm. "Did you plan all this? Was I deliberately trapped into coming with you?"

"No," came the reply. "Remember, you were coming here yourself. We merely came along. We intended to anyhow. You made it easy for us. Besides, I wasn't sure anything would happen this time."

"You should have warned me," Storm rebuked angrily.

"Would you have listened? Would you have believed me? You'd have demanded facts, explanations, proofs. I had nothing but wild guesses."

"I'll believe you now. The question is, how do we get out of here?"

Frazier's voice was stubborn, brutally matter of fact, blunt. "We don't," he said. "Not till we find Morlake. Someone has to look for him. He's in trouble—or he'd have returned. We can't get out unless he shows us a way. I don't know of any..."

In silence, Storm digested the grim facts of the situation. Finally, he said, "How do we go about finding him? Any ideas?"

The shadows moved, drifting closer in that stiff, staggering glide.

"Stand right where you are," warned Frazier. "Don't move. We need a base of operation."

Storm held himself rigidly immovable. He glanced about, trying to force his mind to relax, to accept the rules and standards of unreality. It was like a curiously solid, inescapable dream. He was in a world without perspective, visual or mental. There was no horizon, only limiting, obscuring fog. Within range of sight was no familiar outline, no bulk of recognizable form, no object that could be exactly labeled.

Redfield spoke: "I was just outside the door, waiting to see what happened. I did not go for the police. As you fell, you vanished. We had trouble getting through, finding the right plane. There are a lot of them. We might never have found you. It was just luck. Even then, we couldn't be sure. You were hard to—to identify."

The shadows ranged themselves beside Storm. One of them touched him. The sensation was oddly normal, reassuring. "Stop fighting it, Prof." said Frazier. "It's not so bad. But you still don't quite believe it. So you aren't completely through. The worst part is being caught between two dimensions. You've got to accept it. One illusion is very like another. Accept it, and it works...at least as far as you are concerned."

"Sure, Prof," amended Redfield. "Establishing a beachhead is never fun. I know. But it's better to hit the sand and dig yourself a hole in it than to stand outside, getting your feet wet."

It was Roman counsel; strong, tough-minded, but good if you could take it. Storm remembered that both Frazier and Redfield were G.I. students. They knew something about beachheads. After all, this was one, really, a beachhead into the unknown.

The same rules might apply.

The thought was comforting. Storm had been unaware of his own strangling suspicion that no rules would apply. He relaxed and the light grew stronger, more compelling. Some of the blurring mists cleared. Objects stood out more sharply. The two near shadows were more obviously human, but with disturbing overtones of color and a wavering luminosity of outline.

They were men.

SLOWLY at first, then with a rush, surroundings changed. He stood on a steep slope of bare, jagged rock. There was no sign of weathering, nothing but a blank surface of grainy-textured gray, incredibly rough and pointed like a vastly magnified picture of some abrasive compound, Frazier and Redfield solidified, like a motion picture coming into focus.

"That's better," approved Frazier. He fished a coil of fine, tough nylon cord from his pocket and bent to attach it firmly to a projection of rock. "I hope this serves us better than it did Dr. Morlake. He used it the first two times, and came back. I found this on a bench in the shop. Maybe he forgot it, unless he had another like it. This is the starting point; we'll have to find our way back to it. Or—"

He shrugged. It wasn't necessary to complete the thought.

Paying out the cord, Frazier cautiously descended the slope. Storm followed, and Redfield brought up the rear. Time lost all substance. They secured hours going down a long, slanting shelf of featureless gray rocks. Light waxed and waned. At times, the gray surface lost appearance of solidity, became crystalline, transparent, and they seemed to hang suspended in a titanic abyss of empty space. Again the footing clouded, resumed its original appearance.

Despite the intensity of light, it was like walking in thick darkness. Storm collided with things which were not there, hulks too diffuse to refuse his passage, but which yielded reluctantly under pressure. Invisible semi-solids, which seemed alive, or at least capable of movement, clung about him, resisting, like blobs of very dense gas. It required definite exertion to move against the vague pressure.

He was breathing heavily, and became slowly aware of alien tastes and smells in the atmosphere. Vague whisperings came and went about him. He grew confused. It seemed they had changed directions, but the slope still angled steeply downward. Surrounding pressures eased slightly, and they went more swiftly.

Abruptly the slope broke into a steep and dangerous descent. Loose rock rolled beneath his groping foot, rolled and fell and rattled, then dropped into the silence of free fall. For a full minute it fell, then came an echoing crash far below. Straining his eyes until corkscrews seemed to revolve in his brain, Storm made out details of a cliff face which plunged almost sheer to a dark valley.

There were shadows below, many shadows. Dark shadows that moved restlessly like the patterns wind draws on a field of dry, waving grain. They moved in heaving billows, in irregular tossing swirls. But like the grain, they moved as if somehow attached at one end to a solid, unmoving surface.

Of that fearful descent, Storm could remember little. Down they went, and down, clawing for handholds, reaching blindly below for crevice or cranny in which to wedge feet aching with fatigue. At one place they locked hands to each other's ankles and lowered themselves as on a living rope. None too soon, they reached the valley floor.

Here, the light was very bad. Even objects near at hand were so distorted and so difficult to see clearly that Storm doubted the sureness of his footing. Progress became a · groping for solidity across treacherous, uneasy ground. Had it not been for a constant flicker of vague lights and shadows, they would have moved like blind men, tapping the surface each time before putting a foot down. Near the ground were curious currents, almost like invisible running water, which tugged at feet and legs.

Still paying out the nylon cord, Frazier thrust his way ahead.

"That must be a long cord," Storm growled.

"Not so long," came the sharp answer. "Distance is different here. Either space itself, or our perception of it, is warped I remember Morlake saying something about that after his first trip. You'll find how far it seems when we try to go back."

"If we ever go hack," muttered Storm.

Redfield pressed forward to Storm's side, thrusting a solid small hulk toward him.

"I brought my service revolver," Redfield said. "If it will make you feel better, Prof, you carry it."

Storm rejected the offer. "Keep it. I wouldn't know how to use it."

"What do they teach people in schools?" Frazier laughed. The sound was hideously distorted, like a caricature of laughter. They plodded on in silence.

In the valley shadows were denser, more substantial. Even the atmosphere hung heavy, and there was sharp tang in the nostrils and tingling in the lungs as one breathed. It was stimulating but nerve-wracking. Smell identified it as ozone or something similar; and ozone in sufficient concentration can be toxic. The thought was not pleasant to Storm, but mired in a mixture of embarrassment and hot resentment, he did not mention it to the others.

They trod aisles in a forest of crystal shafts where odd lights moved and beckoned, and soft colors glowed. On the ground were the moving patterns of light and dark, like shadows of invisible living forms. Storm did not like to think about what beings might cast such shadows. In another place, where darkness thickened and sound grew into a vast outpouring of weird harmonies, the shadows stirred and some stood upright like solid bodies. Bodies that moved in response to what might have been fluctuations in the music, bobbing, nodding, swaying sometimes in unison, sometimes singly again the whole mass spinning in the mad gyrations of a group dance. Always there was an appearance of intelligent violation, a hideous lifelike quality of controlled movement.

The shadows were three dimensional, but utterly unhuman. It was a mathematical nightmare, with every form known to geometric science. Cubes, cylinders, cones, pyramids, irregular many-faceted blocks. If solids they were immeasurably elastic, expanding into grotesque elongations, foreshortening into dwarfed, bulging blobs, always transparent, or at least translucent, but distorting light strangely as it flowed through them.

Utter weariness weighed down Storm. Movement became almost mechanical. He trudged as one does in endless nightmare, and there was an illusion of repetition in everything he did.

Mind and muscles revolted at once. From sheer exhaustion he stopped and refused to continue the hopeless task.

"This nonsense has gone far enough," he said defiantly. "We don't stand a chance to find Morlake. If there are infinite planes, as you say, he may be on anyone of them. We don't know that he's on this one. I must have been crazy to come this far."

Frazier and Redfield stared at him. They looked like badly photographed motion pictures.

"I guess you're right," admitted Frazier hopelessly. "The line has run out anyhow. We can find where we were all right. But what then? It's not like opening a door. We don't know how to get out."

Following the cord, reeling it up as they went, Frazier led the way back toward the cliff. He stopped, so suddenly that Storm, following close behind, bumped into him. Frazier, held up the end of the cord. It seemed to have been burned in two. In widening circles, panic mounting, they searched for the opposite end. A few oddly scorched and raveling fragments were found. Redfield touched one and screamed. It had burned like a hot wire. There was no sign of a continuing cord.

THE THREE stood and looked at one another. Catastrophe was beyond comment. Redfield shrugged, rubbed injured fingers on his coat.

"We can't stay here," he said dismally.

Selecting a direction at random, he started walking. The others followed.

Fear strained itself through Storm's consciousness. Loss of the guiding cord seemed to cut him adrift. The nodding and waving shadows had disturbed, but without frightening him. They seemed too evanescent, too insubstantial, unreal. But being lost in this utter strangeness was terrifying. Panic rang in his brain like the muted vibrations of a cracked bell. He felt compelling urge to run, but there was no place to run. In all the pervading grayness, there was no hiding place.

Redfield strode swiftly, as if he sought escape from the terror, which dogged all of them.

Light shifted rapidly, sliding up and down scaled octaves of illumination. It kept pace with their racing emotions, was keyed to the rising crescendo of stark fear. Surroundings also were altered subtly, becoming harsher, more stark and bleak of outline. Objects assumed tantalizing suggestion of familiar forms, but the illusion vanished quickly upon closer approach.

Shadows seemed to draw together behind them. The huddled things made gestures, dimly perceived, vaguely menacing. From all sides came a suggestion of whispering; of furtive, haunted urging. A feeling of deadly pursuit increased from an ugly suspicion into hideous certainty. Bodiless entities, seen only by the shadows they cast, were herding the three fugitives toward some unseen goal.

A defile opened ahead, revealing the place to which the three were being driven. *A city!*

CHAPTER FOUR
Dark Doorway

DESOLATE as the moon, a great plain stretched beyond visible distance. In a near wedge of it, thrusting like a salient into a jumbled mass of broken rock, was a cluster of huge, obviously artificial structures. It must be a city. There were ruins of towering semisolid walls, a tangle of twisted buildings, a maze of threading streets, some partially blocked with curious rubble. In the center, overpowering the disorderly mass of the city, rose gigantic cones, taller by far than the highest surrounding piles.

Light played over the cones, weaving webs of lightnings from apex to apex. The cones themselves were glowing cores of vivid white, but color crawled upon the surfaces. Color, which broke and flowed in constantly changing patterns, melting, resolving, running through complete spectrums and suggesting invisible spectrums beyond. There was sound, sound which seemed integral with the color, sound which flowed with it in audible patterns, which ranged its own spectrums and vanished into contorted and nerve-straining vibrations beyond hearing. It was as if one had struck an accidental chord upon some great color organ, blending harmonies and dissonance into a cluster of tones at once beautiful and maddening to hear.

Like a sheet of glimmering water, light moved outward from the city, enveloped the men who stood too stunned to move and drew them swiftly into the very confines of mystery.

Things moved about the city, things that cast multiform and monstrous shadows of their being...

In that intolerable light and sound, planes shifted oddly, readjusted. It was like a book of colored pictures, flipped through so rapidly that impressions flowed, fused, became moving patterns in a new and startlingly different order of reality. It was like blindness resolving into the world of light, vision so stark and painful, so hideous that Storm cringed, writhing in instinctive denial.

It was then that he first saw the...inhabitants.

If the shadows had suggested nightmare, the reality was beyond nightmare. It was sheer horror, mathematical in form, luminous, living—intelligent.

The frightening part was the perception, instantaneous and complete, of alien intelligence. Had they been mindless beings, creatures of mere existence, he could have stood the utter loathing, which rocked his being. But these...these had mind and will, strong, alert, contemptuous, interested. Not cruel; emotionless, but with unbounded curiosity...

Storm felt like an impaled insect, being examined. For a timeless interval, he felt the idle probing of alien intelligence, he felt the searching thrust of curious thought against his; it was like the touch of sharp but delicate instruments. He was held high, wriggling, poked and jabbed by thin beams of light, while he strove to blank out his mind against the cold insolence of examination.

There was a moment of baffled indecision, followed by curious emotions which he sensed indistinctly, too unfamiliar to identify.

Then he was being flung carelessly aside.

There was a familiar sensation, recognized instantly. He was grateful for the familiarity. But it was pain, sheer outrage of physical pain. Mercifully, he lost consciousness...

Awakening brought further doubt of sanity. He was lying on a hard surface in comparative darkness. He was bound by invisible but solid lines of force. Someone bent over him, fumbling at the network which secured him. It was Morlake.

"Quiet," said Morlake. "They threw us together to see what reactions we would have. Don't give anything away."

"You—saw—them?"

"Oh, yes. A good deal more of them than you did. They're not what you think. Or maybe they are, I don't know. I believe each one of us sees them differently; each brain translates their appearance into something related to itself, its training. The real appearance may be something else again."

"I saw cubes and pyramids and cylinders and gemlike figures with facets reflecting light."

"Then I was right. They are too alien even for perception in the ordinary sense. You imagined mathematical figures. It was an escape for your brain into terms of familiar reality. We strain vision through preconceived ideas, as a protection to sanity. Here there is no sanity—but theirs. They're sane enough, intelligent, even wildly curious about us. They've tried to learn from me about our world, where we came from, what it's like, what people are like—above all, how we got here. They're too damn curious about that. The possibilities frighten me—"

"You should have thought of that before," Storm reproved.

"Good Lord, man! I didn't create this place. It was here before I stumbled on it. With the cyclotron operating, anyone could have blundered here, anytime. Such things are bound to happen. With all the gadgets we've dreamed up, most of them imperfectly understood, mankind is asking for trouble. We don't know what happens when we start cooking with atoms; it's highly probable that we'll unlock a lot of doors, doors that open blindly into the unknown. This is one. The cyclotron is a freak, but there may be others like it. Who knows? Blindness first—the groping and blundering—then the terrible vision. If it's only a vision, we're lucky..."

Morlake stopped, his voice strange with passion.

"I'm no better than the rest," he went on. "I looked into the darker mental closets behind our ghosts and found ugly reality. But you can't shut all the closet doors. Man is too curious. But other things—these or others—may be equally curious. The barriers of mind are too thin. The barriers of matter scarcely exist. We are only pioneers in a new field of exploration. Others will follow very soon, one way or another. Even if we get back and try to warn them of what we have found—"

Storm remembered saying something, but his mind was not working clearly. Shock of his experience had been too great.

Then Morlake was talking again, swiftly, as if time ran through his fingers.

"Getting out is fairly simple. I'm surprised you didn't think of it. Go back to your point of initial contact. I'm sure Frazier can find the way. He's good at orientation. You'll have to find the two of them. They were brought here, as you were. I don't know where, and haven't time to look. *They'll* come for me soon. It's a matter of mental adjustment, helped by the li—"

Words faded into curious rustling hiss. Fainter and fainter as if distance separated him from the source of the sound. Then Storm was conscious of supreme mental effort by Morlake. Sound came again, revolving into speech; but the syllables were flat and metallic, run together.

"Don't think about me. Escape...if you can. Smash the cyclotron...as if accident. I stayed to learn something which may help out...if..."

That was all. Morlake was gone.

THE cell was small, like the hollow interior of a cone. It had never been intended for human occupancy. Weak and shaken, Storm moved about, exploring. He seemed free. In the dimness he reached out and felt a tangle of something like invisible cords.

Above the floor, on one slanting side of the cone, was a spot of lighter darkness. As Storm investigated, he found it to be an oval aperture which expanded as he moved toward it, shrank as he backed away, operating according to his proximity in a manner that suggested a door opening and closing to the control of an electric eye. With an animal's fear of a trap, Storm eyed the oval dubiously. It seemed the only possible exit. He would have to risk it.

Outside was a constantly curving hallway, which wandered up and down and sidewise, with no apparent direction or intention. He followed it cautiously. Off the hallway, opened many cells similar to the one he had vacated. They were all alike, all empty. In any man-made structure, the waste of space would have been criminal—unless here there were more dimensions than three, with consequent variant ideas about space.

It was a vast hive of cone-like cells; the passageways endless complicated warrens, which roved aimlessly at the whims of alien designers. Some ended abruptly at blank walls that might be no barriers to the inhabitants. There was the intricate and meaningless unreality of dreams. It was a maze without pattern or conceivable plan.

Hosts of faint, floorbound shadows swayed and gestured about him. But now their urging whispers and rustlings seemed friendly, worried, warning...

They were as frightened as he.

Storm stopped and tried to grasp at meaning in the half-sounds. But the sound itself was illusory: as fragmentary and unrelated as the mindless patter of wind-stirred leaves.

He went on.

In another cell, bound by the invisible cords, were Frazier and Redfield. Both seemed dazed or asleep. They roused, reluctantly, as he worked over them. They stared at him with dazed, uncomprehending eyes.

Words came unsteadily, vaguely, as if minds worked sluggishly and resisted stimulus. At his insistence, the men stood up and followed him, moving as if drugged or in hypnotic trance.

In an immense, soaring room, built on the lines of ellipsoid, hollow and filled with brilliance of flaky light and chiming sound, they found Morlake.

He still lived after a dreadful fashion. Mounted on a frame of luminous solidity he had apparently been the object of extreme curiosity. The body was turned inside out, all things hideous to see had been done with dispassionate skill at vivisection. Beings, whatever they were, still milled about and hovered over the glowing framework in attitudes of detached impersonal interest. Figures like involved intricacies of intersecting planes; other figures like solids composed of jumbled assemblies of angles difficult to resolve into individual entities; figures that were the mathematics of nightmare—all whirled about in the eerie gyrations of a dance of death.

In the madness that followed, clear impressions were impossible.

Redfield came suddenly alive. He fired bullet after bullet into the writhing obscenity, which was Morlake—with no apparent effect, for the inhuman writhing continued.

There was a fearful outburst of sound, a blinding violence of light, exploding intolerably into brilliance beyond that of fissioning atoms. Cones shattered, and the showering uproar of their fragments was like a deluge of fragile glass.

As they fled through it, the city was crumbling in swift decay, building toppling, the walls shuddering, collapsing into oozing mass, the plain rocked and heaved, while lightnings raved overhead. In the narrow dark valley, the earthbound shadows danced and flapped and crackled like wind-whipped flames. Then they were climbing the precipice, scrambling endlessly upward, while loose rocks rolled and fell and clattered around them. The long slope upward was now ablaze with quivering livid flames, which licked at the fugitives, and strong, invisible currents flowed over their numbed feet, clinging, impeding, attempting to drag down and destroy them.

There was a cord at last, still attached to the projecting rock, its loose end smoldering as the hungry flames licked at it.

Gasping, the three flung themselves on the ground, hugging the hard-bought advantage, as condemned prisoners cling to a dwindling hope.

Fog swirled down and enveloped the exposed barren height. The harshly metallic sky leaned close, while rivers of lightning poured from it. After the dazzling flashes of lightning came flowing soft darkness. Darkness, filled with a rustling and crackling and whispering, as if legions of ghosts besieged the mist-wreathed slopes. Groping blindly, Storm found his way to Frazier and Redfield, seized and held them firmly.

"The light," he whispered hoarsely. "That's the secret. If only there were some way to reach it—"

"The light! Of course," mumbled Frazier.

Temperature dropped rapidly. In a black, seething ocean of darkness, they huddled together. The ground stirred, heaved, moved uneasily beneath their feet.

"I remember now," Frazier cried wildly. "He always tied the cord first. Near the switch, so he'd know where to reach. If we had done that—"

Redfield groaned. "I'd got the replacement tubes, but I did not have time to fit them in. They're still out in the corridor, leaning against the wall. What's the use?"

Horror became tangible. The mists thinned, and something like an army of shadows moved steadily, stealthily up the lower slopes.

Suddenly the darkness was riven. It split wide open as walls of brilliant light became a solid, expanding cube. Magically, the gray bleakness of pitted rock was erased. The advancing armies of shadows faltered, vanished.

There was a moment of awful suspension. Then falling. In a heap, the three tumbled into the corridor of the Physics building. The splintered door crashed heavily against the wall. Hinges gave way; unsupported, the door tottered and fell with shattering noise.

Silence hung in the corridor like layers of invisible smoke.

Light streamed from the doorway of the room housing the haunted cyclotron. It was blocked by a dark, solid silhouette. The watchman stood and blinked solemnly at the tangle of oddly disarrayed bodies on the floor. One stirred and sat up. It was Storm. He gasped, his face was red and swollen with exertion. The savage ferocity of his glance startled the watchman. The others were disentangling themselves noisily.

"That door will have to be replaced," said the watchman. "I must have missed you before. The lights were out for a while. I've replaced the tubes in here. I found them in the hall." He was crackling the corrugated boxes, which had held fluorescent tubing; his thin hands were nervous and wrenched at the paper viciously as he went on.

"I came down to check. Thought maybe you'd be here. The police are upstairs. Want to talk to you. They've found Morlake."

"Morlake!" Storm's voice was completely dazed.

The watchman nodded. "Yes. Over at the power plant. Nobody knows why he went there or when. Or how he got in. The body was across some exposed terminals. It was burned...almost beyond..." the man gulped, "...almost beyond recognition."

Now on their feet, Frazier and Redfield exchanged glances with Storm—glances that bound all three to an unspoken conspiracy of silence. Someday—soon—something would happen to a cyclotron—an accident, unavoidable. He nodded binding himself to the pact.

Foot on the first step, Storm hesitated, nerved himself to look back. They were still standing as he left them, a tableau of suddenly frozen figures. The watchman crumpled the elongated hollow tubing of corrugated paper. Redfield had nervously put the revolver back in his pocket. Frazier looked as if he had been about to say something and then had thought better of it.

From above came the sound of Frudey's voice, shrill, angry, demanding. It would be like the faculty meeting, but worse. There would be more questions, still unanswerable, and he could never offer the truth—which was perhaps the worst possible solution of the mystery. Hand on the aluminum rail, Storm hesitated, dreading to go up and face the battery of alien and unfriendly eyes.

From the basement corridor, and from the vault like room beyond, opening off it through a wrenched and splintered frame doorway, came a faint sound.

It was a series of faint popping noises, followed by a jingling rain of fine particles of glass.

The doorway became a rectangle of darkness. Even before the luminous, geometric figures came swirling into the corridor, Storm knew that he would never again have to ascend into the world of reality.

At the bottom of the curving stairway, he waited...

THE END

Zeritsky's Law

By ANN GRIFFITH

Why bother building a time machine when there's something much easier to find right in your own kitchen?

SOMEBODY someday will make a study of the influence of animals on history. Although not as famous as Mrs. O'Leary's cow, Mrs. Graham's cat should certainly be included in any such study. It has now been definitely established that the experiences of this cat led to the idea of quick-frozen people, which, in turn, led to the passage of Zeritsky's Law.

We must go back to the files of the Los Angeles newspapers for 1950 to find the story. In brief, a Mrs. Fred C. Graham missed her pet cat on the same day that she put a good deal of food down in her home deep-freeze unit. She suspected no connection between the two events. The cat was not to be found until six days later, when its owner went to fetch something from the deep-freeze. Much as she loved her pet, we may imagine that she was more horror-than grief-stricken at her discovery. She lifted the little ice-encased body out of the deep-freeze and set it on the floor. Then she managed to run as far as the next door neighbor's house before fainting.

Mrs. Graham became hysterical after she was revived, and it was several hours before she could be quieted enough to persuade anybody that she hadn't made up the whole thing. She prevailed upon her neighbor to go back to the house with her. In front of the deep-freeze they found a small pool of water, and a wet cat, busily licking itself. The neighbor subsequently told reporters that the cat was concentrating its licking on one of its hind legs, where some ice still remained, so that she, for one, believed the story.

A follow-up dispatch, published a week later, reported that the cat was unharmed by the adventure. Further, Mrs. Graham was quoted as saying that the cat had had a large meal just before its disappearance; that as soon after its rescue as it had dried itself off,

36

it took a long nap, precisely as it always did after a meal; and that it was not hungry again until evening. It was clear from the accounts that the life processes had been stopped dead in their tracks, and had, after defrosting, resumed at exactly the point where they left off.

Perhaps it is unfair to put all the responsibility on one luckless cat. Had such a thing happened anywhere else in the country, it would have been talked about, believed by a few, disbelieved by most, and forgotten. But as the historic kick of Mrs. O'Leary's cow achieved significance because of the time and place that it was delivered, so the falling of Mrs. Graham's cat into the deep-freeze became significant because it occurred in Los Angeles. There, and probably only there, the event was anything but forgotten; the principles it revealed became the basis of a hugely successful business.

How shall we regard the Zeritsky Brothers? As arch villains or pioneers? In support of the latter view, it must be admitted that the spirit of inquiry and the willingness to risk the unknown were indisputably theirs. However, their pioneering—if we agree to call it that—was, equally indisputably, bound up with the quest for a fast buck.

Some of their first clients paid as high as $15,000 for the initial freezing, and the exorbitant rate of $1,000 per year as a storage charge. The Zeritsky Brothers owned and managed one of the largest quick-freezing plants in the world, and it was their claim that converting the freezing equipment and storage facilities to accommodate humans was extremely expensive, hence the high rates.

When the early clients who paid these rates were defrosted years later, and found other clients receiving the same services for as little as $3,000, they threatened a row and the Zeritskys made substantial refunds. By that time they could easily afford it, and since any publicity about their enterprise was unwelcome to them, all refunds were made without a whimper. $3,000 became the standard rate, with $100 per year the storage charge, and no charge for defrosting.

The Zeritskys were businessmen, first and last. Anyone who had the fee could put himself away for whatever period of time he wished, and no questions asked. The ironclad rule that full payment must be made in advance was broken only once, as far as the records show.

A certain young man had a very wealthy uncle, residing in Milwaukee, whose heir he was, but the uncle was not getting along in years fast enough. The young man, then 18 years old, did not wish to waste the "best years of his life" as a poor boy. He wanted the money while he was young, but his uncle was as healthy as he was wealthy. The Zeritskys were the obvious answer to his problem.

The agreement between them has been preserved. They undertook to service the youth without advance payment. They further undertook to watch the Milwaukee papers until the demise of the uncle should be reported, whereupon they would defrost the boy. In exchange for this, the youth, thinking of course that money would be no object when he came out, agreed to pay double.

The uncle lived 17 years longer, during which time he seems to have forgotten his nephew and to have become deeply interested in a mystic society, to which he left his entire fortune. The Zeritskys duly defrosted the boy, and whether they or he were the more disappointed is impossible to imagine. They never forgot the lesson, and never made another exception to their rule.

He, poor fellow, spent, the rest of his life, including the best years, paying off his debt, which, at $3,000 plus 17 years at $100 per year, and the whole doubled, amounted to $9,400. The books record his slow but regular payments over the next 43 years, and indicate that he had only $250 left to pay when he died. We may, I think, assume that various underworld characters who were grateful ex-clients of the Zeritskys were instrumental in persuading the boy to keep up his payments.

Criminals were the first to apply for Quick-freezing, and formed the mainstay of the Zeritskys' business through the years. What more easy than to rob, hide the loot (except for that all-important advance payment), present yourself to the Zeritskys and remain in their admirable chambers for five or ten years, emerge to find the hue and cry long since died down and the crime forgotten, recover your haul and live out your life in luxury?

Due to the shady character of most of their patrons, the Zeritskys kept all records by a system of numbers. Names never appeared on the books, and anonymity was guaranteed.

Law enforcement agents, looking for fugitives from justice, found no way to break down this system, nor any law which they could interpret as making it illegal to quick-freeze. Perhaps the truth is that they did not search too diligently for a law that could be made to apply. As long as the Zeritskys kept things quiet and did not advertise or attract public attention, they could safely continue their bizarre business.

City officials of Los Angeles, and particularly members of the police force, enjoyed a period of unparalleled prosperity. Lawyers and other experts who thought they were on the track of legal means by which to liquidate the Zeritsky empire found themselves suddenly able to buy a ranch or a yacht or both, and retire forever from the arduous task of earning a living.

Even with a goodly part of the population of Los Angeles as permanent pensioners, the Zeritsky fortune grew to incredible proportions. By the time the Zeritsky Brothers died and left the business to their sons, it was a gold mine, and an inexhaustible one at that.

During these later years, the enterprise began to attract a somewhat better class of people. Murderers and other criminals continued to furnish the bulk of the business, but as word of this amazing service seeped through the country, others began to see in it an easy way of solving their problems. They were encouraged, too, by the fact that the process was painless, and the firm completely reliable. There were no risks, no accidents, no fatalities. One could, in short, have confidence in the Zeritskys.

Soon after Monahan's great exposure rocked the nation, however, many of these better-type clients leaped into print to tell their experiences.

One of the most poignant stories came from the daughter of a Zeritsky client. Her father was still, at the age of one hundred and two, passionately interested in politics, but the chances of his lasting until the next election were not good. The daughter herself suggested the deep freeze, and he welcomed the idea. He decided on a twenty-year stay because, in his own words, "If the

Republicans can't get into the White House in twenty years, I give up." Upon his return, he found that his condition had not been fulfilled. His daughter described him as utterly baffled by the new world. He lived in it just a week before he left it, this time for good. She states his last words were, "How do you people stand it?"

Some professional people patronized the Zeritskys, chiefly movie stars. After the expose, fan magazines were filled with accounts of how the stars had kept youthful. The more zealous ones had prolonged their screen lives for years by the simple expedient of storing themselves away between pictures. We may imagine the feelings of their public upon discovering that the seemingly eternal youth of their favorites was due to the Zeritskys and not, as they had been led to believe, to expensive creams, lotions, diet and exercise. There was a distinctly unfavorable reaction, and the letter columns of the fan magazines bristled with angry charges of cheating.

But next to criminals, the majority of people who applied for quick-freezing seem to have been husbands or wives caught in insupportable marital situations. Their experiences were subsequently written up in the confession magazines. It was usually the husband who fled to Los Angeles and incarcerated himself for an appropriate number of years, at the end of which time his unamiable spouse would have died or made other arrangements. If we can believe the magazines, this scheme worked out very well in most cases.

There was, inevitably, one spiteful wife who divined her husband's intentions. By shrewd reasoning, she figured approximately the number of years he had chosen to be absent, and put herself away for a like period. In a TV dramatization rather pessimistically entitled *You Can't Get Away*, the husband described his sensations upon being defrosted after 15 years, only to find his wife waiting for him, right there in the reception room of the Zeritsky plant.

"She was as perfectly preserved as I was," he said. "Every irritating habit that had made my life unbearable with her was absolutely intact."

The sins of the fathers may be visited on the sons, but how

often we see repeated the old familiar pattern of the sons destroying the lifework of the fathers! The Zeritsky Brothers were fanatically meticulous. They supervised every detail of their operations, and kept their records with an elaborate system of checks and double-checks. They were shrewd enough to realize that complete dependability was essential to their business. A satisfied Zeritsky client was a silent client. One dissatisfied client would be enough to blow the business apart.

The sons, in their greed, overexpanded to the point where they could not, even among the four of them, personally supervise each and every detail. A fatal mistake was bound to occur sooner or later. When it did, the victim broadcast his grievance to the world.

The story appeared in a national magazine, every copy of which was sold an hour after it appeared on the stands. Under the title *They Put the Freeze on Me!* John A. Monahan told his tragic tale. At the age of 37, he had fallen desperately in love with a girl of 16. She was immature and frivolous and wanted to "play around" a little more before she settled down.

"She told me," he wrote, "to come back in five years, and that started me thinking. In five years I'd be 42, and what would a girl of 21 want with a man twice as old as her?"

John Monahan moved in circles where the work of the Zeritskys was well known. Not only did he see an opportunity of being still only 37 when his darling reached 21, but he foresaw a painless way of passing the years, which he must endure without her. Accordingly, he presented himself for the deep-freeze, paid his $3,000 and the $500 storage charge in advance, and left, he claimed, "written instructions to let me out in five years, so there'd be no mistakes."

Nobody knows how the slip happened, but somehow John A. Monahan, or rather the number assigned to him, was entered on the books for 25 years instead of five years. Upon being defrosted, and discovering that a quarter of a century had elapsed, his rage was awesome. Along with everything else, his love for his sweetheart had been perfectly preserved, but she had given up waiting for him and was a happy mother of two boys and six girls.

Monahan's accusation that the Zeritskys had "ruined his life" may be taken with a grain of salt. He was still a young man, and the rumor that he received a hundred thousand for the magazine rights to his story was true.

As most readers are aware, what has come to be known, as "Zeritsky's Law" was passed by Congress and signed by the President three days after Monahan's story broke.

Seventy-five years after Mrs. Graham's cat fell into the freezer, it became the law of the land that the mandatory penalty for anyone applying quick-freezing methods to any living thing, human or animal, was death. Also, all quick-frozen people were to be defrosted immediately.

Los Angeles papers reported that beginning on the day Monahan's story appeared, men by the thousands poured into the city. They continued to come, choking every available means of transport, for the next two days—until, that is, Zeritsky's Law went through.

When we consider the date, and remember that due to the gravity of the international situation, a bill had just been passed drafting all men from 16 to 60, we realize why Congress had to act.

The Zeritskys, of course, were among the first to be taken. Because of their experience, they were put in charge of a military warehouse for dehydrated foods, and warned not to get any ideas for a new business.

THE END

With These Hands

By C. M. KORNBLUTH

No self-respecting artist can object to suffering for his art...but not in a society where art is outdated by technology!

CHAPTER ONE

HALVORSEN waited in the Chancery office while Monsignor Reedy disposed of three persons who had preceded him. He was a little dizzy with hunger and noticed only vaguely that the prelate's secretary was beckoning to him. He started to his feet when the secretary pointedly opened the door to Monsignor Reedy's inner office and stood waiting beside it.

The artist crossed the floor, forgetting that he had leaned his portfolio against his chair, remembered at the door and went back for it, flushing. The secretary looked patient.

"Thanks," Halvorsen murmured to him as the door closed.

There was something wrong with the prelate's manner.

"I've brought the designs for the Stations, Padre," he said, opening the portfolio on the desk.

"Bad news, Roald," said the monsignor. "I know how you've been looking forward to the commission—"

"Somebody else get it?" asked the artist faintly, leaning against the desk. "I thought his eminence definitely decided I had the—"

"It's not that," said the monsignor. "But the Sacred Congregation of Rites this week made a pronouncement on images of devotion. Stereopantograph is to be licit within a diocese at the discretion of the bishop. And his eminence—"

"S.P.G.—slimy imitations," protested Halvorsen. "Real as a plastic eye. No texture. No guts. You know that, Padre!" he said accusingly.

"I'm sorry, Roald," said the monsignor. "Your work is better than we'll get from a stereopantograph—to my eyes, at least. But there are other considerations."

"Money!" spat the artist.

"Yes, money," the prelate admitted. "His eminence wants to see the St. Xavier U. building program through before he dies. Is that a mortal sin? And there are our schools, our charities, our Venus mission. S.P.G. will mean a considerable saving on procurement and maintenance of devotional images. Even if I could, I would not disagree with his eminence on adopting it as a matter of diocesan policy."

The prelate's eyes fell on the detailed drawings of the Stations of the Cross and lingered.

"Your St. Veronica," he said abstractedly. "Very fine. It suggests one of Caravaggio's careworn saints to me. I would have liked to see her in the bronze."

"So would I," said Halvorsen hoarsely. "Keep the drawings, Padre." He started for the door.

"But I can't—"

"That's all right."

The artist walked past the secretary blindly and out of the Chancery into Fifth Avenue's spring sunlight. He hoped Monsignor Reedy was enjoying the drawings and was ashamed of himself and sorry for Halvorsen. And he was glad he didn't have to carry the heavy portfolio any more. Everything seemed so heavy lately—chisels, hammer, wooden palette. Maybe the padre would send him something and pretend it was for expenses or an advance, as he had in the past.

Halvorsen's feet carried him up the Avenue. No, there wouldn't be any advances any more. The last steady trickle of income had just been dried up, by an announcement in *Osservatore Romano*. Religious conservatism had carried the church as far as it would go in its ancient role of art patron.

When all Europe was writing on the wonderful new vellum, the church stuck to good old papyrus. When all Europe was writing on the wonderful new paper, the church stuck to good old vellum. When all architects and municipal monument committees and portrait bust clients were patronizing the stereopantograph, the church stuck to good old expensive sculpture. But not any more.

He was passing an S.P.G. salon now, where one of his Tuesday night pupils worked: one of the few men in the classes. Mostly they consisted of lazy, moody, irritable girls. Halvorsen, surprised at himself, entered the salon, walking between asthenic seminude stereos executed in transparent plastic that made the skin of his neck and shoulders prickle with gooseflesh.

Slime! he thought. *How can they*—

"May I help—oh, hello, Roald. What brings you here?"

He knew suddenly what had brought him there. "Could you make a little advance on next month's tuition, Lewis? I'm strapped." He took a nervous look around the chamber of horrors, avoiding the man's condescending face.

"I guess so, Roald. Would ten dollars be any help? That'll carry us through to the 25th, right?"

"Fine, right, sure," he said, while he was being unwillingly towed around the place.

"I know you don't think much of S.P.G., but it's quiet now, so this is a good chance to see how we work. I don't say it's Art with a capital A, but you've got to admit it's an art, something people like at a price they can afford to pay. Here's where we sit them. Then you run out the feelers to the reference points on the face. You know what they are?"

He heard himself say dryly: "I know what they are. The Egyptian sculptors used them when they carved statues of the pharaohs."

"Yes? I never knew that. There's nothing new under the Sun, is there? But *this* is the heart of the S.P.G." The youngster proudly swung open the door of an electronic device in the wall of the portrait booth. Tubes winked sullenly at Halvorsen.

"The esthetikon?" he asked indifferently. He did not feel indifferent, but it would be absurd to show anger, no matter how much he felt it, against a mindless aggregation of circuits that could calculate layouts, criticize and correct pictures for a desired effect—and that had put the artist of design out of a job.

"Yes. The lenses take sixteen profiles, you know, and we set the esthetikon for whatever we want—cute, rugged, sexy, spiritual, brainy, or a combination. It fairs curves from profile to profile to give us just what we want, distorts the profiles themselves within limits if it has to, and there's your portrait stored in the memory tank waiting to be taped. You set your ratio for any enlargement or reduction you want and play it back. I wish we were reproducing today; it's fascinating to watch. You just pour in your cold-set plastic, the nozzles ooze out a core and start crawling over to scan—a drop here, a worm there, and it begins to take shape.

"We mostly do portrait busts here, the Avenue trade, but Wilgus, the foreman, used to work in a monument shop in Brooklyn. He did that heroic-size war memorial on the East River Drive—hired Garda Bouchette, the TV girl, for the central figure. And what a figure! He told me he set the esthetikon plates for three-quarter sexy, one-quarter spiritual. Here's something interesting—standing figurine of Orin Ryerson, the banker. He ordered twelve. Figurines are coming in. The girls like them because they can show their shapes. You'd be surprised at some of the poses they want to try—"

SOMEHOW, Halvorsen got out with the ten dollars, walked to Sixth Avenue and sat down hard in a cheap restaurant. He had coffee and dozed a little, waking with a guilty start at a racket across the street. There was a building going up. For a while he watched the great machines pour walls and floors, the workmen rolling here and there on their little chariots to weld on a wall panel, stripe on an electric circuit of conductive ink, or spray plastic finish over the "wired" wall, all without leaving the saddles of their little mechanical chariots.

Halvorsen felt more determined. He bought a paper from a vending machine by the restaurant door, drew another cup of coffee and turned to the help wanted ads.

The tricky trade-school ads urged him to learn construction work and make big money. Be a plumbing-machine setup man. Be a house-wiring machine tender. Be a servotruck driver. Be a lumber-stacker operator. Learn pouring-machine maintenance.

Make big money!

A sort of panic overcame him. He ran to the phone booth and dialed a Passaic number. He heard the *ring-ring-ring* and strained to hear old Mr. Krehbeil's stumping footsteps growing louder as he neared the phone, even though he knew he would hear nothing until the receiver was picked up.

RING—ring—ring. "Hello?" grunted the old man's voice, and his face appeared on the little screen. "Hello, Mr. Halvorsen. What can I do for you?"

Halvorsen was tongue-tied. He couldn't possibly say: I just wanted to see if you were still there. I was afraid you weren't there any more. He choked and improvised: "Hello, Mr. Krehbeil. It's about the banister on the stairs in my place. I noticed it's pretty shaky. Could you come over sometime and fix it for me?"

Krehbeil peered suspiciously out of the screen. "I could do that," he said slowly. "I don't have much work nowadays. But you can carpenter as good as me Mr. Halvorsen, and frankly you're very slow pay and I like cabinetwork better. I'm not a young man and climbing around on ladders takes it out of me. If you can't find anybody else, I'll take the work, but I got to have some of the money first, just for the materials. It isn't easy to get good wood any more."

"All right," said Halvorsen. "Thanks, Mr. Krehbeil. I'll call you if I can't get anybody else."

He hung up and went back to his table and newspaper. His face was burning with anger at the old man's reluctance and his own foolish panic. Krehbeil didn't realize they were both in the same leaky boat. Krehbeil, who didn't get a job in a month, still thought with senile pride that he was a journeyman carpenter and cabinetmaker who could make his solid way anywhere with his toolbox and his skill, and that he could afford to look down on anything as disreputable as an artist—even an artist who could carpenter as well as he did himself.

Labuerre had made Halvorsen learn carpentry, and Labuerre had been right. You build a scaffold so you can sculpt up high, not so it will collapse and you break a leg. You build your platforms so they hold the rock steady, not so it wobbles and chatters at every blow of the chisel. You build your armatures so they hold the plasticine you slam onto them.

But the help-wanted ads wanted no builders of scaffolds, platforms and armatures. The factories were calling for setup men and maintenance men for the production and assembly machines.

From upstate, General Vegetables had sent a recruiting team for farm help—harvest setup and maintenance men, a few openings for experienced operators of tank-caulking machinery. Under "office and professional" the demand was heavy for computer men, for girls who could run the I.B.M. Letteriter, esp. familiar sales and collections corresp., for office machinery maintenance and repairmen. A job-printing house wanted an esthetikon operator for letterhead layouts and the like. A.T.&T wanted trainees to earn while learning telephone maintenance. A direct-mail advertising outfit wanted an artist—no, they wanted a sales-executive who could scrawl picture-ideas that would be subjected to the criticism and correction of the esthetikon.

Halvorsen leafed tiredly through the rest of the paper. He knew he wouldn't get a job, and if he did he wouldn't hold it. He knew it was a terrible thing to admit to yourself that you might starve to death because you were bored by anything except art, but he admitted it.

It had happened often enough in the past—artists undergoing preposterous hardships, not, as people thought, because they were devoted to art, but because nothing else was interesting. If there were only some impressive, sonorous word that summed up the aching, oppressive futility that overcame him when he tried to get out of art—only there wasn't.

He thought he could tell which of the photos in the tabloid had been corrected by the esthetikon.

There was a shot of Jink Bitsy, who was to star in a remake of *Peter Pan.* Her ears had been made to look not pointed but pointy, her upper lip had been lengthened a trifle, her nose had been pugged a little and tilted quite a lot, her freckles were cuter than cute, her brows were innocently arched, and her lower lip and eyes were nothing less than pornography.

There was a shot, apparently uncorrected, of the last Venus ship coming in at La Guardia and the average-looking explorers grinning. Caption: "Austin Malone and crew smile relief on safe arrival. Malone says Venus colonies need men, machines. See story p, 2."

Petulantly, Halvorsen threw the paper under the table and walked out. What had space travel to do with him? Vacations on the Moon and expeditions to Venus and Mars were part of the deadly encroachment on his livelihood and no more.

CHAPTER TWO

HE took the subway to Passaic and walked down a long-still traffic beltway to his studio, almost the only building alive in the slums near the rusting railroad freight yard.

A sign that had once said "F. Labuerre, Sculptor—Portraits and Architectural Commissions" now said "Roald Halvorsen; Art Classes—Reasonable Fees." It was a grimy two-story frame building with a shopfront in which were mounted some of his students' charcoal figure studies and oil still-lifes. He lived upstairs, taught downstairs front, and did his own work downstairs, back behind dirty, ceiling-high drapes.

Going in, he noticed that he had forgotten to lock the door again. He slammed it bitterly. At the noise, somebody called from behind the drapes: "Who's that?"

"Halvorsen!" he yelled in a sudden fury. "I live here. I own this place. Come out of there! What do you want?"

There was a fumbling at the drapes and a girl stepped between them, shrinking from their dirt.

"Your door was open," she said firmly, "and it's a shop. I've just been here a couple of minutes. I came to ask about classes, but I don't think I'm interested if you're this bad-tempered."

A pupil. Pupils were never to be abused, especially not now.

"I'm terribly sorry," he said. "I had a trying day in the city." Now turn it on. "I wouldn't tell everybody a terrible secret like this, but I've lost a commission. You understand? I thought so. Anybody who'd traipse out here to my dingy abode would be *simpatica*. Won't you sit down? No, not there—humor an artist and sit over there. The warm background of that still-life brings out your color—quite good color. Have you ever been painted? You've a very interesting face, you know. Some day I'd like to— but you mentioned classes.

"We have figure classes, male and female models alternating, on Tuesday nights. For that I have to be very stern and ask you to sign up for an entire course of twelve lessons at sixty dollars. It's the models' fees—they're exorbitant. Saturday afternoons we have still-life classes for beginners in oils. That's only two dollars a class, but you might sign up for a series of six and pay ten dollars in advance, which saves you two whole dollars. I also give private instructions to a few talented amateurs."

The price was open on that one—whatever the traffic would bear. It had been a year since he'd had a private pupil and she'd taken only six lessons at five dollars an hour.

"The still-life sounds interesting," said the girl, holding her head self-consciously the way they all did when he gave them the patter. It was a good head, carried well up. The muscles clung close, not yet slacked into geotropic loops and lumps. The line of youth is heliotropic, he confusedly thought. "I saw some interesting things back there. Was that your own work?"

She rose, obviously with the expectation of being taken into the studio. Her body was one of those long-lined, small-breasted, coltish jobs that the pre-Raphaelites loved to draw.

"Well—" said Halvorsen. A deliberate show of reluctance and then a bright smile of confidence. *"You'll* understand," he said positively and drew aside the curtains.

"What a curious place!" She wandered about, inspecting the drums of plaster, clay and plasticene, the racks of tools, the stands, the stones, the chisels, the forge, the kiln, the lumber, the glaze bench.

"I *like* this," she said determinedly, picking up a figure a half-meter tall, a Venus he had cast in bronze while studying under Labuerre, some years ago. "How much is it?"

An honest answer would scare her off, and there was no chance in the world that she'd buy. "I hardly ever put my things up for sale," he told her lightly. "That was just a little study. I do work on commission only nowadays."

Her eyes flicked about the dingy room, seeming to take in its scaling plaster and warped floor and see through the wall to the abandoned slum in which it was set. There was amusement in her glance.

I am not being honest, she thinks. She thinks that is funny. Very well, I will be honest. "Six hundred dollars," he said, flatly.

THE girl set the figurine on its stand with a rap and said, half-angry and half-amused: "I don't understand it. That's more than a month's pay for me. I could get an S.P.G. statuette just as pretty as this for ten dollars. Who do you artists think you are, anyway?"

Halvorsen debated with himself about what he could say in reply:

An S.P.G. operator spends a week learning his skill and I spend a lifetime learning mine.

An S.P.G. operator makes a mechanical copy of a human form distorted by formulae mechanically arrived at from psychotests of population samples. I take full responsibility for my work; it is mine, though I use what I see fit from Egypt, Greece, Rome, the Middle Ages, the Renaissance, the Augustan and Romantic and Modern Eras.

An S.P.G. operator works in soft, homogeneous plastic; I work in bronze that is more complicated than you dream, which is cast and acid-dipped today so it will slowly take on rich and subtle coloring many years from today.

An S.P.G. operator could not make an Orpheus Fountain—

He mumbled, "Orpheus," and keeled over.

HALVORSEN awoke in his bed on the second floor of the building. His fingers and toes buzzed electrically and he felt very clear-headed. The girl and a man, unmistakably a doctor, were watching him.

"You don't seem to belong to any Medical Plans, Halvorsen," the doctor said irritably. "There weren't any cards on you at all. No Red, no Blue, no Green, no Brown."

"I used to be on the Green Plan, but I let it lapse," the artist said defensively.

"And look what happened!"

"Stop nagging him!" the girl said. "I'll pay you your fee."

"It's supposed to come through a Plan," the doctor fretted.

"We won't tell anybody," the girl promised. "Here's five dollars. Just stop nagging him."

"Malnutrition," said the doctor. "Normally I'd send him to a hospital, but I don't see how I could manage it. He isn't on any Plan at all. Look, I'll, take the money and leave some vitamins. That's what he needs—vitamins. And food."

"I'll see that he eats," the girl said, and the doctor left.

"How long since you've had anything?" she asked Halvorsen.

"I had some coffee today," he answered, thinking back. "I'd been working on detail drawings for a commission and it fell through. I told you that. It was a shock."

"I'm Lucretia Grumman," she said, and went out.

He dozed until she came back with an armful of groceries.

"It's hard to get around down here," she complained.

"It was Labuerre's studio," he told her defiantly. "He left it to me when he died. Things weren't so rundown in his time. I studied under him; he was one of the last. He had a joke— They don't really want my stuff, but they're ashamed to let me starve.' He warned me that they wouldn't be ashamed to let me starve, but I insisted and he took me in."

Halvorsen drank some milk and ate some bread. He thought of the change from the ten dollars in his pocket and decided not to mention it. Then he remembered that the doctor had gone through his pockets.

"I can pay you for this," he said. "It's very kind of you, but you mustn't think I'm penniless. I've just been too preoccupied to take care of myself."

"Sure," said the girl. "But we can call this an advance. I want to sign up for some classes."

"Be happy to have you."

"Am I bothering you?" asked the girl. "You said something odd when you fainted—'Orpheus.'"

"Did I say that? I must have been thinking of Milles' Orpheus Fountain in Copenhagen. I've seen photos, but I've never been there."

"Germany? But there's nothing left of Germany."

"Copenhagen's in Denmark. There's quite a lot of Denmark left. It was only on the fringes. Heavily radiated, but still there."

"I want to travel, too," she said. "I work at La Guardia and I've never been off, except for an orbiting excursion. I want to go to the Moon on my vacation. They give us a bonus in travel vouchers. It must be wonderful dancing under the low gravity."

Spaceport? Off? Low gravity? Terms belonging to the detested electronic world of the stereopantograph in which he had no place.

"Be very interesting," he said, closing his eyes to conceal disgust.

"I *am* bothering you. I'll go away now, but I'll be back Tuesday night for the class. What time do I come and what should I bring?"

"Eight. It's charcoal—I sell you the sticks and paper. Just bring a smock."

"All right. And I want to take the oils class, too. And I want to bring some people I know to see your work. I'm sure they'll see something they like. Austin Malone's in from Venus—he's a special friend of mine."

"Lucretia," he said. "Or do some people call you Lucy?"

"Lucy."

"Will you take that little bronze you liked? As a thank you?"

"I can't do that!"

"Please. I'd feel much better about this. I really mean it."

She nodded abruptly, flushing, and almost ran from the room.

Now why did I do that? he asked himself. He hoped it was because he liked Lucy Grumman very much. He hoped it wasn't a cold-blooded investment of a piece of sculpture that would never be sold, anyway, just to make sure she'd be back with class fees and more groceries.

CHAPTER THREE

SHE was back on Tuesday, a half-hour early and carrying a smock. He introduced her formally to the others as they arrived: a dozen or so bored young women who, he suspected, talked a great deal about their art lessons outside, but in class used any excuse to stop sketching.

He didn't dare show Lucy any particular consideration. There were fierce little miniature cliques in the class. Halvorsen knew they laughed at him and his line among themselves, and yet, strangely, were fiercely jealous of their seniority and right to individual attention.

The lesson was an ordeal, as usual. The model, a muscle-bound young graduate of the barbell gyms and figure-photography studios, was stupid and argumentative about ten minute poses.

Two of the girls came near a hair-pulling brawl over the rights to a preferred sketching location. A third girl had discovered Picasso's cubist period during the past week and proudly announced that she didn't *feel* perspective in art.

But the two interminable hours finally ticked by. He nagged them into cleaning up—not as bad as the Saturdays with oils—and stood by the open door. Otherwise they would have stayed all night, cackling about absent students and snarling sulkily among themselves. His well-laid plans went sour, though. A large and flashy car drove up as the girls were leaving.

"That's Austin Malone," said Lucy. "He came to pick me up and look at your work."

That was all the wedge her fellow-pupils needed.

*"Aus-*tin Ma-*lone! Well!"*

"Lucy, darling. I'd love to meet a real *spaceman.*"

"Roald, darling, would you mind very much if I stayed a moment."

"I'm certainly not going to miss this and I don't care if you mind or not, Roald, darling!"

Malone was an impressive figure. Halvorsen thought: he looks as though he's been run through an esthetikon set for 'brawny' and 'determined.' Lucy made a hash of the introductions and the spaceman didn't rise to conversational bait dangled enticingly by the girls.

In a clear voice, he said to Halvorsen: "I don't want to take up too much of your time. Lucy tells me you have some things for sale. Is there any place we can look at them where it's quiet?"

The students made sulky exits.

"Back here," said the artist.

The girl and Malone followed him through the curtains. The spaceman made a slow circuit of the studio, seeming to repel questions.

He sat down at last and said; "I don't know what to think, Halvorsen. This place stuns me. Do you know you're in the Dark Ages?"

People who never have given a thought to Chartres and Mont St. Michel usually call it the Dark Ages, Halvorsen thought wryly. He asked, "Technologically, you mean? No, not at all. My plaster's better, my colors are better, my metal is better—tool metal, not casting metal, that is."

"I mean *hand* work," said the spaceman. "Actually working by *hand.*"

The artist shrugged. "There have been crazes for the techniques of the boiler works and the machine shop," he admitted. "Some interesting things were done, but they didn't stand up well. Is there anything here that takes your eye?"

"I like those dolphins." said the spaceman, pointing to a perforated terra-cotta relief on the wall. They had been commissioned by an architect, then later refused for reasons of economy when the house had run way over estimate. "They'd look bully over the fireplace in my town apartment. Like them, Lucy?"

"I think they're wonderful," said the girl.

Roald saw the spaceman go rigid with the effort not to turn and stare at her. He loved her and he was jealous.

Roald told the story of the dolphins and said: "The price that the architect thought was too high was three hundred and sixty dollars."

Malone grunted. "Doesn't seem unreasonable—if you set a high store on inspiration."

"I don't know about inspiration," the artist said evenly. "But I was awake for two days and two nights shoveling coal and adjusting drafts to fire that thing in my kiln."

The spaceman looked contemptuous. "I'll take it," he said. "Be something to talk about during those awkward pauses. Tell me, Halvorsen, how's Lucy's work? Do you think she ought to stick with it?"

"Austin," objected the girl, "don't be so blunt. How can he possibly know after one day?"

"She can't draw yet," the artist said cautiously. "It's all coordination, you know—thousands of hours of practice, training your eye and hand to work together until you can put a line on paper where you want it. Lucy, if you're really interested in it, you'll learn to draw well. I don't think any of the other students will. They're in it because of boredom or snobbery, and they'll stop before they have their eye-hand coordination."

"I *am* interested," she said firmly.

Malone's determined restraint broke. "Damned right you are. In—" He recovered himself and demanded of Halvorsen: "I understand your point about coordination. But thousands of hours when you can buy a camera? It's absurd."

"I was talking about drawing, not art," replied Halvorsen. "Drawing is putting a line on paper where you want it, I said." He took a deep breath and hoped the great distinction wouldn't sound ludicrous and trivial. "So let's say that art is knowing how to put the line in the right place."

"Be practical. There isn't any art. Not any more. I get around quite a bit and I never see anything but photos and S.P.G.'s. A few heirlooms, yes, but nobody's painting or carving any more."

"There's some art, Malone. My students—a couple of them in the still-life class—are quite good. There are more across the country. Art for occupational therapy, or a hobby, or something to do with the hands. There's trade in their work. They sell them to each other, they give them to their friends, they hang them on their walls. There are even some sculptors like that. Sculpture is prescribed by doctors. The occupational therapists say it's even better than drawing and painting, so some of these people work in plasticene and soft stone, and some of them get to be good."

"Maybe so. I'm an engineer, Halvorsen. We glory in doing things the easy way. Doing things the easy way got me to Mars and Venus and it's going to get me to Ganymede. You're doing things the hard way, and your inefficiency has no place in this world. Look at you! You've lost a fingertip—some accident, I suppose."

"I never noticed—" said Lucy, and then let out a faint. "Oh!"

Halvorsen curled the middle finger of his left hand into the palm, where he usually carried it to hide the missing first joint.

"Yes," he said softly. "An accident."

"Accidents are a sign of inadequate mastery of material and equipment," said Malone sententiously. "While you stick to your methods and I stick to mine, *you can't compete with me.*"

His tone made it clear that he was talking about more than engineering.

"Shall we go now, Lucy? Here's my card, Halvorsen. Send those dolphins along and I'll mail you a check."

CHAPTER FOUR

THE artist walked the half-dozen blocks to Mr. Krehbeil's place the next day. He found the old man in the basement shop of his fussy house, hunched over his bench with a powerful light overhead. He was trying to file a saw.

"Mr. Krehbeil!" Halvorsen called over the shriek of metal.

The carpenter turned around and peered with watery eyes. "I can't see like I used to," he said querulously. "I go over the same teeth on this damn saw, I skip teeth, I can't see the light shine off it when I got one set. The glare." He banged down his three-cornered file petulantly. "Well, what can I do for you?"

"I need some crating stock. Anything. I'll trade you a couple of my maple four-by-fours."

The old face became cunning.

"And will you set my saw? My saws, I mean. It's nothing to you—an hour's work. You have the eyes."

Halvorsen said bitterly, "All right." The old man had to drive his bargain, even though he might never use his saws again. And then the artist promptly repented of his bitterness, offering up a quick prayer that his own failure to conform didn't make him as much of a nuisance to the world as Krehbeil was.

The carpenter was pleased as they went through his small stock of wood and chose boards to crate the dolphin relief. He was pleased enough to give Halvorsen coffee and cake before the artist buckled down to filing the saws.

Over the kitchen table, Halvorsen tried to probe. "Things pretty slow now?"

It would be hard to spoil Krehbeil's day now. "People are always fools. They don't know good handwork. Some day," he said apocalyptically, "I laugh on the other side of my face when their foolish machine-buildings go falling down in a strong wind, all of them, all over the country. Even my boy—I used to beat him good, almost every day—he works a foolish concrete machine and his house should fall on his head like the rest."

Halvorsen knew it was Krehbeil's son who supported him by mail, and changed the subject. "You get some cabinet work?"

"Stupid women! What they call antiques—they don't know Meissen, they don't know Biedermeier. They bring me trash to repair sometimes. I make them pay; I swindle them good."

"I wonder if things would be different if there were anything left over in Europe..."

"People will still be fools, Mr. Halvorsen," said the carpenter positively. "Didn't you say you were going to file those saws today?"

So the artist spent two noisy hours filing before he carried his crating stock to the studio.

LUCY was there. She had brought some things to eat. He dumped the lumber with a bang and demanded: "Why aren't you at work?"

"We get days off," she said vaguely. "Austin thought he'd give me the cash for the terracotta and I could give it to you."

She held out an envelope while he studied her silently. The farce was beginning again. But this time he dreaded it.

It would not be the first time that a lonesome, discontented girl chose to see him as a combination of romantic rebel and lost pup, with the consequences you'd expect.

He knew from books, experience and Labuerre's conversation in the old days that there was nothing novel about the comedy— that there had even been artists, lots of them, who had counted on endless repetitions of it for their livelihood.

The girl drops in with groceries and the artist is pleasantly surprised; the girl admires this little thing or that after payday and buys it and the artist is pleasantly surprised; the girl brings her friends to take lessons or make little purchases and the artist is pleasantly surprised. The girl may be seduced by the artist or vice versa, which shortens the comedy, or they get married, which lengthens it somewhat.

It had been three years since Halvorsen had last played out the farce with a manic-depressive divorcee from Elmira: three years during which he had crossed the mid-point between thirty and forty; three more years to get beaten down by being unwanted and working too much and eating too little.

Also, he knew, he was in love with this girl.

He took the envelope, counted three hundred and twenty dollars and crammed it into his pocket. "That was your idea," he said. "Thanks. Now get out, will you? I've got work to do."

She stood there, shocked.

"I said get out. I have work to do."

"Austin was right," she told him miserably. "You don't care how people feel. You just want to get things out of them."

She ran from the studio, and Halvorsen fought with himself not to run after her.

He walked slowly into his workshop and studied his array of tools, though he paid little attention to his finished pieces. It would be nice to spend about half of this money on open-hearth steel rod and bar stock to forge into chisels; he thought he knew where he could get some—but she would be back, or he would break and go to her and be forgiven and the comedy would be played out, after all.

He couldn't let that happen.

CHAPTER FIVE

AALESUND, on the Atlantic side of the Dourefeld mountains of Norway, was in the lee of the blasted continent. One more archeologist there made no difference, as long as he had the sense to recognize the propeller-like international signposts that said with their three blades, *Radiation Hazard,* and knew what every schoolboy knew about protective clothing and reading a personal Geiger counter.

The car Halvorsen rented was for a brief trip over the mountains to study contaminated Oslo. Well-muffled, he could make it and back in a dozen hours and no harm done.

But he took the car past Oslo, Wennersborg and Goteborg, along the Kattegat coast to Helsingborg, and abandoned it there, among the three-bladed polyglot signs, crossing to Denmark. Danes were as unlike Prussians as they could be, but their unfortunate little peninsula was a sprout off Prussia which radio-cobalt dust couldn't tell from the real thing. The three-bladed signs were most specific.

With a long way to walk along the rubble-littered highways, he stripped off the impregnated coveralls and boots. He had long since shed the noisy counter and the uncomfortable gloves and mask.

The silence was eerie as he limped into Copenhagen at noon. He didn't know whether the radiation was getting to him or whether he was tired and hungry and no more. As though thinking of a stranger, he liked what he was doing.

I'll be my own audience, he thought. God knows I learned there isn't any other, not any more. You have to know when to stop. Rodin, the dirty old, wonderful old man, knew that. He taught us not to slick it and polish it and smooth it until it looked like liquid instead of bronze and stone. Van Gogh was crazy as a loon, but he knew when to stop and varnish it, and he didn't care if the paint looked like paint instead of looking like sunset clouds or moonbeams. Up in Hartford, Browne and Sharpe stop when they've got a turret lathe; they don't put caryatids on it. I'll stop while my life is a life, before it becomes a thing with distracting embellishments such as a wife who will come to despise me, a succession of gradually less worthwhile pieces that nobody will look at.

Blame nobody, he told himself, light-headedly.

And then it was in front of him, terminating a vista of weeds and bomb rubble—Milles' Orpheus Fountain.

It took a man, he thought. Esthetikon circuits couldn't do it. There was a gross mixture of styles, a calculated flaw that the esthetikon couldn't be set to make. Orpheus and the souls were classic or later; the three-headed dog was archaic. That was to tell you about the antiquity and invincibility of Hell, and that Cerberus knows Orpheus will never go back into life with his bride.

There was the heroic, tragic central figure that looked mighty enough to battle with the gods, but battle wasn't any good against the grinning, knowing, hateful three-headed dog it stood on. You don't battle the pavement where you walk or the floor of the house you're in; you can't. So Orpheus, his face a mask of controlled and suffering fury, crashes a great chord from his lyre that moved trees and stones. Around him the naked souls in Hell start at the chord, each in its own way: the young lovers down in death; the mother down in death; the musician, deaf and down in death, straining to hear.

Halvorsen, walking uncertainly toward the fountain, felt something break inside him, and a heaviness in his lungs. As he pitched forward among the weeds, he thought he heard the chord from the lyre and didn't care that the three-headed dog was grinning its knowing, hateful grin down at him.

CHAPTER SIX

WHEN Halvorsen awoke, he supposed he was in Hell. There were the young lovers' arms about each others' waists, solemnly looking down at him, and the mother was placidly smoothing his brow. He stirred and felt his left arm fall heavily.

"Ah," said the mother, "you mustn't." He felt her pick up his limp arm and lay it across his chest. "Your poor finger!" she sighed. "Can you talk? What happened to it?"

He could talk, weakly. "Labuerre and I," he said. "We were moving a big block of marble with the crane—somehow the finger got under it. I didn't notice until it was too late to shift my grip without the marble slipping and smashing on the floor."

The boy said in a solemn, adolescent croak: "You mean you saved the marble and lost your finger?"

"Marble," he muttered. "It's so hard to get. Labuerre was so old."

The young lovers exchanged a glance and he slept again. He was half-awake when the musician seized first one of his hands and then the other, jabbing them with stubby fingers and bending his lion's head close to peer at the horny callouses left by chisel and mallet.

"*Ja, ja,*" the musician kept saying.

Hell goes on forever, so for an eternity he jolted and jarred, and for an eternity he heard bickering voices: "Why he was so foolish, then?" "A idiot he could be." "Hush, let him rest." "The children told the story." "There only one Labuerre was." "Easy with the tubing." "Let him rest."

Daylight dazzled his eyes. "Why you were so foolish?" demanded a harsh voice. "The sister says I can talk to you now, so that is what I first want to know."

He looked at the face of—not the musician; that had been delirium. But it was a tough old face.

"*Ja,* I am mean-looking; that is settled. What did you think you were doing without coveralls and way over your exposure time?"

"I wanted to die," said Halvorsen. There were tubes sticking in his arms.

The crag-faced old man let out a contemptuous bellow.

"Sister!" he shouted. "Pull the plasma tubes out before more we waste. He says he wants to die."

"Hush," said the nurse. She laid her hand on his brow again.

"Don't bother with him, Sister," the old man jeered. "He is a shrinking little flower, too delicate for the great, rough world. He has done nothing, he can do nothing, so he decides to make of himself a nuisance by dying."

"You lie," said Halvorsen. "I worked. Good God, how I worked! Nobody wanted my work. They wanted me to wear in their buttonholes like a flower. They were getting to me. Another year and I wouldn't have been an artist any more."

"*Ja?*" asked the old man. "Tell me about it."

Halvorsen told him, sometimes weeping with self-pity and weakness, sometimes cursing the old man for not letting him die, sometimes quietly describing this statuette or that portrait head, or raving wildly against the mad folly of the world.

At the last he told the old man about Lucy.

"You cannot have everything, you know," said his listener.

"I can have her," answered the artist harshly. "You wouldn't let me die, so I won't die. I'll go back and I'll take her away from that fathead Malone that she ought to marry. I'll give her a couple of happy years working herself to skin and bones for me before she begins to hate it—before I begin to hate it."

"You can't go back," said the old man. "I'm Cerberus. You understand that? The girl is nothing. The society you come from is nothing. We have a place here... Sister, can he sit up?"

The woman smiled and cranked his bed. Halvorsen saw through a picture window that he was in a mountain-rimmed valley that was very green and dotted with herds and unpainted houses.

"Such a place there had to be," said the old man. "In the whole geography of Europe, there had to be a Soltau Valley with winds and terrain just right to deflect the dust."

"Nobody knows?" whispered the artist.

"We prefer it that way. It's impossible to get some things, but you would be surprised how little difference it makes to the young people. They are great travelers, the young people, in their sweaty coveralls with radiation meters. They think when they see the ruined cities that the people who lived in them must have been mad. It was a little travel party like that which found you. The boy was impressed by something you said, and I saw some interesting things in your hands. There isn't much rock around here; we have fine deep topsoil. But the boys could get you stone.

"There should be a statue of the Mayor for one thing, before I die. And from the Rathaus the wooden angels have mostly broken off. Soltau Valley used to be proud of them—could you make good copies? And of course cameras are useless and the best drawings we can do look funny. Could you teach the youngers at least to draw so faces look like faces and not behinds? And like you were saying about you and Labuerre, maybe one younger there will be so crazy that he will want to learn it all, so Soltau will always have an artist and sculptor for the necessary work. And you will find a Lucy or somebody better. I think better."

"Hush," warned the nurse. "You're exciting the patient."

"It's all right," said Halvorsen eagerly. "Thanks, but it's really all right."

THE END

The Trouble With Ants

By CLIFFORD D. SIMAK

*In the Earth's distant future, Man has seemingly vanished. There were dogs
and robots in his place—and ants...*

ARCHIE, the little renegade raccoon, crouched on the hillside,
trying to catch one of the tiny, scurrying things running in the
grass.   Rufus, Archie's robot, tried to talk to Archie, but the
raccoon was too busy and he did not answer.

Homer did a thing no Dog had ever done before. He crossed
the river and trotted into the wild robots' camp and he was scared,
for there was no telling what the wild robots might do to him when
they turned around and saw him. But he was worried worse than
he was scared, so he trotted on.

Deep in a secret nest, ants dreamed and planned for a world
they could not understand. And pushed into that world, hoping
for the best, aiming at a thing no Dog, or robot, or man could
understand.

In Geneva, Jon Webster rounded out his ten-thousandth year of
suspended animation and slept on, not stirring.   In the street
outside, a wandering breeze rustled the leaves along the boulevard,
but no one heard and no one saw.

Jenkins strode across the hill and did not look to either left or
right, for there were things he did not wish to see. There was a tree
that stood where another tree had stood in another world. There
was the lay of ground that had been imprinted on his brain with a
billion footsteps across ten thousand years.

And, if one listened closely one might have heard laughter
echoing down the ages...the sardonic laughter of a man named
Joe.

ARCHIE caught one of the scurrying things and held it
clutched within his tight-shut paw. Carefully he lifted the paw and
opened it and the thing was there, running madly, trying to escape.

"Archie," said Rufus, "you aren't listening to me."

The scurrying thing dived into Archie's fur, streaked swiftly up his forearm.

"Might have been a flea," said Archie. He sat up and scratched his belly.

"New kind of flea," he said. "Although I hope it wasn't. Just the ordinary kind are bad enough."

"You aren't listening," said Rufus.

"I'm busy," said Archie. "The grass is full of them things. Got to find out what they are."

"I'm leaving you, Archie."

"You're what!"

"Leaving you," said Rufus. "I'm going to the Building."

"You're crazy," fumed Archie. "You can't do a thing like that to me. You've been tetched ever since you fell into that ant hill…"

"I've had the Call," said Rufus. "I just got to go."

"I've been good to you," the raccoon pleaded. "I've never overworked you. You've been like a pal of mine instead of like a robot. I've always treated you just like an animal."

Rufus shook his head stubbornly. "You can't make me stay," he said. "I couldn't stay, no matter what you did. I got the Call and I got to go."

"It isn't like I could get another robot," Archie argued. "They drew my number and I ran away. I'm a deserter and you know I am. You know I can't get another robot with the wardens watching for me."

Rufus just stood there.

"I need you," Archie told him. "You got to stay and help me rustle grub. I can't go near none of the feeding places or the wardens will nab me and drag me up to Webster Hill. You got to help me dig a den. Winter's coming on and I will need a den. It won't have heat or light, but I got to have one. And you've got to…"

Rufus had turned around and was walking down the hill, heading for the river trail. Down the river trail…traveling toward the dark smudge above the far horizon.

Archie sat hunched against the wind that ruffled through his fur, tucked his tail around his feet. The wind had a chill about it, a chill it had not held an hour or so before. And it was not the chill of the weather, but the chill of other things.

His bright, beady eyes searched the hillside and there was no sign of Rufus.

No food, no den, no robot. Hunted by the wardens. Eaten up by fleas.

And the Building, a smudge against the farther hills across the river valley.

A hundred years ago, so the records said, the Building had been no bigger than the Webster House.

But it had grown since...a place that never was completed. First it had covered an acre. And then a square mile. Now finally a township. And still it grew, sprawling out and towering up.

A smudge above the hills and a cloudy terror for the little, superstitious forest folks who watched it. A word to frighten kit and whelp and cub into sudden quiet.

FOR THERE was evil in it...the evil of the unknown, an understood evil, an evil sensed and attributed rather than seen or heard or smelled. A sensed evil, especially in the dark of night, when the lights were out and the wind keened in the den's mouth and the other animals were sleeping, while one lay awake and listened to the pulsing *otherness* that sang between the worlds.

Archie blinked in the autumn sunlight, scratched furtively at his side.

Maybe someday, he told himself, someone will find a way to handle fleas. Something to rub on one's fur so they will stay away. Or a way to reason with them, to reach them and talk things over with them. Maybe set up a reservation for them, a place where they could stay and be fed and not bother animals. Or something of the sort.

As it was, there wasn't much that could be done. You scratched yourself. You had your robot pick them off, although the robot usually got more fur than fleas. You rolled in the sand or dust. You went for a swim and drowned some of them...well, you really didn't drown them; you just washed them off and if some of them drowned that was their own tough luck.

You had your robot pick them off...but now there was no robot.

No robot to pick off fleas.

No robot to help him hunt for food.

But, Archie remembered there was a black haw tree down in the river bottom and last night's frost would have touched the fruit. He smacked his lips, thinking of the haws. And there was a cornfield just over the ridge. If one was fast enough and bided his time and was sneaky about it, it was no trouble at all to get an ear of corn. And if worse came to worse there always would be roots and wild acorns and that patch of wild grapes over on the sand bar.

"Let Rufus go," said Archie, mumbling to himself. Let the Dogs keep their feeding stations. Let the wardens go on watching.

He would live his own life. He would eat fruit and grub for roots and raid the cornfields, even as his remote ancestors had eaten fruit and grubbed for roots and raided fields.

He would live as the other raccoons had lived before the Dogs had come along with their ideas about the Brotherhood of Beasts. Like animals had lived before they could talk with words, before they could read the printed books that the Dogs provided, before they had robots that served in lieu of hands, before there was warmth and light for dens.

Yes, and before there was a drawing that told you if you stayed on Earth or went to another world.

The Dogs, Archie remembered, had been quite persuasive about it, very reasonable and suave. Some animals, they said, had to go to the other worlds or there would be too many animals on Earth. Earth wasn't big enough, they said, to hold everyone. And a drawing, they pointed out, was the fair way to decide which of them would go to the other worlds.

And, after all, they said, the other worlds would be almost like the Earth. For they were just extensions of the Earth. Just other worlds following in the track of Earth. Not quite like it, perhaps, but very close. Just a minor difference here and there. Maybe no tree where there was a tree on Earth. Maybe an oak tree where Earth had a walnut tree. Maybe a spring of fresh, cold water where there was no such spring on Earth.

Maybe, Homer had told him, growing very enthusiastic...maybe the world he would be assigned to would be a better world than Earth.

Archie hunched against the hillside, felt the warmish sun of autumn cutting through the cold chill of autumn's wind. He thought about the black haws. They would be soft and mushy and there would be some of them lying on the ground. He would eat those that were on the ground, then he'd climb the tree and pick some more and then he'd climb down again and finish off the ones he had shaken loose with his climbing of the tree.

He'd eat them and take them in his paws and smear them on his face. He might even roll in them.

Out of the corner of one eye, he saw the scurrying things running in the grass. Like ants, he thought, only they weren't ants. At least, not like any ants he'd ever seen before.

Fleas, maybe. A new kind of flea.

His paw darted out and snatched one up. He felt it running in his palm. He opened the paw and saw it running there and closed the paw again.

He raised his paw to his ear and listened.

The thing he'd caught was ticking!

THE WILD robot camp was not at all the way Homer had imagined it would be. It was not a camp and it was not a city. It was scarcely anything. There were no buildings and there were no streets. Just launching ramps and three spaceships and half a dozen robots working on one of the ships.

Although, come to think of it, Homer told himself, one should have known there would be no buildings in a robot camp. For the robots would have no use of shelter and that was all a building was.

Homer was scared, but he tried hard not to show it. He curled his tail over his back and carried his head high and his ears well forward and trotted toward the little group of robots, never hesitating. When he reached them, he sat down and lolled out his tongue and waited for one of them to speak.

But when none of them did, he screwed up his courage and spoke to them, himself.

"My name is Homer," he said, "and I represent the Dogs. If you have a head robot, I would like to talk to him."

The robots kept on working for a minute, but finally one of them turned around and came over and squatted down beside Homer so that his head was level with the dog's head. All the other robots kept on working as if nothing had happened.

"I am a robot called Andrew," said the robot squatting next to Homer, "and I am not what you would call the head robot, for we have no such thing among us. But I can speak with you."

"I came to you about the Building," Homer told him.

"I take it," said the robot called Andrew, "that you are speaking of the structure to the northeast of us. The one you can see from here if you just turn around."

"That's the one," said Homer. "I came to ask why you are building it."

"But we aren't building it," said Andrew.

"We have seen robots working on it."

"Yes, there are robots working there. But we are not building it."

"You are helping someone else?"

Andrew shook his head. "Some of us get a call...a call to go and work there. The rest of us do not try to stop them, for we are all free agents."

"But who is building it?" asked Homer.

"The ants," said Andrew.

Homer's jaw dropped slack. "Ants? You mean the insects. The little things that live in ant hills?"

"Precisely," said Andrew. He made the fingers of one hand run across the sand like a harried ant.

"But they couldn't build a place like that," protested Homer. "They are stupid."

"Not any more," said Andrew.

Homer sat stock still, frozen to the sand and felt the chilly feet of terror run along his nerves.

"Not any more," said Andrew, talking to himself. "Not stupid any more. You see once upon a time, there was a man named Joe..."

"A man? What's that?" asked Homer.

The robot made a clucking noise, as if gently chiding Homer.

"Men were animals," he said. "Animals that went on two legs. They looked very much like us except they were flesh and we are metal."

"You must mean the websters," said Homer. "We know about things like that, but we call them websters."

The robot nodded slowly. "Yes, the websters could be men. There was a family of them by that name. Lived just across the river."

"There's a place called Webster House," said Homer. "It stands on Webster Hill."

"That's the place," said Andrew.

"We keep it up," said Homer. "It's a shrine to us, but we don't understand just why. It is the word that has been passed down to us...we must keep Webster House."

"The Websters," Andrew told him, "were the ones that taught you Dogs to speak."

Homer stiffened. "No one taught us to speak. We taught ourselves. We developed in the course of many years. And we taught the other animals."

ANDREW, the robot sat hunched in the sun, nodding his head as if he might be thinking to himself.

"Ten thousand years," he said. "No, I guess it's nearer twelve. Around eleven, maybe."

Homer waited and as he waited he sensed the weight of years that pressed against the hills...the years of river and of sun, of sand and wind and sky.

And the years of Andrew.

"You are old," he said. "You can remember that far back?"

"Yes," said Andrew. "Although I am one of the last of the man-made robots. I was made just a few years before they went to Jupiter."

Homer sat silently, tumult stirring in his brain.

Man...a new word.

An animal that went on two legs.

An animal that made the robots, that taught the Dogs to talk.

And, as if he might be reading Homer's mind, Andrew spoke to him.

"You should not have stayed away from us," he said. "We should have worked together. We worked together once. We both would have gained if we had worked together."

"We were afraid of you," said Homer. "I am still afraid of you."

"Yes," said Andrew. "Yes, I suppose you would be. I suppose Jenkins kept you afraid of us. For Jenkins was a smart one. He knew that you must start afresh. He knew that you must not carry the memory of Man as a dead weight on your necks."

Homer sat silently.

"And we," the robot said, "are nothing more than the memory of Man. We do the things he did, although more scientifically, for, since we are machines, we must be scientific. More patiently than Man, because we have forever and he had a few short years."

Andrew drew two lines in the sand, crossed them with two other lines. He made an X in the open square in the upper left-hand corner.

"You think I'm crazy," he said. "You think I'm talking through my hat."

Homer wriggled his haunches deeper into the sand.

"I don't know what to think," he said. "All these years..."

Andrew drew an O with his finger in the center square of the crosshatch he had drawn in the sand.

"I know," he said. "All these years you have lived with a dream. The idea that the Dogs were the prime movers. And the facts are hard to understand, hard to reconcile. Maybe it would be just as well if you forgot what I said. Facts are painful things at times. A robot has to work with them, for they are the only things he has to work with. We can't dream, you know. Facts are all we have."

"We passed fact long ago," Homer told him. "Not that we don't use it, for there are times we do. But we work in other ways. Intuition and cobbling and listening."

"You aren't mechanical," said Andrew. "For you, two and two are not always four, but for us it must be four. And sometimes I wonder if tradition doesn't blind us. I wonder sometimes if two and two may not be something more or less than four."

They squatted in silence, watching the river, a flood of molten silver tumbling down a colored land.

Andrew made an X in the upper right-hand corner of the crosshatch, an O in the center upper space, and X in the center lower space. With the flat of his hand, he rubbed the sand smooth.

"I never win," he said. "I'm too smart for myself."

"You were telling me about the ants," said Homer. "About them not being stupid any more."

"Oh, yes," said Andrew. "I was telling you about a man named Joe..."

JENKINS strode across the hill and did not look to either left or right, for there were things he did not wish to see, things that struck too deeply into memory. There was a tree that stood where another tree had stood in another world. There was the lay of ground that had been imprinted on his brain with a billion footsteps across ten thousand years.

The weak winter sun of afternoon flickered in the sky, flickered like a candle guttering in the wind, and when it steadied and there was no flicker it was moonlight and not sunlight at all.

Jenkins checked his stride and swung around and the house was there...low-set against the ground, sprawled across the hill, like a sleepy young thing that clung close to mother earth.

Jenkins took a hesitant step and as he moved his metal body glowed and sparkled in the moonlight that had been sunlight a short heartbeat ago.

From the river valley came the sound of a night bird crying and a raccoon was whimpering in a cornfield just below the ridge. Jenkins took another step and prayed the house would stay...although he knew it couldn't because it wasn't there. For this was an empty hilltop that had never known a house. This was another world in which no house existed.

The house remained, dark and silent, no smoke from the chimneys, no light from the windows, but with remembered lines that one could not mistake.

Jenkins moved slowly, carefully, afraid the house would leave, afraid that he would startle it and it would disappear.

But the house stayed put. And there were other things. The tree at the corner had been an elm and now it was an oak, as it had been before. And it was autumn moon instead of winter sun. The breeze was blowing from the west and not out of the north.

Something happened, thought Jenkins. The thing that has been growing on me. The thing I felt and could not understand. An ability developing? Or a new sense finally reaching light? Or a power I never dreamed I had.

A power to walk between the worlds at will. A power to go anywhere I choose by the shortest route that the twisting lines of force and happenstance can conjure up for me.

He walked less carefully and the house still stayed, unfrightened, solid and substantial.

He crossed the grass-grown patio and stood before the door.

Hesitantly, he put out a hand and laid it on the latch. And the latch was there. No phantom thing, but substantial metal.

Slowly he lifted it and the door swung in and he stepped across the threshold.

After five thousand years, Jenkins had come home...back to Webster House.

SO THERE was a man named Joe. Not a webster, but a man. For a webster was a man. And the Dogs had not been first.

Homer lay before the fire, a limp pile of fur and bone and muscle, with his paws stretched out in front of him and his head resting on his paws. Through half closed eyes he saw the fire and shadow, felt the heat of the blazing logs reach out and fluff his fur.

But inside his brain he saw the sand and the squatting robot and the hills with the years upon them.

Andrew had squatted in the sand and talked, with the autumn sun shining on his shoulders...had talked of men and dogs and ants. Of a thing that had happened when Nathaniel was alive, and that was a time long gone, for Nathaniel was the first Dog.

There had been a man named Joe...a mutant-man, a more-than-man...who had wondered about ants twelve thousand years ago. Wondered why they had progressed so far and then no farther, why they had reached the dead end of destiny.

Hunger, perhaps, Joe had reasoned...the ever-pressing need to garner food so that they might live. Hibernation, perhaps, the stagnation of the winter sleep, the broken memory chain, the starting over once again, each year a genesis for ants.

So, Andrew said, his baldpate gleaming in the sun, Joe had picked one hill, had set himself up as a god to change the destiny of ants. He had fed them, so that they need not strive with hunger. He had enclosed their hill in a dome of glassite and had heated it so they need not hibernate.

And the thing had worked. The ants advanced. They fashioned carts and they smelted ore. This much one could know, for the carts were on the surface and acrid smelting smoke came from the chimneys that thrust up from the hill. What other things they did, what other things they learned, deep down in their tunnels, there was no way of knowing.

Joe was crazy, Andrew said. Crazy...and yet, maybe not so crazy either.

For one day he broke the dome of glassite and tore the hill asunder with his foot, then turned and walked away, not caring any more what happened to the ants.

But the ants had cared.

The hand that broke the dome, the foot that ripped the hill had put the ants on the road to greatness. It had made them fight...fight to keep the things they had, fight to keep the bottleneck of destiny from closing once again.

A kick in the pants, said Andrew. A kick in the pants for ants. A kick in the right direction.

Twelve thousand years ago a broken, trampled hill. Today a mighty building that grew with each passing year. A building that had covered a township in one short century, that would cover a hundred townships in the next. A building that would push out and take the land. Land that belonged, not to ants, but animals.

A building...and that was not quite right, although it had been called the Building from the very start. For a building was a shelter, a place to hide from storm and cold. The ants would have no need of that, for they had their tunnels and their hills.

Why would an ant build a place that sprawled across a township in a hundred years and yet that kept on growing? What possible use could an ant have for a place like that?

Homer nuzzled his chin deep into his paws, growled inside his throat.

There was no way of knowing. For first you had to know how an ant would think. You would have to know her ambition and her goal. You would have to probe her knowledge.

Twelve thousand years of knowledge. Twelve thousand years from a starting point that itself was unknowable.

But one had to know. There must be a way to know.

FOR, YEAR after year, the Building would push out. A mile across, and then six miles and after that a hundred. A hundred miles and then another hundred and after that the world.

Retreat, thought Homer. Yes, we could retreat. We could migrate to those other worlds, the worlds that follow us in the stream of time, the worlds that tread on one another's heels. We could give the Earth to ants and there still would be space for us.

But this is home. This is where the Dogs arose. This is where we taught the animals to talk and think and act together. This is the place where we created the Brotherhood of Beasts.

For it does not matter who came first...the webster or the dog. This place is home. Our home as well as webster's home. Our home as well as ants.

And we must stop the ants.

There must be a way to stop them. A way to talk to them, find out what they want. A way to reason with them. Some basis for negotiation. Some agreement to be reached.

Homer lay motionless on the hearth and listened to the whisperings that ran through the house, the soft, far-off padding of robots on their rounds of duties, the muted talk of Dogs in a room upstairs, the crackling of the flames as they ate along the log.

"A good life," said Homer, muttering to himself. A good life and we thought we were the ones who made it. Although Andrew says it wasn't us. Andrew says we have not added one iota to the mechanical skill and mechanical logic that was our heritage...and that we have lost a lot. He spoke of chemistry and he tried to explain, but I couldn't understand. The study of elements, he said, and things like molecules and atoms. And electronics...although he said we did certain things without the benefit of electronics more wonderfully than man could have done with all his knowledge. You might study electronics for a million years, he said, and not reach those other worlds, not even know they're there...and we did it, we did a thing a webster could not do.

Because we think differently than a webster does. No, it's man, not webster.

And the robots. The robots are no better than the ones that were left to us by man. A minor modification here and there...an obvious modification, but no real improvement.

Who ever would have dreamed there could be a better robot?

A better ear of corn, yes. Or a better walnut tree. Or a wild rice that would grow a fuller head. A better way to make the yeast that substitutes for meat.

But a better robot...why, a robot does everything we might wish that it could do. Why should it be better?

And yet...the robots receive a call and go off to work on the Building, to build a thing that will push us off the Earth.

We do not understand. Of course, we cannot understand. If we knew our robots better, we might understand. Understanding, we might fix it so that the robots would not receive the call, or, receiving it, would pay it no attention.

And that, of course, would be the answer. If the robots did not work, there would be no building. For the ants, without the aid of robots, could not go on with their building.

A flea ran along Homer's scalp and he twitched his ear.

Although Andrew might be wrong, he told himself. We have our legend of the rise of the Brotherhood of Beasts and the wild robots have their legend of the fall of man. At this date, who is there to tell which of the two is right?

But Andrew's story does tie in. There were Dogs and there were robots and when man fell they went their separate ways...although we kept some of the robots to serve as hands for us. Some robots stayed with us, but no dogs stayed with the robots.

A LATE autumn fly buzzed out of a corner, bewildered in the firelight. It buzzed around Homer's head and settled on his nose. Homer glared at it and it lifted its legs and insolently brushed its wings. Homer dabbed at it with a paw and it flew away.

A knock came at the door.

Homer lifted his head and blinked at the knocking sound.

"Come in," he finally said. It was the robot, Hezekiah.

"They caught Archie," Hezekiah said.

"Archie?"

"Archie, the raccoon."

"Oh, yes," said Homer. "He was the one that ran away."

"They have him out here now," said Hezekiah. "Do you want to see him?"

"Send them in," said Homer.

Hezekiah beckoned with his finger and Archie ambled through the door. His fur was matted with burs and his tail was dragging. Behind him stalked two robot wardens.

"He tried to steal some corn," one of the wardens said, "and we spotted him, but he led us quite a chase."

Homer sat up ponderously and stared at Archie. Archie stared straight back.

"They never would have caught me," Archie said, "if I'd still had Rufus. Rufus was my robot and he would have warned me."

"And where is Rufus now?"

"He got the call today," said Archie, "and left me for the Building."

"Tell me," said Homer. "Did anything happen to Rufus before he left—? Anything unusual? Out of the ordinary?"

"Nothing," Archie told him. "Except that he fell into an ant hill. He was a clumsy robot. A regular stumble bum...always tripping himself, getting tangled up. He wasn't co-ordinated just the way he should be. He had a screw loose someplace."

Something black and tiny jumped off of Archie's nose, raced along the floor. Archie's paw went out in a lightning stroke and scooped it up.

"You better move back a ways," Hezekiah warned Homer. "He's simply dripping fleas."

"It's not a flea," said Archie, puffing up in anger. "It is something else. I caught it this afternoon. It ticks and it looks like an ant, but it isn't one."

The thing that ticked oozed between Archie's claws and tumbled to the floor. It landed right side up and was off again. Archie made a stab at it, but it zigzagged out of reach. Like a flash it reaches Hezekiah and streaked up his leg.

Homer came to his feet in a sudden flash of knowledge.

"Quick!" he shouted. "Get it! Catch it! Don't let it…"

But the thing was gone.

Slowly Homer sat down again. His voice was quiet now, quiet and almost deadly.

"Wardens," he said, "take Hezekiah into custody. Don't leave his side, don't let him get away. Report to me everything he does."

Hezekiah backed away.

"But I haven't done a thing."

"No," said Homer, softly. "No, you haven't yet. But you will. You'll get the Call and you'll try to desert us for the Building. And before we let you go, we'll find out what it is that made you do it. What it is and how it works."

Homer turned around, a doggish grin wrinkling up his face.

"And, now, Archie…"

But there was no Archie.

There was an open window. And there was no Archie.

HOMER stirred on his bed of hay, unwilling to awake, a growl gurgling in his throat.

Getting old, he thought. Too many years upon me, like the years upon the hills. There was a time when I'd be out of bed at the first sound of something at the door, on my feet, with hay sticking in my fur, barking my head off to let the robots know.

The knock came again and Homer staggered to his feet.

"Come in," he yelled. "Cut out the racket and come in."

The door opened and it was a robot, but a bigger robot than Homer had ever seen before. A gleaming robot, huge and massive, with a polished body that shone like slow fire even in the dark. And riding on the robot's shoulder was Archie, the raccoon.

"I am Jenkins," said the robot. "I came back tonight."

Homer gulped and sat down very slowly.

"Jenkins," he said. "There are stories...legends...from the long ago."

"No more than a legend?" Jenkins asked.

"That's all," said Homer. "A legend of a robot that looked after us. Although Andrew spoke of Jenkins this afternoon as if he might have known him. And there is a story of how the Dogs gave you a body on your seven thousandth birthday and it was a marvelous body that..."

His voice ran down...for the body of the robot that stood before him with the raccoon perched on his shoulder...that body could be none other than the birthday gift.

"And Webster House?" asked Jenkins. "You still keep Webster House?"

"We still keep Webster House," said Homer. "We keep it as it is. It's a thing we have to do."

"The websters?"

"There aren't any websters."

Jenkins nodded at that. His body's hair-trigger sense had told him there were no websters. There were no webster vibrations. There was no thought of websters in the minds of things he'd touched.

And that was as it should be.

He came slowly across the room, soft-footed as a cat despite his mighty weight, and Homer felt him moving, felt the friendliness and kindness of the metal creature, the protectiveness of the ponderous strength within him.

Jenkins squatted down beside him.

"You are in trouble," Jenkins said.

Homer stared at him.

"The ants," said Jenkins. "Archie told me. Said you were troubled by the ants."

"I went to Webster House to hide," said Archie. "I was scared you would hunt me down again and I thought that Webster House..."

"Hush, Archie," Jenkins told him. "You don't know a thing about it. You told me that you didn't. You just said the Dogs were having trouble with the ants."

He looked at Homer.

"I suppose they are Joe's ants," he said.

"So you know about Joe," said Homer. "So there was a man called Joe."

Jenkins chuckled. "Yes, a troublemaker. But likeable at times. He had the devil in him."

Homer said: "They're building. They get the robots to work for them and they are putting up a building."

"Surely," said Jenkins, "even ants have the right to build."

"But they're building too fast. They'll push us off the Earth. Another thousand years or so and they'll cover the whole Earth if they keep on building at the rate they've been."

"And you have no place to go? That's what worries you."

"Yes, we have a place to go. Many places. All the other worlds. The cobbly worlds."

JENKINS nodded gravely. "I was in a cobbly world. The first world after this. I took some websters there five thousand years ago. I just came back tonight. And I know the way you feel. No other world is home. I've hungered for the Earth for almost every one of those five thousand years. I came back to Webster House and I found Archie there. He told me about the ants and so I came up here. I hope you do not mind."

"We are glad you came," said Homer, softly.

"These ants," said Jenkins. "I suppose you want to stop them."

Homer nodded his head.

"There is a way," said Jenkins. "I know there is a way. The websters had a way if I could just remember. But it's so long ago. And it's a simple way, I know. A very simple way."

His hand came up and scraped back and forth across his chin.

"What are you doing that for?" Archie asked.

"Eh?"

"Rubbing your face that way. What do you do it for?"

Jenkins dropped his hand. "Just a habit, Archie. A webster gesture. A way they had of thinking. I picked it up from them."

"Does it help you think?"

"Well, maybe. Maybe not. It seemed to help the websters. Now what would a webster do in a case like this? The websters could help us. I know they could..."

"The websters in the cobbly world," said Homer.

Jenkins shook his head. "There aren't any websters there."

"But you said you took some back."

"I know. But they aren't there now. I've been alone in the cobbly world for almost four thousand years."

"Then there aren't websters anywhere. The rest went to Jupiter. Andrew told me that. Jenkins, where is Jupiter?"

"Yes, there are," said Jenkins. "There are some websters left, I mean. Or there used to be. A few left at Geneva."

"It won't be easy," Homer said. "Not even for a webster. Those ants are smart. Archie told you about the flea he found."

"It wasn't any flea," said Archie.

"Yes, he told me," Jenkins said. "Said it got onto Hezekiah."

"Not onto," Homer told them. "Into is the word. It wasn't a flea...it was a robot, a tiny robot. It drilled a hole in Hezekiah's skull and got into his brain. It sealed the hole behind it."

"And what is Hezekiah doing now?"

"Nothing," said Homer. "But we are pretty sure what he will do as soon as the ant robot gets the setup fixed. He'll get the Call. He'll get the call to go and work on the Building."

Jenkins nodded. "Taking over," he said. "They can't do a job like that themselves, so they take control of things that can."

He lifted his hand again and scraped it across his chin.

"I wonder if Joe knew," he mumbled. "When he played god to the ants I wonder if he knew."

But that was ridiculous. Joe never could have known. Even a mutation like Joe could not have looked twelve thousand years ahead.

SO LONG ago, thought Jenkins. So many things have happened. Bruce Webster was just starting to experiment with dogs, had no more than dreamed his dream of talking, thinking dogs that would go down the path of destiny paw in hand with Man...not knowing then that Man within a few short centuries would scatter to the four winds of eternity and leave the Earth to robot and to dog. Not knowing then that even the name of Man would be forgotten in the dust of years, that the race would come to be known by the name of a single family.

And yet, thought Jenkins, if it was to be any family, the Websters were the ones. I can remember them as if it were yesterday. Those were the days when I thought of myself as a Webster, too.

Lord knows, I tried to be. I did the best I could. I stood by the Webster dogs when the race of men had gone and finally I took the last bothersome survivors of that madcap race into another world to clear the way for Dogs...so that the Dogs could fashion the Earth in the way they planned.

And now even those last bothersome survivors have gone...someplace, somewhere...I wish that I could know. Escaped into some fantasy of the human mind. And the men on Jupiter are not even men, but something else. And Geneva is shut off...blocked off from the world.

Although it can't be farther away or blocked more tightly than the world from which I came. If only I could learn how it was I traveled from the exile cobbly world back to Webster House...then, maybe, perhaps, somehow or other, I could reach Geneva.

A new power, he told himself. A new ability. A thing that grew upon me without my knowing that it grew. A thing that every man and every robot...and perhaps every dog...could have if he but knew the way.

Although it may be my body that made it possible...this body that the Dogs gave me on my seven thousandth birthday. A body that has more than any body of flesh and blood has ever quite attained. A body that can know what a bear is thinking or a fox is dreaming...that can feel the happy little mouse thoughts running in the grass.

Wish fulfillment. That might be it. The answer to the strange, illogical yearnings for things that seldom are and often cannot be. But all of which are possible if one knows the way, if one can grow or develop or graft onto oneself the new ability that directs the mind and body to the fulfillment of the wish.

I walked the hill each day, he remembered. Walked there because I could not stay away, because the longing was so strong, steeling myself against looking too closely, for there were differences I did not wish to see.

I walked there a million times and it took that many times before the power within me was strong enough to take me back.

For I was trapped. The word, the thought, the concept that took me into the cobbly world was a one way ticket and while it took me there it could not take me back. But there was another way, a way I did not know. That even now I do not know.

"You said there was away," urged Homer.

"A way?"

"Yes, a way to stop the ants."

Jenkins nodded. "I am going to find out. I'm going to Geneva."

JON WEBSTER awoke. And this is strange, he thought, for I said eternity.

I was to sleep forever and forever has no end.

All else was mist and the greyness of sleep forgetfulness, but this much stood out with mind-sharp clarity. Eternity, and this was not eternity.

A word ticked at his mind, like feeble tapping on a door that was far away.

He lay and listened to the tapping and the word became two words...words that spoke his name:

"Jon Webster. Jon Webster." On and on, on and on. Two words tapping at his brain.

"Jon Webster."

"Jon Webster."

"Yes," said Webster's brain and the words stopped and did not come again.

Silence and the thinning of the mists of forgetfulness. And the trickling back of memory. One thing at a time.

There was a city and the name of the city was Geneva.

Men lived in the city, but men without a purpose.

The Dogs lived outside the city...in the whole world outside the city. The Dogs had purpose and a dream.

Sara climbed the hill to take a century of dreams.

And I...I, thought Jon Webster, climbed the hill and asked for eternity. This is not eternity.

"This is Jenkins, Jon Webster."

"Yes, Jenkins," said Jon Webster, and yet he did not say it, not with lip and tongue and throat, for he felt the fluid that pressed around his body inside its cylinder, fluid that fed him and kept him from dehydrating. Fluid that sealed his lips and eyes and ears.

"Yes, Jenkins," said Webster, speaking with his mind. "I remember you. I remember you now. You were with the family from the very first. You helped us teach the Dogs. You stayed with them when the family was no more."

"I am still with them," said Jenkins.

"I sought eternity," said Webster. "I closed the city and sought eternity."

"We often wondered," Jenkins told him. "Why did you close the city?"

"The Dogs," said Webster's mind. "The Dogs had to have their chance. Man would have spoiled their chance."

"The dogs are doing well," said Jenkins.

"But the city is open now?"

"No, the city still is closed."

"But you are here."

"Yes, but I'm the only one who knows the way. And there will be no others. Not for a long time, anyway."

"Time," said Webster. "I had forgotten time. How long is it, Jenkins?"

"Since you closed the city? Ten thousand years or so."

"And there are others?"

"Yes, but they are sleeping."

"And the robots? The robots still keep watch?"

"The robots still keep watch."

Webster lay quietly and a peace came upon his mind. The city still was closed and the last of men were sleeping. The Dogs were doing well and the robots stayed on watch.

"You should not have wakened me," he said. "You should have let me sleep."

"There was a thing I had to know. I knew it once, but I have forgotten and it is very simple. Simple and yet terribly important."

Webster chuckled in his brain. "What is it, Jenkins?"

"It's about ants," said Jenkins. "Ants used to trouble men. What did you do about it?"

"Why, we poisoned them," said Webster.

Jenkins gasped. "Poisoned them!"

"Yes," said Webster. "A very simple thing. We used a base of syrup, sweet, to attract the ants. And we put poison in it, a poison that was deadly to ants. But we did not put in enough of it to kill them right away. A slow poison, you see, so they would have time to carry it to the nest. That way we killed many instead of just two or three."

Silence hummed in Webster's head...the silence of no thought, no word.

"Jenkins," he said. "Jenkins, are you..."

"Yes, Jon Webster, I am here."

"That is all you want?"

"That is all I want."

"I can go to sleep again."

"Yes, Jon Webster. Go to sleep again."

JENKINS stood upon the hilltop and felt the first rough forerunning wind of winter whine across the land. Below him the slope that ran down to the river was etched in black and grey with the leafless skeletons of trees.

To the northeast rose the shadow-shape, the cloud of evil omen that was called the Building. A growing thing spawned in the mind of ants, built for what purpose and to what end no thing but an ant could even closely guess.

But there was a way to deal with ants.

The human way.

The way Jon Webster had told him after ten thousand years of sleep. A simple way and a fundamental way, a brutal, but efficient way. You took some syrup, sweet, so the ants would like it, and you put some poison in it...slow poison so it wouldn't work too fast.

The simple way of poison, Jenkins said. The very simple way.

Except it called for chemistry and the Dogs knew no chemistry.

Except it called for killing and there was no killing.

Not even fleas, and the Dogs were pestered plenty by the fleas. Not even ants...and the ants threatened to dispossess the animals of the world they called their birthplace.

There had been no killing for five thousand years or more. The idea of killing had been swept from the minds of things.

And it is better that way, Jenkins told himself. Better that one should lose a world than go back to killing.

He turned slowly and went down the hill.

Homer would be disappointed, he told himself.

Terribly disappointed when he found the websters had no way of dealing with the ants...

THE END

The Isolationists

By GEORGE OSBORNE

Consider the far tomorrow, when benevolent Earthmen cruise around creation, offering culture to all intelligent aliens they can find—particularly those aliens whose own culture is hopelessly bemired in peace and stability. Macintyre is one of these happy Earthmen with a mission but—mistake not—his task is not always an easy one!

AS THE SMALL planet took shape in his screens, Macintyre felt the usual twinge of anticipation. Once, as a boy on Earth twenty years before, Macintyre had contemplated a boulder by the side of a swift-flowing stream for a long moment, then tipped it over. Revealed in the moist soil beneath the boulder were wonders: white grubs three inches long, with sparkling green eyes and furious little mandibles.

Macintyre had never forgotten that incident. It was written large on his mind every time he prepared to make first landing on an unexplored planet; one never knew what gaudy surprises might lie hidden and waiting.

Macintyre checked his charts. The planet was the fourth of a fourteen-planet system, but it was the only one of the fourteen that looked habitable. The Mapping Corps had ticketed it for future survey. The calibrating computer keyed into his ship's mass-detector told Macintyre that the planet was of .75 Earthmass: a 7000-mile diameter, but therefore lower in density and short of heavy elements. Macintyre set up landing coordinates at once. His instructions were to visit every reasonably Earthtype planet along the sine-wave curve of his tracking course; he was to file a report on the status of the planet's inhabitants, if intelligent, and on the feasibility of Terran colonization, there.

The planet was inhabited—the little red star on his master chart told him that much. Macintyre wondered what particular grubs would lay underneath this stone. Inhabited planets were always full of surprises, and first contact came as a different sort of shock to different kinds of beings.

HIS SHIP dropped lower. It swung into a landing orbit, and roared through the thickening atmosphere toward the tawny land below. He wondered if the alien beings of this world were gathering to mark his blazing path through their skies.

He selected a continent on his tenth orbital pass, activated the braking jets. The small ship's tail dropped into landing position.

A stretch of clear flat land beckoned. Macintyre jabbed the landing buttons, and flames sprouted beneath his ship. He dropped gently down on a fiery cushion. The ship seated itself to a square upright landing.

He had arrived. The stone had been tipped. Now to see what was beneath!

THE ALIENS did not arrive on the scene for nearly ten minutes, which allowed Macintyre something of a breather in which to look around. He did not roam far from his ship. The samplers had shown him that the planet's atmosphere was a chlorine one, with lesser quantities of nitrogen and the inerts. He wore a breathing-helmet strapped over his uniform, since no more than two good whiffs of that atmosphere would be enough to scald his throat and rot his lungs.

The sky was a light yellow—due partly, Macintyre decided, to the murky wisps of chlorine drifting above, and partly to some refractive trick of the atmosphere. It was an oddly attractive effect, at any rate. The landscape was strangely rugged, with bare rock scooped into shell-like depressions by erosive action. Strange, almost surrealistic trees sprang up high, jointed and involute, twisted grotesquely, crested with bizarre and disturbing-looking flowers. In the distance, Macintyre saw buildings, sleek and colorfully fashioned, evidently, from some form of pink coral. A few birds drifted in the sky. Macintyre watched one come to light in an angular tree; the bird landed on a spatulate limb in an inverted position, as if it had sucker-pads instead of claws, and began to nibble on the pendulous fruits.

AFTER HIS first detailed glance at the landscape, Macintyre unshipped the portable Translator and set it up. He busied himself over the installation, jacking the input to his instrument belt and rigging a booster in case the aliens refused to approach near enough for the Translator's amplifier to reach them.

But his precautions were unnecessary. A voice said in crisp and unaccented Terran, "There will be no need of that machine, Earthman. We will be able to understand you fully."

The nine-year-old Macintyre had gasped in awed delight at the sight of the writhing grubs beneath the stone. The twenty-nine-year-old Macintyre whirled like a stung cat when the firm voice spoke.

"Who said that?"

"We did."

Macintyre turned and saw the aliens. There were seven of them in a tight group about a hundred yards to his left. Macintyre had not seen them approach. And, he thought, at this distance and in this sort of atmosphere it was odd that he had heard them so clearly.

They were beings as angular as the trees—six and a half or seven feet tall. Macintyre estimated, with rich purple skins. He doubted if any of them would weigh as much as a hundred pounds under Terran gravity; here, they were even lighter.

They did not seem to have any flesh; they were merely skin stretched over bone, and light bone at that. Their heads were diamond-shaped and hairless, with long solemn chins and tapering pointed skulls; their nostrils were but slits, their mouths dark slashes, their eyes cold and hooded, their ears nonexistent. Macintyre guessed that they were a cold-blooded race. There was something reptilian about them. Their legs were like sticks, terminating in splayed claws.

They walked toward Macintyre in a body.

THE EARTHMAN looked uncertainly at the advancing aliens, then at his Translator. "You speak my language?"

"We speak all languages." It was impossible to tell which member of the group had spoken. Perhaps none of them had; perhaps all.

"You must be telepaths, then."

"Yes."

Can you understand what I'm saying? Macintyre thought. There was no response.

"I've just thought a message at you," said the Earthman. "Didn't you get it?"

"We can only respond to supraliminal projection from you, Earthman. We reach the deep layer of your mind, but cannot detect surface thoughts."

Macintyre frowned. He didn't care for that sort of arrangement. But, after all, he *had* dealt with telepathic races before. In a way, this made things a good deal easier, for if they could see the deep layers of his mind they would not have to worry about his sincerity. They could tell whenever he was lying, and Macintyre did not intend to lie.

HE SAID, "I'm not a telepath myself."

"Of course. But we can communicate with you."

"Good. Since you've looked deep into my mind, you know I've come here for peaceful purposes." There was no reply, and Macintyre went on with somewhat less assurance: "You *do* know that I'm here for peaceful purposes. I'm a representative of the Terran Confederation, a group of one hundred ninety worlds of the galaxy, offering mutual benefits and harmonious fellowship. Now, since this is the first landing an Earthman has made on your planet, you undoubtedly want time to think matters over, and…"

Macintyre was on the verge of launching into the standard *take-me-to-your-leader* pitch when the calm voice of the aliens—he saw now that the voice was collectively emanating from the group—interrupted him. "You are not the first Earthman to land here."

The statement, taken at its face value, made no sense. According to the charts, the planet was unexplored. Had the Mapping Corps outfit made a planetary landing? Unlikely. Had a previous Surveyor visited the planet and neglected to report the fact? Implausible. Had an unauthorized Earthman made an independent landing on an unexplored world? Impossible.

"I don't understand," Macintyre said. "How could other Earthmen have landed here? I mean…"

"YOU ARE the third one. The other two came in ships just like yours."

"When?"

"The first was eleven years ago. The second was five years after that."

"Local years?"

"Terran years."

Macintyre frowned, deeply troubled. Unreported visits by Survey men? What possible reason could a Survey man have for not reporting a planetfall? And why would it happen twice, years apart?

He took a deep breath. "At any rate, the Terran Confederation offers you…"

"We are not interested."

"At least let me tell you…"

The implacable mental voice cut him off once again. "We will join no Confederations. We do not want Earthmen landing on our planet."

MACINTYRE took a deep breath. He had run up across this sort of insularity and intransigence before, and he had special persuasive techniques to overcome it. Earth was geared to an infinitely expanding economy; it needed an infinitely expanding market as well, and with such conditions prevailing it was imperative that all possible avenues of trade be opened.

He said. "Please don't be hasty. At least let me explain the value of entering into friendly relationship with our Confederation. For instance, it would be possible to carry on trade without the necessity of a single space ship landing on your soil. If…"

"We are not interested."

"Give me a few minutes. In my ship I have solido slides that will be helpful in…"

"No."

Macintyre began to feel exasperated. "Why won't you listen to me?"

"We have maintained our independence for many thousands of years. Our economy and ecology are balanced with equal precision. We are self-sufficient. We have no need of Earth and its Confederation."

"What would you do if we *forced* you to trade with us?" Macintyre said rashly. He doubted that Earth would go along with him on the use of force but he wanted to see the alien reaction.

It was a mild one. "You would not do such a thing."

"Suppose we did?"

"You would not succeed."

"Why not?"

"You *could* not succeed."

MACINTYRE scowled. The seven aliens had not changed expression once during the colloquy, indeed had hardly as much as moved—yet, the door was slammed firmly in his face. These people wanted to remain in isolation. That much was abundantly clear. But Macintyre did not give up easily.

"You owe a debt to the universe," he began, taking an abstract approach. "Your planet, your solar system, are all part of the great celestial machine. Do you think you can withdraw yourself totally from that machine? No planet is an island, friends. There has to be an intermeshing of gears. Otherwise you'll pay the price of cultural decadence. You'll go the way of all..."

"We have survived successfully for many thousands of years. Our society is stable. We are not interested in the meddling ways of Earthmen. We made this clear to the other Earthmen who visited us."

"I don't know anything about them."

"They were like you. Stubborn, self-willed, convinced of their own possession of eternal truth. Spouting generalizations about the universe, fuzzy analogies, crude and pathetic syllogisms. Leave us, Earthman."

"Hold on a second," Macintyre burst out. "I'm a duly-accredited ambassador from the Terran Confederation. I don't intend to be brushed off this way. I demand to be taken to someone in authority on this planet!"

"We are all equals here," said the alien voice. It sounded tired; impatient, perhaps. "Return to your ship. Depart. Do not return."

"I won't leave until I've spoken to someone who…"

"You will leave immediately."

"What if I don't?"

MACINTYRE felt the equivalent of a mental shrug. "We are peaceful and passive people. We would not take direct steps to harm you. But if you fail to leave, you will cause harm to come to yourself."

"Please," Macintyre wheedled. "Don't fly off the handle. Let me try to tell you…!"

"You have been warned," came the weary reply.

"But…"

Macintyre heard two gentle plopping sounds above him. For an instant, he did not understand; then he swiveled his head upward and he understood.

A chill quivered through him. He realized in that single panicky instant that he was about to die.

"YOU WILL not be harmed if you return to your ship at once," came the alien voice.

Macintyre stared. One of the birds he had seen in the strange trees had plummeted down and landed atop his breathing-helmet. Its sucker-equipped feet were firmly attached to the plastic dome. The bird was the size of a small hen, blue, with a bright red crest and glittering beady eyes. A conspicuous feature of the bird was its sharp and imposing beak.

At the moment, that beak was clamped around Macintyre's left-hand breathing-tube. One switch of the creature's jaws and the rubber tube would be severed; his air would rush out, and the deadly alien atmosphere come filtering in.

Macintyre tentatively reached his left arm up to pluck the bird away.

The alien voice said quietly, "The bird will sever your breathing-tube before you are able to remove him. You will die almost immediately."

Macintyre stared with popping eyes. The bird had made no attempt to bite into the tube yet; it simply sat there on Macintyre's helmet, grasping the tube in its beak and remaining motionless.

Macintyre froze. Any motion, he felt, might disturb the bird.

"Get him off me," he whispered harshly.

"The tube of your helmet closely resembles the large green worm of the flatlands which is this bird's chief food," the aliens remarked. "The bird is anxious to feed. Only our control is preventing him from doing so."

SWEAT TRICKLED down Macintyre's forehead faster than his air-conditioners could pump his helmet dry. "What do you want me to do?"

"Walk slowly toward your ship."

"And if I don't?"

"We will order the bird to sever the tube. You see, the choice is entirely in your hands. Refusal to enter your ship would be tantamount to suicide."

"You'll—*order*—the bird?"

"All life on this planet is in harmony, Earthman. This is why we have no need of your Confederation. The bird understands our orders—but the bird is hungry, Earthman."

Macintyre did not need further hints. He began to edge across the flat terrain, slowly, cautiously, as if the creature perched on his helmet were highly explosive. He was twenty feet from his ship. The twenty feet seemed to last forever.

At length he reached the open hatch of the ship. His alien tormentors were eyeing him gravely from where they stood.

"All right," Macintyre growled, "I'm back at my ship. Call off your bird!"

"Enter the ship."

"With the bird?"

"The bird will leave you."

BITTERLY, Macintyre grabbed the handhold and pulled himself up into the hatchway. Just before he drew himself back into the ship, he heard two loud popping sounds, and saw the blue bird fluttering up into the air.

He exhaled feelingly. Having those pincers on his air-tube had been like having a hand round his throat.

The bird hovered ominously in the air a few feet above Macintyre's ship, flying in a tight little circle, obviously ready to pounce once again if Macintyre should attempt to quit his ship. But Macintyre knew that this time the beak would close, and he remained where he was.

"Is your answer final?" he said to the aliens.

"Our ecology is a closed cycle and our economy is stable. We value our stability. We have no desire for contact, Earthman."

Macintyre nodded. The door had slammed shut. Short of coercion, there was no way to make these beings see reason.

He glowered at the hovering bird. He scowled at the motionless knot of aliens. He frowned at the whole weird landscape and yellow sky.

Failure.

Macintyre's hand grasped the actuating lever of the airlock control. He yanked. The metal sheath rolled smoothly into place, blotting out bird and aliens and landscape and sky.

Minutes later, his ship was streaking out of the chlorinated atmosphere and heading for space.

MACINTYRE knew now why the two previous Survey men had neglected to mention the fact of their visits to the small world. Obviously, they had been too humiliated to care to record their encounter in the official record. The planet was an ecological whole; apparently the lean purple humanoids were merely first among equals. And the planet's inhabitants wanted to remain as they were—isolated.

They would have cooperated to repulse any invasion. They had driven Macintyre away with a bird the size of a hen—it isn't easy to sell Confederation when your air-tube is in imminent danger of puncture—and no doubt they had been equally imaginative in driving away the two previous Survey men. Macintyre amused himself by trying to picture the scene. A cloud of gnats? A horde of small lizards? It didn't matter. Humanity could not hope to win a conflict waged against the total inhabitants of a world. Defeating humanoids is possible; but when the birds and insects—and perhaps even the filterable viruses—join the fray, victory for the Confederation would become impossible.

MACINTYRE brooded long and hard before he tapped out his report on the planet. The easiest thing to do would be simply to neglect to mention the stop, as his predecessors had done; but Macintyre was too conscientious for that. He had to file a report.

He filed it.

Report of Survey Scout J. F. Macintyre on World Four of System 107b332.

Planet is inhabited by intelligent life. Contact was made but dominant life-forms show little interest in galactic affairs. Hostile non-intelligent life-forms make the planet highly undesirable. This operative nearly lost his life in an encounter with a dangerous native life-form. Probability of other hostile life-forms is high.

Recommendation: This planet's inhabitants are not promising members of the Confederation nor is the planet itself suitable for Terran habitation. Therefore it seems unwise to attempt further contact with this world.

Macintyre typed the report out on the black-bordered paper used for negative reports, and dropped the completed report in the polar facsimilizer. An electronic impulse flickered out along the subspace channels, and an instant later a reproduction of his report had arrived at the main headquarters of the Survey Corps, on Earth.

Macintyre knew the procedure. The report would be filed in the *negative* bank and all references to World Four of System 107b332 would be altered to show the planet as not suitable for contact. In the course of events, Macintyre's negative report would come up for review, as regulations provided. He would be called upon to explain his reasons for filing such a report.

But, at last word, the Central Board was fifty years behind on reviewing. Macintyre shrugged and set up the coordinates for his next stop. By the time they got around to calling him up for an explanation, he would be pensioned off and no longer concerned with matters of pride. But, just for now, Macintyre thought with a red face, it was better that no one found out that on World Four of System 107b332 the mighty Terran Confederation had been repulsed by a bright-colored bird the size of a small hen.

THE END

Venus Is A Man's World

By WILLIAM TENN

Actually, there wouldn't be too much difference if women took over the Earth altogether. But not for some men and most boys!

I'VE always said that even if Sis is seven years older than me—and a girl besides—she don't always know what's best. Put me on a spaceship jam-packed with three hundred females just aching to get themselves husbands in the one place they're still to be had—the planet Venus—and you know I'll be in trouble.

Bad trouble. With the law, which is the worst a boy can get into.

Twenty minutes after we lifted from the Sahara Spaceport, I wriggled out of my acceleration hammock and started for the door of our cabin.

"Now you be careful, Ferdinand," Sis called after me as she opened a book called *Family Problems of the Frontier Woman.* "Remember you're a nice boy. Don't make me ashamed of you."

I tore down the corridor. Most of the cabins had purple lights on in front of the doors, showing that the girls were still inside their hammocks. That meant only the ship's crew was up and about. Ship's crews are men; women are too busy with important things like government to run ships. I felt free all over—and happy. Now was my chance to really see the *Eleanor Roosevelt!*

IT WAS hard to believe I was traveling in space at last. Ahead and behind me, all the way up to where the companionway curved in out of sight, there was nothing but smooth black wall and smooth white doors—on and on and on. *Gee,* I thought excitedly, *this is one big ship!*

Of course; every once in a while I would run across a big scene of stars in the void set in the wall; but they were only pictures. Nothing that gave the feel of great empty space like I'd read about in *The Boy Rocketeers,* no portholes, no visiplates, nothing.

So when I came to the crossways, I stopped for a second, then turned left. To the right, see, there was Deck Four, then Deck Three, leading inward past the engine fo'c'sle to the main jets and the grav helix going *purr-purr-purrty-purr* in the comforting way big machinery has when it's happy and oiled. But to the left, the crossway led all the way to the outside level, which ran just under the hull. There were portholes on the hull.

I'd studied all that out in our cabin, long before we'd lifted, on the transparent model of the ship hanging like a big cigar from the ceiling. Sis had studied it too, but she was looking for places like the dining salon and the library and Lifeboat 68 where we should go in case of emergency. I looked for the *important* things.

As I trotted along the crossway, I sort of wished that Sis hadn't decided to go after a husband on a luxury liner. On a cargo ship, now, I'd be climbing from deck to deck on a ladder instead of having gravity underfoot all the time just like I was home on the bottom of the Gulf of Mexico. But women always know what's right, and a boy can only make faces and do what they say, same as the men have to do.

Still, it was pretty exciting to press my nose against the slots in the wall and see the sliding panels that could come charging out and block the crossway into an airtight fit in case a meteor or something smashed into the ship. And all along there were glass cases with spacesuits standing in them, like those knights they used to have back in the Middle Ages.

"In the event of disaster affecting the oxygen content of companionway," they had the words etched into the glass, "break glass with hammer upon wall, remove spacesuit and proceed to don it in the following fashion."

I read the "following fashion" until I knew it by heart. *Boy,* I said to myself. *I hope we have that kind of disaster. I'd sure like to get into one of those! Bet it would be more fun than those diving suits back in Undersea.*

And all the time I was alone. That was the best part.

THEN I passed Deck Twelve and there was a big sign. "Notice! Passengers not permitted past this point!" A big sign in red.

I peeked around the corner. I knew it—the next deck was the hull. I could see the portholes. Every twelve feet, they were, filled with the velvet of space and the dancing of more stars than I'd ever dreamed existed in the Universe.

There wasn't anyone on the deck, as far as I could see. And this distance from the grav helix, the ship seemed mighty quiet and lonely. If I just took one quick look...

But I thought of what Sis would say and I turned around obediently. Then I saw the big red sign again. "Passengers not permitted—"

Well! Didn't I know from my civics class that only women could be Earth Citizens these days? Sure, ever since the Male Desuffrage Act. And didn't I know that you had to be a citizen of a planet in order to get an interplanetary passport? Sis had explained it all to me in the careful, patient way she always talks politics and things like that to men.

"Technically, Ferdinand, I'm the only passenger in our family. You can't be one, because, not being a citizen, you can't acquire an Earth Passport. However, you'll be going to Venus on the strength of this clause—'Miss Evelyn Sparling and all dependent male members of family, this number not to exceed the registered quota of sub-regulations pertaining'—and so on. I want you to understand these matters, so that you will grow into a man who takes an active interest in world affairs. No matter what you hear, women really like and appreciate such men."

Of course, I never pay much attention to Sis when she says such dumb things. I'm old enough, I guess, to know that it isn't what *Women* like and appreciate that counts when it comes to people, getting married. If it were, Sis and three hundred other pretty girls like her wouldn't be on their way to Venus to hook husbands.

Still, if I wasn't a passenger, the sign didn't have anything to do with me. I knew what Sis could say to *that,* but at least it was an argument I could use if it ever came up. So I broke the law.

I was glad I did. The stars were exciting enough, but away off to the left, about five times as big as I'd ever seen it, except in the movies, was the Moon, a great blob of gray and white pockmarks holding off the black of space. I was hoping to see the Earth, but I figured it must be on the other side of the ship or behind us. I pressed my nose against the port and saw the tiny flicker of a spaceliner taking off, Mars bound, I wished I was on that one!

Then I noticed, a little farther down the companionway, a stretch of blank wall where there should have been portholes. High up on the wall in glowing red letters were the words, "Lifeboat: 47. Passengers: Thirty-two. Crew: Eleven. Unauthorized personnel keep away!"

Another one of those signs.

I CREPT up to the porthole nearest it and could just barely make out the stern jets where it was plastered against the hull. Then I walked under the sign and tried to figure the way you were supposed to get into it. There was a very thin line going around in a big circle that I knew must be the door. But I couldn't see any knobs or switches to open it with. Not even a button you could press.

That meant it was a sonic lock like the kind we had on the outer keeps back home in Undersea. But knock or voice? I tried the two knock combinations I knew, and nothing happened. I only remembered one voice key—might as well see if that's it, I figured.

"Twenty. Twenty-three. Open Sesame."

For a second, I thought I'd hit it just right out of all the million possible combinations— The door clicked inward toward a black hole, and a hairy hand as broad as my shoulders shot out of the hole. It closed around my throat and plucked me inside as if I'd been a baby sardine.

I bounced once on the hard lifeboat floor. Before I got my breath and sat up, the door had been shut again. When the light came on, I found myself staring up the muzzle of a highly polished blaster and into the cold blue eyes of the biggest man I'd ever seen.

He was wearing a one-piece suit made of some scaly green stuff that looked hard and soft at the same time.

His boots were made of it too, and so was the hood hanging down his back.

And his face was brown. Not just ordinary tan, you understand, but the deep, dark, burned-all-the-way-in brown I'd seen on the lifeguards in New Orleans whenever we took a surface vacation—

the kind of tan that comes from day after broiling day under a really hot Sun. His hair looked as if it had once been blond, but now there were just long combed-out waves with a yellowish tinge that boiled all the way down to his shoulders.

I hadn't seen hair like that on a man except maybe in history books; every man I'd ever known had his hair cropped in the fashionable soup-bowl style. I was staring at his hair, almost forgetting about the blaster which I knew it was against the law for him to have at all, when I suddenly got scared right through.

His eyes.

They didn't blink and there seemed to he no expression around them. Just coldness. Maybe it was the kind of clothes he was wearing that did it, but all of a sudden I was reminded of a crocodile I'd seen in a surface zoo that had stared quietly at me for twenty minutes until it opened two long tooth-studded jaws.

"Green shatas!" he said suddenly. "Only a tadpole. I must be getting jumpy enough to splash."

Then he shoved the blaster away in a holster made of the same scaly leather, crossed his arms on his chest and began to study me. I grunted to my feet, feeling a lot better. The coldness had gone out of his eyes.

I held out my hand the way Sis had taught me. "My name is Ferdinand Sparling. I'm very pleased to meet you, Mr.—Mr.—"

"Hope for your sake," he said to me, "that you aren't what you seem—tadpole brother to one of them husbandless anura."

"What?"

"A 'nuran is a female looking to nest. Anura is a herd of same. Come from Flatfolk ways."

"Flatfolk are the Venusian natives, aren't they? Are you a Venusian? What part of Venus do you come from? Why did you say you hope—"

He chuckled and swung me up into one of the bunks that lined the lifeboat. "Questions you ask," he said in his soft voice. "Venus is a sharp enough place for a dryhorn, let alone a tadpole dryhorn with a boss-minded sister."

"I'm not a dryleg," I told him proudly. *"We're* from Undersea."

"Dry*horn*, I said, not dryleg. And what's Undersea?"

"Well, in Undersea we called foreigners and newcomers drylegs. Just like on Venus, I guess, you call them dryhorns." And then I told him how Undersea had been built on the bottom of the Gulf of Mexico, when the mineral resources of the land began to give out and engineers figured that a lot could still be reached from the sea bottoms.

HE NODDED. He'd heard about the sea-bottom mining cities that were bubbling under protective domes in everyone of the Earth's oceans just about the same time settlements were springing up on the planets.

He looked impressed when I told him about Mom and Pop being one of the first couples to get married in Undersea. He looked thoughtful when I told him how Sis and I had been born there and spent half our childhood listening to the pressure pumps. He raised his eyebrows and looked disgusted when I told how Mom, as Undersea representative on the World Council, had been one of the framers of the Male Desuffrage Act after the Third Atomic War had resulted in the Maternal Revolution.

HE ALMOST squeezed my arm when I got to the time Mom and Pop were blown up in a surfacing boat.

"Well, after the funeral, there was a little money, so Sis decided we might as well use it to migrate. There was no future for her on Earth, she figured. You know, the three-out-of-four."

"How's that?"

"The three-out-of-four. No more than three women out of every four on Earth can expect to find husbands. Not enough men to go around. Way back in the Twentieth Century, it began to be felt, Sis says, what with the wars and all. Then the wars went on and a lot more men began to die or get no good from the radioactivity. Then the best men went to the planets, Sis says, until by now even if a woman can scrounge a personal husband, he's not much to boast about."

The stranger nodded violently. "Not on Earth, he isn't. Those busybody anura make sure of that. What a place! Suffering gridniks, I had a bellyful!"

He told me about it. Women were scarce on Venus, and he hadn't been able to find any who were willing to come out to his lonely little islands; he had decided to go to Earth where there was supposed to be a surplus. Naturally, having been born and brought up on a very primitive planet, he didn't know "it's a woman's world," like the older boys in school used to say.

The moment he landed on Earth he was in trouble. He didn't know he had to register at a government operated hotel for transient males; he threw a bartender through a thick plastic window for saying something nasty about the length of his hair; and *imagine!*—he not only resisted arrest, resulting in three hospitalized policemen, but he sassed the judge in open court!

"Told me a man wasn't supposed to say anything except through female attorneys. Told *her* that where *I* came from, a man spoke his piece when he'd a mind to; and his woman walked by his side."

"What happened?" I asked breathlessly.

"Oh, Guilty of This and Contempt of That. That blown-up brinosaur took my last munit for fines, then explained that she was remitting the rest because I was a foreigner and uneducated." His eyes grew dark for a moment. He chuckled again. "But I wasn't going to serve all those fancy little prison sentences. Forcible Citizenship Indoctrination, they call it? Shook the dead-dry dust of the misbegotten, God forsaken mother world from my feet forever. The women on it deserve their men. My pockets were folded from the fines, and the paddlefeet were looking for me so close I didn't dare radio for more munit. So I stowed away."

FOR a moment, I didn't understand him. When I did, I was almost ill. "Y-you mean," I choked, "th-that you're b-breaking the law right now? And I'm with you while you're doing it?"

He leaned over the edge of the bunk and stared at me very seriously. "What breed of tadpole are they turning out these days? Besides, what business do *you* have this close to the hull?"

After a moment of sober reflection, I nodded. "You're right. I've also become a male outside the law. We're in this together."

He guffawed. Then he sat up and began cleaning his blaster. I found myself drawn to the bright killer-tube with exactly the fascination Sis insists such things have always had for men.

"Ferdinand your label? That's not right for a sprouting tadpole. I'll call you Ford. My name's Butt. Butt Lee Brown."

I liked the sound of Ford. "Is Butt a nickname, too?"

"Yeah. Short for Alberta, but I haven't found a man who can draw a blaster fast enough to call me that. You see, Pop came over in the eighties—the big wave of immigrants when they evacuated Ontario. Named all us boys after Canadian provinces. I was the youngest, so I got the name they were saving for a girl."

"You had a lot of brothers, Mr. Butt?"

He grinned with a mighty set of teeth. "Oh, a nestful. Of course, they were all killed in the Blue Chicago Rising by the MacGregor boys—all except me and Saskatchewan. Then Sas and me hunted the Macgregor's down. Took a heap of time; we didn't float Jock MacGregor's ugly face down the Tuscany till both of us were pretty near grown up."

I walked up close to where I could see the tiny bright copper coils of the blaster above the firing button. "Have you killed a lot of men with that, Mr. Butt?"

"Butt. Just plain Butt to you, Ford." He frowned and sighted at the light globe. "No more'n twelve—not counting five government paddlefeet, of course. I'm a peaceable planter. Way I figure it, violence never accomplishes much that's important. My brother Sas, now—"

HE HAD just begun to work into a wonderful anecdote, about his brother when the dinner gong rang. Butt told me to scat. He said I was a growing tadpole and needed my vitamins. And he mentioned, very off-hand, that he wouldn't at all object if I brought him some fresh fruit. It seemed there was nothing but processed foods in the lifeboat and Butt was used to a farmer's diet.

Trouble was, he was a special kind of farmer. Ordinary fruit would have been pretty easy to sneak into my pockets at meals. I even found a way to handle the kelp and giant watercress Mr. Brown liked, but things like seaweed salt and Venusian mudgrapes just had too strong a smell. Twice, the mechanical hamper refused to accept my jacket for laundering and I had to wash it myself. But I learned so many wonderful things about Venus every time I visited that stowaway...

I learned three wild-wave songs of the Flatfolk and what it is that the native Venusians hate so much; I learned how you tell the difference between a lousy government paddlefoot from New Kalamazoo and the slap-toe slinker who is the planter's friend. After a lot of begging, Butt Lee Brown explained the workings of his blaster, explained it so carefully that I could name every part and tell what it did from the tiny round electrodes to the long spirals of transformer.

But no matter what, he would never let me hold it.

"Sorry, Ford, old tad," he would drawl, spinning around and around in the control swivel chair at the nose of the lifeboat. "But way I look at it, a man who lets somebody else handle his blaster is like the giant whose heart was in an egg that an enemy found. When you've grown enough so's your pop feels you ought to have a weapon, why, then's the time to learn it and you might's well learn fast. Before then, you're plain too young to be even near it."

"I don't have a father to give me one when I come of age. I don't even have an older brother as head of my family like your brother Labrador. All I have is Sis. And *she*—"

"She'll marry some fancy dryhorn who's never been farther South than the Polar Coast. And she'll stay head of the family, if I know her breed of green shata. *Bossy, opinionated.* By the way, Fordie," he said, rising and stretching so the fish-leather bounced and rippled off his biceps, "that sister. She ever..."

And he'd be off again, cross-examining me about Evelyn. I sat in the swivel chair he'd vacated and tried to answer his questions. But there was a lot of stuff I didn't know. Evelyn was a healthy girl, for instance; how healthy, exactly, I had no way of finding out. Yes, I'd tell him, my aunts on both sides of my family each had had more than the average number of children. No, we'd never done any farming to speak of, back in Undersea, but—yes, I'd guess Evelyn knew about as much as any girl there when it came to diving equipment and pressure pump regulation.

How would I know that stuff would lead to trouble for me?

SIS had insisted I come along to the geography lecture. Most of the other girls who were going to Venus for husbands talked to each other during the lecture, but not *my* sister! She hung on every word, took notes even, and asked enough questions to make the perspiring purser really work in those orientation periods.

"I am very sorry, Miss Sparling," he said with pretty heavy sarcasm, "but I cannot remember any of the agricultural products of the Macro Continent. Since the human population is well below one per thousand square miles, it can readily be understood that the quantity of tilled soil, land or sub-surface, is so small that— Wait, I remember something. The Macro Continent exports a fruit though not exactly an edible one. The wild *dunging* drug is harvested there by criminal speculators. Contrary to belief on Earth, the traffic has been growing in recent years. In fact—"

"Pardon me, sir," I broke in, "but doesn't *dunging* come only from Leif Erickson Island off the Moscow Peninsula of the Macro Continent? You remember, purser—Wang Li's third exploration, where he proved the island and the peninsula didn't meet for most of the year?"

The purser nodded slowly. "I forgot," he admitted. "Sorry, ladies, but the boy's right. Please make the correction in your notes."

But Sis was the only one who took notes, and she didn't take that one. She stared at me for a moment, biting her lower lip thoughtfully, while I got sicker and sicker. Then she shut her pad with the final gesture of the right hand that Mom used to use just before challenging the opposition to come right down on the Council floor and debate it out with her.

"Ferdinand," Sis said, "let's go back to our cabin."

The moment she sat me down and walked slowly around me, I knew I was in for it. "I've been reading up on Venusian geography in the ship's library," I told her in a hurry.

"No doubt," she said dryly. She shook her night-black hair out. "But you aren't going to tell me that you read about *dunging* in the ship's library. The books there have been censored by a government agent of Earth against the possibility that they might be read by susceptible young male minds like yours. She would not have allowed—this Terran Agent—"

"Paddlefoot," I sneered.

Sis sat down hard in our zoom-air chair. "Now that's a term," she said carefully, "that is used only by Venusian riffraff."

"They're not!"

"Not what?"

"Riffraff," I had to answer, knowing I was getting in deeper all the time and not being able to help it. I mustn't give Mr. Brown away! "They're trappers and farmers, pioneers and, explorers, who're building Venus. And it takes a real man to build on a hot, hungry hell like Venus."

"Does it, now?" she said, looking at me as if I were beginning to grow a second pair of ears. "Tell me more."

"You can't have meek, law-abiding, women-ruled men when you start civilization on a new planet. You've got to have men who aren't afraid to make their own law if necessary—with their own guns. That's where law begins; the books get written up later."

"You're going to *tell,* Ferdinand, what evil, criminal male is speaking through your mouth!"

"Nobody!" I insisted. "They're my own ideas!"

"They are remarkably well-organized for a young boy's ideas. A boy, who I might add, has previously shown a ridiculous but nonetheless entirely masculine boredom with political philosophy. I plan to have a government career on that new planet you talk about, Ferdinand—after I have found a good, steady husband, of course—and I don't look forward to a masculinist radical in the family. Now, who has been filling your head with all this nonsense?"

I WAS sweating. Sis has that deadly bulldog approach, when she feels someone is lying. I pulled my pulpast handkerchief from my pocket to wipe my face. Something rattled to the floor.

"What is this picture of me doing in your pocket, Ferdinand?"

A trap seemed to be hinging noisily into place. "One of the passengers wanted to see how you looked in a bathing suit."

"The passengers on this ship are all female. I can't imagine any of them that curious, about my appearance. Ferdinand, it's a man who has been giving you these anti-social ideas, isn't it? A war-mongering masculinist like all the frustrated men who want to engage in government and don't have the vaguest idea how. Except, of course, in their ancient, bloody ways. Ferdinand, who has been perverting that sunny and carefree soul of yours?"

"Nobody! *Nobody.*"

"Ferdinand, there's no point in lying! I demand—"

"I told you, Sis. I told you! And don't call me Ferdinand. Call me Ford."

"Ford? *Ford?* Now, you listen to me, Ferdinand…"

After that it was all over but the confession. That came in a few moments. I couldn't fool Sis. She just knew me too well, I decided miserably. Besides, she was a girl.

All the same, I wouldn't get Mr. Butt lee Brown into trouble if I could help it. I made Sis promise she wouldn't turn him in, if I took her to him. And the quick, nodding way she said she would made me feel just a little better.

The door opened on the signal, "Sesame." When Butt saw somebody was with me, he jumped and the ten-inch blaster barrel grew out of his fingers. Then he recognized Sis from the pictures.

He stepped to one side and, with the same sweeping gesture, holstered his blaster and pushed his green hood off. It was Sis's turn to jump when she saw the wild mass of hair rolling down his back.

"An honor, Miss Sparling," he said in that rumbly voice. "Please come right in. There's a hurry-up draft."

So Sis went in and I followed right after her. Mr. Brown closed the door. I tried to catch his eye so I could give him some kind of hint or explanation, but he had taken a couple of his big strides and was in the control section with Sis. She didn't give ground, though; I'll say that for her. She only came to his chest, but she had her arms crossed sternly.

"First, Mr. Brown," she began, like talking to a cluck of a kid in class, "you realize that you are not only committing the political crime of traveling without a visa, and the criminal one of stowing away without paying your fare, but the moral delinquency of consuming stores intended for the personnel of this ship solely in emergency?"

HE OPENED his mouth to its maximum width and raised an enormous hand. Then he let the air out and dropped his arm.

"I take it you either have no defense or care to make none," Sis added caustically.

Butt laughed slowly and carefully as if he were going over each word. "Wonder if all the anura talk like that. And *you* want to foul up Venus."

"We haven't done so badly on Earth, after the mess you men made of politics. It needed a revolution of the mothers before—"

"Needed nothing. Everyone wanted peace. Earth is a weary old world."

"It's a world of strong moral fiber compared to yours; Mr. Alberta lee Brown." Hearing his rightful name made him move suddenly and tower over her. Sis said with a certain amount of hurry and change of tone, "What *do* you have to say about stowing away and using up lifeboat stores?"

HE COCKED his head and considered a moment. "Look," he said finally, "I have more than enough munit to pay for round trip tickets, but I couldn't get a return visa because of that brinosaur judge and all the charges she hung on me. Had to stowaway. Picked the *Eleanor Roosevelt* because a couple of the boys in the crew are friends of mine and they were willing to help. But this lifeboat—don't you know that every passenger ship carries four times as many lifeboats as it needs? Not to mention the food I didn't eat because it stuck in my throat?"

"Yes," she said bitterly. "You had this boy steal, fresh fruit for you. I suppose you didn't know that under space regulations that makes him equally guilty?"

"No, Sis, he didn't," I was beginning to argue. "All he wanted—"

"Sure I knew. Also know that if I'm picked up as a stowaway, I'll be sent back to Earth to serve out those fancy little sentences."

"Well, you're guilty of them, aren't you?"

He waved his hands at her impatiently. "I'm not talking law, female; I'm talking sense. Listen! I'm in trouble because I went to Earth to look for a wife. You're standing here right now because you're on your way to Venus for a husband. So let's."

Sis actually staggered back. "Let's? Let's *what?* Are—are you daring to suggest that—that—"

"Now, Miss Sparling, no hoopla. I'm saying let's get married, and you know it. You figured out from what the boy told you that I was chewing on you for a wife. You're healthy and strong, got good heredity, you know how to operate sub-surface machinery, you've lived underwater, and your disposition's no worse than most of the anura I've seen. Prolific stock, too."

I was so excited I just had to yell: "Gee, Sis, say *yes!"*

MY SISTER'S voice was steaming with scorn. "And what makes you think that I'd consider you a desirable husband?"

He spread his hands genially.

"Figure if you wanted a poodle, you're pretty enough to pick one up on Earth. Figure if you charge off to Venus, you don't want a poodle, you want a man. I'm one. I own three islands in the Galertan Archipelago that'll be good oozing mudgrape land when they're cleared. Not to mention the rich berzeliot beds offshore. I got no bad habits outside of having my own way. I'm also passable good-looking for a slap-toe planter. Besides, if you marry me you'll be the first mated on this ship—and that's a splash most nesting females like to make."

There was a longish stretch of quiet. Sis stepped back and measured him slowly with her eyes; there was a lot to look at. He waited patiently while she covered the distance from his peculiar green boots to that head of hair. I was so excited I was gulping instead of breathing. Imagine having Butt for a brother-in-law and living on a wet-plantation in Flatfolk country! But then I remembered Sis's level head and I didn't have much hope any more.

"You know," she began, "there's more to marriage than just—"

"So there is," he cut in. "Well, we can try each other for taste." And he pulled her in, both of his great hands practically covering her slim, straight back.

Neither of them said anything for a bit after he let go. Butt spoke up first.

"Now, me," he said, "I'd vote yes."

Sis ran the tip of her tongue kind of delicately from side to side of her mouth. Then she stepped back slowly and looked at him as if she were figuring out how many feet high he was. She kept on moving backward, tapping her chin, while Butt and I got more and more impatient. When she touched the lifeboat door, she pushed it open and jumped out.

BUTT ran over and looked down the crossway. After a while, he shut the door and came back beside me. "Well," he said, swinging to a bunk, "that's sort of it."

"You're better off, Butt," I burst out. "You shouldn't have a woman like Sis for a wife. She looks small and helpless, but don't forget she was trained to run an underwater city!"

"Wasn't worrying about that," he grinned. "*I* grew up in the fifteen long years of the Blue Chicago Rising. Nope." He turned over on his back and clicked his teeth at the ceiling. "Think we'd have nested out nicely."

I hitched myself up to him and we sat on the bunk, glooming away at each other. Then we heard the tramp of feet in the crossway.

Butt swung down and headed for the control compartment in the nose of the lifeboat. He had his blaster out and was cursing very interestingly. I started after him, but he picked me up by the seat of my jumper and tossed me toward the door. The Captain came in and tripped over me.

I got all tangled up in his gold braid and million-mile space buttons. When we finally got to our feet and sorted out right, he was breathing very hard. The Captain was a round little man with a plump, golden face and a very scared look on it. He *humphed* at me, just the way Sis does; and lifted me by the scruff of my neck. The Chief Mate picked me up and passed me to the Second Assistant Engineer.

Sis was there, being held by the purser on one side and the Chief Computer's Mate on the other. Behind them, I could see a flock of wide-eyed female passengers.

"You cowards!" Sis was raging. "Letting your Captain face a dangerous outlaw all by himself!"

"I dunno, Miss Sparling," the Computer's Mate said, scratching the miniature slide-rule insignia on his visor with his free hand. "The Old Man would've been willing to let it go with a log entry, figuring the spaceport paddlefeet could pry out the stowaway when we landed. But you had to quote the Mother Anita Law at him, and he's in there doing his duty. He figures the rest of us are family men, too, and there's no sense making orphans."

"You promised, Sis," I told her through my teeth. "You promised you wouldn't get Butt into trouble!"

She tossed her spiral curls at me and ground a heel into the purser's instep. He screwed up his face and howled, but he didn't let go of her arm.

"*Shush,* Ferdinand, this is serious!"

It was. I heard the Captain say, "I'm not carrying a weapon, Brown."

"Then *get* one," Butt's low, lazy voice floated out.

"No, thanks. You're as handy with that thing as I am with a rocketboard." The Captain's words got a little fainter as he walked forward. Butt growled like a gusher about to blow.

"I'm counting on your being a good guy, Brown." The Captain's voice quavered just a bit. "I'm banking on what I heard about the blast-happy Browns every time I lifted gravs in New Kalamazoo; they have a code, they don't burn unarmed men."

JUST about this time, events in the lifeboat went down to a mumble. The top of my head got wet and I looked up. There was sweat rolling down the Second Assistant's forehead; it converged at his nose and bounced off the tip in a sizable stream. I twisted out of the way.

"What's happening?" Sis gritted, straining toward the lock.

"Butt's trying to decide whether he wants him fried or scrambled," the Computer's Mate said, pulling her back. "Hey, purse, remember when the whole family with their pop at the head went into Heatwave to argue with Colonel Leclerc?"

"Eleven dead, sixty-four injured;" the purser answered mechanically. "And no more army stationed south of Icebox." His right ear twitched irritably. "But what're they saying?"

Suddenly we heard. "By authority vested in me under the Pomona College Treaty," the Captain was saying very loudly, "I arrest you for violation of Articles Sixteen to Twenty-one inclusive of the Space Transport Code, and order your person and belongings impounded for the duration of this voyage as set forth in Sections Forty-one and Forty-five—"

"Forty-three and Forty-five," Sis groaned. "Sections Forty-three and Forty-five; I told him. I even made him repeat it after me!"

"—of the Mother Anita Law, SC 2136, Emergency Interplanetary Directives."

WE ALL waited breathlessly for Butt's reply. The seconds ambled on and there was no clatter of electrostatic discharge, no smell of burning flesh.

Then we heard some feet walking. A big man in a green suit swung out into the crossway. That was Butt. Behind him came the Captain, holding the blaster gingerly with both hands. Butt had a funny, thoughtful look on his face.

The girls surged forward when they saw him, scattering the crew to one side. They were like a school of sharks that had just caught sight of a dying whale.

"M-m-m-m! Are all Venusians built like that?"

"Men like that are worth the mileage!"

"I want him!" "I want him!" "I want him!"

Sis had been let go. She grabbed my free hand and pulled me away. She was trying to look only annoyed, but her eyes had bright little bubbles of fury popping in them.

"The cheap extroverts! And they call themselves responsible women!"

I was angry, too. And I let her know, once we were in our cabin. "What about that promise, Sis? You said you wouldn't turn him in. You *promised!*"

She stopped walking around the room as if she had been expecting to get to Venus on foot. "I know I did, Ferdinand, but he forced me."

"My name is Ford and I don't understand."

"Your name is Ferdinand and stop trying to act forcefully like a girl. It doesn't become you. In just a few days, you'll forget all this and be your simple, carefree self again. I really truly meant to keep my word. From what you'd told me, Mr. Brown seemed to be a fundamentally decent chap despite his barbaric notions on equality between the sexes—or worse. I was positive I could shame him into a more rational social behavior and make him give himself up. Then he—he—"

She pressed her fingernails into her palms and let out a long, glaring sigh at the door. "Then he kissed me! Oh, it was a good enough kiss—Mr. Brown has evidently had a varied and colorful background—but the galling idiocy of the man, trying that! I was just getting over the colossal impudence involved in *his* proposing marriage—as if *he* had to bear the children!—and was considering the offer seriously, on its merits, as one should consider *all* suggestions, when he deliberately dropped the pretense of reason. He appealed to me as most of the savage ancients appealed to their women, as an emotional machine. Throw the correct sexual switches, says this theory, and the female surrenders herself ecstatically to the doubtful and bloody murk of masculine plans."

THERE was a double knock on the door and the Captain walked in without waiting for an invitation. He was still holding Butt's blaster. He pointed it at me. "Get your hands up, Ferdinand Sparling," he said.

I did.

"I hereby order your detention for the duration of this voyage, for aiding and abetting a stowaway, as set forth in Sections' Forty-one and Forty-five—"

"Forty-three and Forty-five," Sis interrupted him, her eyes getting larger and rounder. "But you gave me your word of honor that no charges would be lodged against the boy!"

"Forty-one and Forty-five," he corrected her courteously, still staring fiercely at me. "I looked it up. Of the Anita Mason law, Emergency Interplanetary Directives. That was the usual promise one makes to an informer, but I made it before I knew it was Butt lee Brown you were talking about. I didn't want to arrest Butt lee Brown. You forced me. So I'm breaking my promise to you, just as, I understand, you broke your promise to your brother. They'll both be picked up at New Kalamazoo Spaceport and sent Terraward for trial."

"But I used all of our money to buy passage," Sis wailed.

"And now you'll have to return with the boy. I'm sorry, Miss Sparling. But as you explained to me; a man who has been honored with an important official position should stay close to the letter of the law for the sake of other men who are trying to break down terrestrial anti-male prejudice. Of course, there's a way out."

"There is? Tell me, please!"

"Can I lower my hands a minute?" I asked.

"No, you can't, son—not according to the armed surveillance provisions of the Mother Anita Law. Miss Sparling, if you'd marry Brown—now, now, don't look at me like that!—we could let the whole matter drop. A shipboard wedding and he goes on your passport as a dependent male member of family, which means, so far as the law is concerned, that he had a regulation passport from the beginning of this voyage. And once we touch Venusian soil he can contact his bank and pay for passage. On the record, no crime was ever committed. He's free, the boy's free, and you—"

"—Are married to an uncombed desperado who doesn't know enough to sit back and let a woman run things. Oh, you should be ashamed!"

THE Captain shrugged and spread his arms wide.

"Perhaps I should be, but that's what comes of putting men into responsible positions, as you would say. See here, Miss Sparling, I didn't want to arrest Brown, and, if it's at all possible, I'd still prefer not to. The crew, officers and men, all go along with me. We may be legal residents of Earth, but our work requires us to be on Venus several times a year. We don't want to be disliked by any members of the highly irritable Brown clan or its collateral branches. Butt Lee Brown himself, for all of his savage appearance in your civilized eyes, is a man of much influence on the Polar Continent. In his own bailiwick, the Galertan Archipelago, he makes, breaks and occasionally readjusts officials. Then there's his brother Saskatchewan who considers Butt a helpless, put-upon youngster—"

"Much influence, you say? Mr. Brown has?" Sis was suddenly thoughtful.

"Power, actually. The kind a strong man usually wields in a newly settled community. Besides, Miss Sparling, you're going to Venus for a husband because the male-female ratio on Earth is reversed. Well, not only is Butt Lee Brown a first class catch, but you can't afford to be too particular in any case. While you're fairly pretty, you won't bring any wealth into a marriage and your high degree of opinionation is not likely to be well received on a backward, masculinist world. Then, too, the woman-hunger is not so great any more, what with the *Marie Curie* and the *Fatima* having already deposited their cargoes, the *Mme. Sun Yat Sen* due to arrive next month…"

SIS nodded to herself, waved the door open, and walked out.

"Let's hope," the Captain said, "like any father used to say, a man who knows how to handle women, how to get around them without their knowing it, doesn't need to know anything else in this life. I'm plain wasted in space. You can lower your hands now, son."

We sat down and I explained the blaster to him. He was very interested. He said all Butt had told him—in the lifeboat when they decided to use my arrest as a club over Sis—was to keep the safety catch all the way up against his thumb. I could see he really had been excited about carrying a lethal weapon around. He told me that back in the old days, captains—sea captains, that is— actually had the right to keep guns in their cabins all the time to put down mutinies and other things our ancestors did.

The telewall flickered, and we turned it on. Sis smiled down. "Everything's all right, Captain. Come up and marry us, please."

"What did you stick him for?" he asked. "What was the price?"

Sis's full lips went thin and hard, the way Mom's used to. Then she thought better of it and laughed. "Mr. Brown is going to see that I'm elected sheriff of the Galertan Archipelago."

"And I thought she'd settle for a county clerkship!" the Captain muttered as we spun up to the brig.

The doors were open and girls were chattering in every corner. Sis came up to the Captain to discuss arrangements. I slipped away and found Butt sitting with folded arms in a corner of the brig. He grinned at me. "Hi, tadpole. Like the splash?"

I shook my head unhappily. "Butt, why did you do it? I'd sure love to be your brother-in-law, but, gosh, you didn't have to marry, Sis." I pointed at some of the bustling females. Sis was going to have three hundred bridesmaids. "Anyone of them would have jumped at the chance to be your wife. And once on any woman's passport, you'd be free. Why Sis?"

"That's what the Captain said in the lifeboat. Told him same thing I'm telling you. I'm stubborn. What I like at first, I keep on liking. What I want at first, I keep on wanting until I get."

"Yes, but making Sis sheriff! And you'll have to back her up with your blaster. What'll happen to that man's world?"

"Wait'll after we nest and go out to my islands." He produced a hard-lipped, smug grin, sighting it at Sis's slender back. "She'll find herself sheriff over a bunch of natives and exactly two Earth males—you and me. I got a hunch that'll keep her pretty busy, though."

THE END

A Gift From Earth

By MANLY BANISTER

Except for transportation, it was absolutely free...but how much would the freight cost?

"IT is an outrage," said Koltan of the House of Masur, "that the Earthmen land among the Thorabians!"

Zotul, youngest of the Masur brothers, stirred uneasily. Personally, he was in favor of the coming of the Earthmen to the world of Zur.

At the head of the long, shining table sat old Kalrab Masur, in his dotage, but still giving what he could of aid and comfort to the Pottery of Masur, even though nobody listened to him any more and he knew it. Around the table sat the six brothers—Koltan, eldest and Director of the Pottery; Morvan, his vice-chief; Singula, their treasurer; Thendro, sales manager; Lubiosa, export chief; and last in the rank of age, Zotul, who was responsible for affairs of design.

"Behold, my sons," said Kalrab, stroking his scanty beard. "What are these Earthmen to worry about? Remember the clay. It is our strength and our fortune. It is the muscle and bone of our trade. Earthmen may come and Earthmen may go, but day goes on forever...and with it, the fame and fortune of the House of Masur."

"It *is* a damned imposition," agreed Morvan, ignoring his father's philosophical attitude. "They could have landed just as easily here in Lor."

"The Thorabians will lick up the gravy," said Singula, whose mind ran rather to matters of financial aspect, "and leave us the grease."

By this, he seemed to imply that the Thorabians would rob the Earthmen, which the Lorians would not. The truth was that all on Zur were panting to get their hands on that marvelous ship, which

118

was all of metal, a very scarce commodity on Zur, worth billions of ken.

LUBIOSA, who had interests in Thorabia, and many agents there, kept his own counsel. His people were active in the matter and that was enough for him. He would report when the time was ripe.

"Doubtless," said Zotul unexpectedly, for the youngest at a conference was expected to keep his mouth shut and applaud the decisions of his elders, "the Earthmen used all the metal on their planet in building that ship. We cannot possibly bilk them of it; it is their only means of transport."

Such frank expression of motive was unheard of, even in the secret conclave of conference. Only the speaker's youth could account for it. The speech drew scowls from the brothers and stern rebuke from Koltan.

"When your opinion is wanted, we will ask you for it. Meantime, remember your position in the family."

Zotul bowed his head meekly, but he burned with resentment.

"Listen to the boy," said the aged father. "There is more wisdom in his head than in all the rest of you. Forget the Earthmen and think only of the clay."

Zotul did not appreciate his father's approval, for it only earned him a beating as soon as the old man went to bed. It was a common enough thing among the brothers Masur, as among everybody, to be frustrated in their desires. However, they had Zotul to take it out upon, and they did.

Still smarting, Zotul went back to his designing quarters and thought about the Earthmen. If it was impossible to hope for much in the way of metal from the Earthmen, what could one get from them? If he could figure this problem out, he might rise somewhat in the estimation of his brothers. That wouldn't take him out of the rank of scapegoat, of course, but the beatings might become fewer and less severe.

BY and by, the Earthmen came to Lor, flying through the air in strange metal contraptions. They paraded through the tile-paved streets of the city, marveled here, as they had in Thorabia, at the buildings all of tile inside and out, and made a great show of themselves for all the people to see. Speeches were made through interpreters, who had much too quickly learned the tongue of the aliens; hence these left much to be desired in the way of clarity, though their sincerity was evident.

The Earthmen were going to do great things for the whole world of Zur. It required but the cooperation—an excellent word, that—of all Zurians, and many blessings would rain down from the skies. This, in effect, was what the Earthmen had to say. Zotul felt greatly cheered, for it refuted the attitude of his brothers without earning him a whaling for it.

There was also some talk going around about agreements made between the Earthmen and officials of the Lorian government, but you heard one thing one day and another the next. Accurate reporting, much less a newspaper, was unknown on Zur.

Finally, the Earthmen took off in their great, shining ship. Obviously, none had succeeded in chiseling them out of it, if, indeed, any had tried. The anti-Earthmen Faction—in any culture complex, there is always an "anti" faction to protest any movement of endeavor—crowed happily that the Earthmen were gone for good, and a good thing, too.

Such jubilation proved premature, however. One day, a fleet of ships arrived and after they had landed all over the planet, Zur was practically a crawl with Earthmen.

Immediately, the Earthmen established what they called "corporations"—Zurian trading companies under terrestrial control. The object of the visit was trade.

In spite of the fact that a terrestrial ship had landed at every Zurian city of major and minor importance, and all in a single day, it took some time for the news to spread.

The first awareness Zotul had was that upon coming home from the pottery one evening, he found his wife Lania proudly brandishing an aluminum pot at him.

"What is that thing?" he asked curiously.

"A pot. I bought it at the market."

"Did you now? Well, take it back. Am I made of money that you spend my substance for some fool's product of precious metal? Take it back, I say!"

THE pretty young wife laughed at him. "Up to your ears in clay, no wonder you hear nothing of news! The pot is very cheap. The Earthmen are selling them everywhere. They're much better than our old clay pots; they're light and easy to handle and they don't break when dropped."

"What good is it?" asked Zotul, interested. "How will it hold heat, being so light?"

"The Earthmen don't cook as we do," she explained patiently. "There is a paper with each pot that explains how it is used. And you will have to design a new ceramic stove for me to use the pots on."

"Don't be idiotic! Do you suppose Koltan would agree to produce a new type of stove when the old has sold well for centuries? Besides, why do you need a whole new stove for one little pot?"

"A dozen pots. They come in sets and are cheaper that way. And Koltan will have to produce the new stove because all the housewives are buying these pots and there will be a big demand for it. The Earthman said so."

"He did, did he? These pots are only a fad. You will soon enough go back to cooking with your old ones."

"The Earthman took them in trade—one reason why the new ones are so cheap. There isn't a pot in the house but these metal ones, and you will have to design and produce a new stove if you expect me to use them."

After he had beaten his wife thoroughly for her foolishness, Zotul stamped off in a rage and designed a new ceramic stove, one that would accommodate the terrestrial pots very well.

And Koltan put the model into production.

"Orders already are pouring in like mad," he said the next day. "It was wise of you to foresee it and have the design ready. Already, I am sorry for thinking as I did about the Earthmen. They really intend to do well by us."

The kilns of the Pottery of Masur fired day and night to keep up with the demand for the new porcelain stoves. In three years, more than a million had been made and sold by the Masurs alone, not counting the hundreds of thousands of copies turned out by competitors in every land.

IN the meantime, however, more things than pots came from Earth. One was a printing press, the like of which none on Zur had ever dreamed. This, for some unknown reason and much to the disgust of the Lorians, was set up in Thorabia. Books and magazines poured from it in a fantastic stream. The populace fervidly brushed up on its scanty reading ability and bought everything available, overcome by the novelty of it. Even Zotul bought a book—a primer in the Lorian language—and learned how to read and write. The remainder of the brothers Masur, on the other hand, preferred to remain in ignorance.

Moreover, the Earthmen brought miles of copper wire—more than enough in value to buy out the governorship of any country on Zur—and set up telegraph lines from country to country and continent to continent. Within five years of the first landing of the Earthmen, every major city on the globe had a printing press, a daily newspaper, and enjoyed the instantaneous transmission of news via telegraph. And the business of the House of Masur continued to look up.

"As I have always said from the beginning," chortled Director Koltan, "this coming of the Earthmen had been a great thing for us, and especially for the House of Masur."

"You didn't think so at first," Zotul pointed out, and was immediately sorry, for Koltan turned and gave him a hiding, single-handed, for his unthinkable impertinence.

It would do no good, Zotul realized, to bring up the fact that their production of ceramic cooking pots had dropped off to about two percent of its former volume. Of course, profits on the line of new stoves greatly overbalanced the loss, so that actually they were ahead; but their business was now dependent upon the supply of the metal pots from Earth.

About this time, plastic utensils—dishes, cups, knives, forks— made their appearance on Zur. It became very stylish to eat with the newfangled paraphernalia...and very cheap, too, because for everything they sold, the Earthmen always took the old ware in trade. What they did with the stuff had been hard to believe at first. They destroyed it, which proved how valueless it really was.

The result of the new flood was that in the following year, the sale of Masur ceramic table service dropped to less than a tenth.

TREMBLING with excitement at this news from their bookkeeper, Koltan called an emergency meeting. He even routed old Kalrab out of his senile stupor for the occasion, on the off chance that the old man might still have a little wit left that could be helpful.

"Note," Koltan announced in a shaky voice, "that the Earthmen undermine our business," and he read off the figures.

"Perhaps," said Zotul, "it is a good thing also, as you said before, and will result in something even better for us."

Koltan frowned, and Zotul, in fear of another beating, instantly subsided.

"They are replacing our high quality ceramic ware with inferior terrestrial junk!" Koltan went on bitterly. "It is only the glamour that sells it, of course, but before the people get the shine out of their eyes, we can be ruined."

The brothers discussed the situation for an hour, and all the while Father Kalrab sat and pulled his scanty whiskers. Seeing that they got nowhere with their wrangle, he cleared his throat and spoke up.

"My sons, you forget it is not the Earthmen themselves at the bottom of your trouble, but the *things* of Earth. Think of the telegraph and the newspaper, how these spread news of every shipment from Earth. The merchandise of the Earthmen is put up for sale by means of these newspapers, which also are the property of the Earthmen. The people are intrigued by these advertisements, as they are called, and flock to buy. Now, if you would pull a tooth from the kwi that bites you, you might also have advertisements of your own."

Alas for that suggestion, no newspaper would accept advertising from the House of Masur; all available space was occupied by the advertisements of the Earthmen.

In their dozenth conference since that first and fateful one, the brothers Masur decided upon drastic steps. In the meantime, several things had happened. For one, old Kalrab had passed on to his immortal rest, but this made no real difference. For another, the Earthmen had procured legal authority to prospect the planet for metals, of which they found a good deal, but they told no one on Zur of this. What they did mention was the crude oil and natural gas they discovered in the underlayers of the planet's crust. Crews of Zurians, working under supervision of the Earthmen, laid pipelines from the gas and oil regions to every major and minor city on Zur.

BY the time ten years had passed since the landing of the first terrestrial ship, the Earthmen were conducting a brisk business in gas-fired ranges, furnaces and heaters...and the Masur stove business was gone. Moreover, the Earthmen sold the Zurians their own natural gas at a nice profit and everybody was happy with the situation except the brothers Masur.

The drastic steps of the brothers applied, therefore, to making an energetic protest to the governor of Lor.

At one edge of the city, an area had been turned over to the Earthmen for a spaceport, and the great terrestrial spaceships came to it and departed from it at regular intervals. As the heirs of the House of Masur walked by on their way to see the governor, Zotul observed that much new building was taking place and wondered what it was.

"Some new devilment of the Earthmen, you can be sure," said Koltan blackly.

In fact, the Earthmen were building an assembly plant for radio receiving sets. The ship now standing on its fins upon the apron was loaded with printed circuits, resistors, variable condensers and other radio parts. This was Earth's first step toward flooding Zur with the natural follow-up in its campaign of advertising: radio programs—with commercials.

Happily for the brothers, they did not understand this at the time or they would surely have gone back to be buried in their own clay.

"I think," the governor told them, "that you gentlemen have not paused to consider the affair from all angles. You must learn to be modern—keep up with the times! We heads of government on Zur are doing all in our power to aid the Earthmen and facilitate their bringing a great, new culture that can only benefit us. See how Zur has changed in ten short years! Imagine the world of tomorrow! Why, do you know they are even bringing *autos* to Zur!"

The brothers were fascinated with the governor's description of these hitherto unheard-of vehicles.

"It only remains," concluded the governor, "to build highways, and the Earthmen are taking care of that."

At any rate, the brothers Masur were still able to console themselves that they had their tile business. Tile served well enough for houses and street surfacing; what better material could be devised for the new highways the governor spoke of? There was a lot of money to be made yet.

RADIO stations went up all over Zur and began broadcasting. The people bought receiving sets like mad. The automobiles arrived and highways were constructed.

The last hope of the brothers was dashed. The Earthmen set up plants and began to manufacture Portland cement.

You could build a house of concrete much cheaper than with tile. Of course, since wood was scarce on Zur, it was no competition for either tile or concrete. Concrete floors were smoother, too, and the stuff made far better road surfacing.

The demand for Masur tile hit rock bottom.

The next time the brothers went to see the governor, he said, "I cannot handle such complaints as yours. I must refer you to the Merchandising Council."

"What is that?" asked Koltan.

"It is an Earthman association that deals with complaints such as yours. In the matter of material progress, we must expect some strain in the fabric of our culture. Machinery has been set up to deal with it. Here is their address; go air your troubles to them."

The business of a formal complaint was turned over by the brothers to Zotul. It took three weeks for the Earthmen to get around to calling him in, as a representative of the Pottery of Masur, for an interview.

All the brothers could no longer be spared from the plant, even for the purpose of pressing a complaint. Their days of idle wealth over, they had to get in and work with the clay with the rest of the help.

Zotul found the headquarters of the Merchandising Council as indicated on their message. He had not been this way in some time, but was not surprised to find that a number of old buildings had been torn down to make room for the concrete Council House and a roomy parking lot, paved with something called "blacktop" and jammed with an array of glittering new automobiles.

An automobile was an expense none of the brothers could afford, now that they barely eked a living from the pottery. Still, Zotul ached with desire at sight of so many shiny cars. Only a few had them and they were the envied ones of Zur.

Kent Broderick, the Earthman in charge of the Council, shook hands jovially with Zotul. That alien custom conformed with, Zotul took a better look at his host. Broderick was an affable, smiling individual with genial laugh wrinkles at his eyes. A man of middle age, dressed in the baggy costume of Zur, he looked almost like a Zurian, except for an indefinite sense of alienness about him.

"Glad to have you call on us, Mr. Masur," boomed the Earthman, clapping Zotul on the back. "Just tell us your troubles and we'll have you straightened out in no time."

ALL the chill recriminations and arguments Zotul had stored for this occasion were dissipated in the warmth of the Earthman's manner.

Almost apologetically, Zotul told of the encroachment that had been made upon the business of the Pottery of Masur.

"Once," he said formally, "the Masur fortune was the greatest in the world of Zur. That was before my father, the famous Kalrab Masur—Divinity protect him—departed this life to collect his greater reward. He often told us, my father did, that the clay is the flesh and bones of our culture and our fortune. Now it has been shown how prone is the flesh to corruption and how feeble the bones. We are ruined, and all because of new things coming from Earth."

Broderick stroked his shaven chin and looked sad. "Why didn't you come to me sooner? This would never have happened. But now that it has, we're going to do right by you. That is the policy of Earth—always to do right by the customer."

"Divinity witness," Zorin said, "that we ask only compensation for damages."

Broderick shook his head. "It is not possible to replace an immense fortune at this late date. As I said, you should have reported your trouble sooner. However, we can give you an opportunity to rebuild. Do you own an automobile?"

"No."

"A gas range? A gas-fired furnace? A radio?"

Zotul had to answer no to all except the radio. "My wife Lania likes the music," he explained. "I cannot afford the other things."

Broderick clucked sympathetically. One who could not afford the bargain-priced merchandise of Earth must be poor indeed.

"To begin with," he said, "I am going to make you a gift of all these luxuries you do not have." As Zotul made to protest, he cut him off with a wave of his hand. "It is the least we can do for you. Pick a car from the lot outside. I will arrange to have the other things delivered and installed in your home."

"To receive gifts," said Zotul, "incurs an obligation."

"None at all," beamed the Earthman cheerily. "Every item is given to you absolutely free—a gift from the people of Earth. All we ask is that you pay the freight charges on the items. Our purpose is not to make profit, but to spread technology and prosperity throughout the Galaxy. We have already done well on numerous worlds, but working out the full program takes time."

He chuckled deeply. "We of Earth have a saying about one of our extremely slow-moving native animals. We say, 'Slow is the tortoise, but sure.' And so with us. Our goal is a long-range one, with the motto, 'Better times with better merchandise.'"

THE engaging manner of the man won Zotul's confidence. After all, it was no more than fair to pay transportation.

He said, "How much does the freight cost?"

Broderick told him.

"It may seem high," said the Earthman, "but remember that Earth is sixty-odd light-years away. After all, we are absorbing the cost of the merchandise. All you pay is the freight, which is cheap, considering the cost of operating an interstellar spaceship."

"Impossible," said Zotul drably. "Not I and all my brothers together have so much money any more."

"You don't know us of Earth very well yet, but you will. I offer you credit!"

"What is that?" asked Zotul skeptically.

"It is how the poor are enabled to enjoy all the luxuries of the rich," said Broderick, and went on to give a thumbnail sketch of the involutions and devolutions of credit, leaving out some angles that might have had a discouraging effect.

On a world where credit was a totally new concept, it was enchanting. Zotul grasped at the glittering promise with avidity. "What must I do to get credit?"

"Just sign this paper," said Broderick, "and you become part of our Easy Payment Plan."

Zotul drew back. "I have five brothers. If I took all these things for myself and nothing for them, they would beat me black and blue."

"Here." Broderick handed him a sheaf of chattel mortgages. "Have each of your brothers sign one of these, then bring them back to me. That is all there is to it."

It sounded wonderful. But how would the brothers take it? Zotul wrestled with his misgivings and the misgivings won.

"I will talk it over with them," he said. "Give me the total so I will have the figures."

The total was more than it ought to be by simple addition. Zotul pointed this out politely.

"Interest," Broderick explained. "A mere fifteen percent. After all, you get the merchandise free. The transportation company has to be paid, so another company loans you the money to pay for the freight. This small extra sum pays the lending company for its trouble."

"I see." Zotul puzzled over it sadly. "It is too much," he said. "Our plant doesn't make enough money for us to meet the payments."

"I have a surprise for you," smiled Broderick. "Here is a contract. You will start making ceramic parts for automobile spark plugs and certain parts for radios and gas ranges. It is our policy to encourage local manufacture to help bring prices down."

"We haven't the equipment."

"We will equip your plant," beamed Broderick. "It will require only a quarter interest in your plant itself, assigned to our terrestrial company."

ZOTUL, anxious to possess the treasures promised by the Earthman, won over his brothers. They signed with marks and gave up a quarter interest in the Pottery of Masur. They rolled in the luxuries of Earth. These, who had never known debt before, were in it up to their ears.

The retooled plant forged ahead and profits began to look up, but the Earthmen took a fourth of them as their share in the industry.

For a year, the brothers drove their shiny new cars about on the new concrete highways the Earthmen had built. From pumps owned by a terrestrial company, they bought gas and oil that had been drawn from the crust of Zur and was sold to the Zurians at a magnificent profit. The food they ate was cooked in Earthly pots on Earth-type gas ranges, served up on metal plates that had been stamped out on Earth. In the winter, they toasted their shins before handsome gas grates, though they had gas-fired central heating.

About this time, the ships from Earth brought steam-powered electric generators. Lines went up, power was generated, and a flood of electrical gadgets and appliances hit the market. For some reason, batteries for the radios were no longer available and everybody had to buy the new radios. And who could do without a radio in this modern age?

The homes of the brothers Masur blossomed on the Easy Payment Plan. They had refrigerators, washers, dryers, toasters, grills, electric fans, air-conditioning equipment and everything else Earth could possibly sell them.

"We will be forty years paying it all off," exulted Zotul, "but meantime we have the things and aren't they worth it?"

But at the end of three years, the Earthmen dropped their option. The Pottery of Masur had no more contracts. Business languished. The Earthmen, explained Broderick, had built a plant of their own because it was so much more efficient—and to lower prices, which was Earth's unswerving policy, greater and greater efficiency was demanded. Broderick was very sympathetic, but there was nothing he could do.

The introduction of television provided a further calamity. The sets were delicate and needed frequent repairs, hence were costly to own and maintain. But all Zurians who had to keep up with the latest from Earth had them. Now it was possible not only to hear about things of Earth, but to see them as they were broadcast from the videotapes.

The printing plants that turned out mortgage contracts did a lush business.

FOR the common people of Zur, times were good everywhere. In a decade and a half, the Earthmen had wrought magnificent changes on this backward world. As Broderick had said, the progress of the tortoise was slow, but it was extremely sure.

The brothers Masur got along in spite of dropped options. They had less money and felt the pinch of their debts more keenly, but television kept their wives and children amused and furnished an anodyne for the pangs of impoverishment.

The pottery income dropped to an impossible low, no matter how Zotul designed and the brothers produced. Their figurines and religious icons were a drag on the market. The Earthmen made them of plastic and sold them for less.

The brothers, unable to meet the payments that were not so easy any more, looked up Zotul and cuffed him around reproachfully.

"You got us into this," they said, emphasizing their bitterness with fists. "Go see Broderick. Tell him we are undone and must have some contracts to continue operating."

Nursing bruises, Zotul unhappily went to the Council House again. Mr. Broderick was no longer with them, a suave assistant informed him. Would he like to see Mr. Siwicki instead? Zotul would.

Siwicki was tall, thin, dark and somber-looking. There was even a hint of toughness about the set of his jaw and the hardness of his glance.

"So you can't pay," he said, tapping his teeth with a pencil. He looked at Zotul coldly. "It is well you have come to us instead of making it necessary for us to approach you through the courts."

"I don't know what you mean," said Zotul.

"If we have to sue, we take back the merchandise and everything attached to them. That means you would lose your houses, for they are attached to the furnaces. However, it is not as bad as that—yet. We will only require you to assign the remaining three-quarters of your pottery to us."

The brothers, when they heard of this, were too stunned to think of beating Zotul, by which he assumed he had progressed a little and was somewhat comforted.

"To fail," said Koltan soberly, "is not a Masur attribute. Go to the governor and tell him what we think of this business. The House of Masur has long supported the government with heavy taxes. Now it is time for the government to do something for us."

THE governor's palace was jammed with hurrying people, a scene of confusion that upset Zotul. The clerk who took his application for an interview was, he noticed only vaguely, a young Earthwoman. It was remarkable that he paid so little attention, for the female terrestrials were picked for physical assets that made Zurian men covetous and Zurian women envious.

"The governor will see you," she said sweetly. "He has been expecting you."

"Me?" marveled Zotul.

She ushered him into the magnificent private office of the governor of Lor. The man behind the desk stood up, extended his hand with a friendly smile.

"Come in, come in! I'm glad to see you again."

Zotul stared blankly. This was not the governor. This was Broderick, the Earthman.

"I—I came to see the governor," he said in confusion.

Broderick nodded agreeably. "I am the governor and I am well acquainted with your case, Mr. Masur. Shall we talk it over? Please sit down."

"I don't understand. The Earthmen..." Zotul paused, coloring. "We are about to lose our plant."

"You were about to say that the Earthmen are taking your plant away from you. That is true. Since the House of Masur was the largest and richest on Zur, it has taken a long time—the longest of all, in fact."

"What do you mean?"

"Yours is the last business on Zur to be taken over by us. We have bought you out."

"Our government..."

"Your governments belong to us, too," said Broderick. "When they could not pay for the roads, the telegraphs, the civic improvements, we took them over, just as we are taking you over."

"You mean," exclaimed Zotul, aghast, "that you Earthmen own everything on Zur?"

"Even your armies."

"But *why?*"

BRODERICK clasped his hands behind back, went to the window and stared down moodily into the street.

"You don't know what an overcrowded world is like," he said. "A street like this, with so few people and vehicles on it, would be impossible on Earth."

"But it's mobbed," protested Zotul. "It gave me a headache."

"And to us it's almost empty. The pressure of population on Earth has made us range the Galaxy for places to put our extra people. The only habitable planets, unfortunately, are populated ones. We take the least populous worlds and—well, buy them out and move in."

"And after that?"

Broderick smiled gently. "Zur will grow. Our people will intermarry with yours. The future population of Zur will be neither true Zurians nor true Earthmen, but a mixture of both."

Zotul sat in silent thought. "But you did not have to buy us out. You had the power to conquer us, even to destroy us. The whole planet could have been yours alone." He stopped in alarm. "Or am I suggesting an idea that didn't occur to you?"

"No," said Broderick, his usually smiling face almost pained with memory. "We know the history of conquest all too well. Our method causes more distress than we like to inflict, but it's better—

and more sure—than war and invasion by force. Now that the unpleasant job is finished, we can repair the dislocations."

"At last I understand what you said about the tortoise."

"Slow but sure." Broderick beamed again and clapped Zotul on the shoulder. "Don't worry. You'll have your job back, the same as always, but you'll be working for us...until the children of Earth and Zur are equal in knowledge and therefore equal partners. That's why we had to break down your caste system."

Zotul's eyes widened. "And that is why my brothers did not beat me when I failed!"

"Of course. Are you ready now to take the assignment papers for you and your brothers to sign?"

"Yes," said Zotul. "I am ready."

THE END

Judas Ram

By SAM MERWIN, JR.

The house was furnished with all luxuries, including women. If it only had a lease that could be broken—

ROGER TENNANT, crossing the lawn, could see two of the three wings of the house, which radiated spoke-like from its heptagonal central portion. The wing on the left was white, with slim square pillars, reminiscent of scores of movie sets of the Deep South. That on the right was sundeck solar house living-machine modern, something like a montage of shoeboxes. The wing hidden by the rest of the house was, he knew, spired, gabled and multicolored, like an ancient building in pre-Hitler Cracow.

Dana was lying under a tree near the door, stretched out on a sort of deck chair with her eyes closed. She wore a golden gown, long and close fitting and slit up the leg like the gown of a Chinese woman. Above it her comely face was sullen beneath its sleek cocoon of auburn hair.

She opened her eyes at his approach and regarded him with nothing like favor. Involuntarily he glanced down at the tartan shorts that were his only garment to make sure that they were on properly. They were. He had thought them up in a moment of utter boredom and they were extremely comfortable. However, the near-Buchanan tartan did not crease or even wrinkle when he moved. Their captors had no idea of how a woven design should behave.

"Waiting for me?" Tennant asked the girl.

She said, "I'd rather be dead. Maybe I am. Maybe we're all dead and this is Hell."

He stood over her and looked down until she turned away her reddening face. He said, "So it's going to be you again, Dana. You'll be the first to come back for a second run."

"Don't flatter yourself," she replied angrily. She sat up, pushed back her hair, got to her feet a trifle awkwardly because of the tight-fitting tubular gown. "If I could do anything about it…"

"But you can't," he told her. "They're too clever."

"Is this crop rotation or did you send for me?" she asked cynically. "If you did, I wish you hadn't. You haven't asked about your son."

"I don't even want to think about him," said Tennant. "Let's get on with it." He could sense the restless stirring of the woman within Dana, just as he could feel the stirring toward her within himself—desire that both of them loathed because it was implanted within them by their captors.

They walked toward the house.

IT DIDN'T look like a prison—or a cage. Within the dome of the barrier, it looked more like a well kept if bizarre little country estate. There was clipped lawn, a scattering of trees, even a clear little brook that chattered unending annoyance at the small stones, which impeded its flow.

But the lawn was not of grass—it was of a bright green substance that might have been cellophane but wasn't, and it sprouted from a fabric that might have been canvas but was something else. The trees looked like trees, only their trunks were bark all the way through—except that it was not bark. The brook was practically water, but the small stones over which it flowed were of no earthly mineral.

They entered the house, which had no roof, continued to move beneath a sky that glowed with light, which did not come from a sun or moon. It might have been a well kept if bizarre little country estate, but it wasn't. It was a prison, a cage.

The other two women were sitting in the heptagonal central hall. Eudalia, who had borne twin girls recently, was lying back, newly thin and dark of skin and hair, smoking a scentless cigarette. A tall woman, thirtyish, she wore a sort of shimmering green strapless evening gown. Tennant wondered how she maintained it in place, for despite her recent double motherhood, she was almost flat of bosom. He asked her how she was feeling.

"Okay, I guess," she said. "The way they manage it, there's nothing to it." She had a flat, potentially raucous voice. Eudalia had been a female foreman in a garment-cutting shop before being captured and brought through.

"Good," he said. "Glad to hear it." He felt oddly embarrassed. He turned to Olga, broad, blonde and curiously vital, who sat perfectly still, regarding him over the pregnant swell of her dirndl-clad waist. Olga had been a waitress in a mining town hash house near Scranton.

Tennant wanted to put an encouraging hand on her shoulder; to say something that might cheer her up, for she was by far the youngest of the three female captives, barely nineteen. But with the eyes of the other two, especially Dana, upon him, he could not.

"I guess I wasn't cut out to be a Turk," he said. "I don't feel at ease in a harem, even when it's supposedly my own."

"You're not doing so badly," Dana replied acidly.

"Layoff—he can't help it," said Eudalia unexpectedly. "He doesn't like it any better than we do."

"But he doesn't have to—have them," objected Olga. She had a trace of Polish accent that was not unpleasant. In fact, Tennant thought, only her laughter was unpleasant, a shrill, uncontrolled burst of staccato sound that jarred him to his heels. Olga had not laughed of late, however. She was too frightened.

"LET'S get the meal ordered," said Dana and they were all silent, thinking of what they wanted to eat but would not enjoy when it came. Tennant finished with his order, then got busy with his surprise.

It arrived before the meal, materializing against one of the seven walls of the roofless chamber. It was a large cabinet on slender straight legs that resembled dark polished wood. Tennant went to it, opened a hingeless door and pushed a knob on the inner surface. At once the air was hideous with the accrete harmony of a singing commercial...

> ...so go soak your head,
> be it gold, brown or red,
> in Any-tone Shampoo!

A disc jockey's buoyant tones cut in quickly as the final *ooooo* faded: "This is Grady Martin, your old night-owl, coming to you with your requests over Station WZZX, Manhattan. Here's a wire from Theresa McManus and the girls in the family entrance of Conaghan's Bar and Grill on West..."

Tennant watched the girls as a sweet-voiced crooner began to play an unfamiliar love lyric to a melody whose similarity to a thousand predecessors doomed it to instant success.

Olga sat up straight, her pale blue eyes round with utter disbelief. She looked at the radio, at Tennant, at the other two women, then back at the machine. She murmured something in Polish that was inaudible, but her expression showed that it must have been wistful.

Eudalia grinned at Tennant and, rising, did a sort of tap dance to the music, then whirled back into her chair, green dress a-shimmer, and sank into it just to listen.

Dana stood almost in the center of the room, carmine-tipped fingers clasped beneath the swell of her breasts. She might have been listening to Brahms or Debussy. Her eyes glowed with the salty brilliance of emotion and she was almost beautiful.

"*Rog!*" she cried softly when the music stopped. "A radio and WZZX! Is it—are they—real?"

"As real as you or I," he told her. "It took quite a bit of doing, getting them to put a set together. And I wasn't sure that radio would get through. TV doesn't seem to. Somehow it brings things closer..."

Olga got up quite suddenly, went to the machine and, after frowning at it for a moment, tuned in another station from which a Polish-speaking announcer was followed by polka music. She leaned against the wall, resting one smooth forearm on the top of the machine. Her eyes closed and she swayed a little in time to the polka beat.

TENNANT caught Dana looking at him and there was near approval in her expression—approval that faded quickly as soon as she caught his gaze upon her. The food arrived then and they sat down at the round table to eat it.

Tennant's meat looked like steak, it felt like steak, but, lacking the aroma of steak, it was almost tasteless. This was so with all of their foods, with their cigarettes, with everything in their prison— or their cage. Their captors were utterly without a human conception of smell, living, apparently, in a world without odor at all.

Dana said suddenly, "I named the boy Tom, after somebody I hate almost as much as I hate you."

Eudalia laid down her fork with a clatter and regarded Dana disapprovingly. "Why take it out on Rog?" she asked bluntly. "He didn't ask to come here any more than we did. He's got a wife back home. Maybe you want him to fall in love with you? Maybe you're jealous because he doesn't? Well, maybe he can't! And maybe it wouldn't work, the way things are arranged here."

"Thanks, Eudalia," said Tennant. "I think I can defend myself. But she's right, Dana. We're as helpless as—laboratory animals. They have the means to make us do whatever they want."

"Rog," said Dana, looking suddenly scared, "I'm sorry I snapped at you. I know it's not your fault. I'm—*changing.*"

He shook his head. "No, Dana, you're not changing. You're adapting. We all are. We seem to be in a universe of different properties as well as different dimensions. We're adjusting. I can do a thing or two myself that seem absolutely impossible."

"Are we really in the fourth dimension?" Dana asked. Of the three of them, she alone had more than a high-school education.

"We may be in the eleventh for all I know," he told her. "But I'll settle for the fourth—a fourth dimension in space, if that makes scientific sense, because we don't seem to have moved in time. I wasn't sure of that, though, till we got the radio."

"Why haven't they brought more of us through?" Eudalia asked, tamping out ashes in a tray that might have been silver.

"I'm not sure," he said thoughtfully. "I think it's hard for them. They have a hell of a time bringing anyone through alive, and lately they haven't brought anyone through—not alive."

"Why do they do it—the other way, I mean?" asked Dana.

Tennant shrugged. "I don't know. I've been thinking about it. I suppose it's because they're pretty human."

"*Human!*" Dana was outraged. "Do you call it human to—"

"Hold on," he said. "They pass through their gateway to Earth at considerable danger and, probably, expense of some kind. Some of them don't come back. They kill those of us who put up a fight. Those who don't—or can't—they bring back with them. Live or dead, we're just laboratory specimens."

"Maybe," Eudalia conceded doubtfully. Then her eyes blazed. "But the things they do—stuffing people, mounting their heads, keeping them on display in their—their whatever they live in. You call that human, Rog?"

"Were you ever in a big-game hunter's trophy room?" Tennant asked quietly. "Or in a Museum of Natural History? A zoo? A naturalist's lab? Or even, maybe, photographed as a baby on a bearskin rug?"

"I was," said Olga. "But that's not the same thing."

"Of course not," he agreed. "In the one instance, *we're* the hunters, the breeders, the trophy collectors. "In the other"—he shrugged—"we're the trophies."

THERE was a long silence. They finished eating and then Dana stood up and said, "I'm going out on the lawn for a while." She unzipped her golden gown, stepped out of it to reveal a pair of tartan shorts that matched his, and a narrow halter.

"You thought those up while we ate," he said. It annoyed him to be copied, though he did not know why. She laughed at him silently, tossed her auburn hair back from her face and went out of the roofless house, holding the gold dress casually over her bare arm.

Eudalia took him to the nursery. He was irritated now in another, angrier way. The infants, protected by cellophane-like coverlets, were asleep.

"They never cry," the thin woman told him. "But they grow— God, how they grow!"

"Good," said Tennant, fighting down his anger. He kissed her, held her close, although neither of them felt desire at the moment. Their captors had seen to that; it wasn't Eudalia's turn. Tennant said, "I wish I could do something about this. I hate seeing Dana so bitter and Olga so scared. It isn't their fault."

"And it's not yours," insisted Eudalia. "Don't let them make you think it is."

"I'll try not to," he said and stopped, realizing the family party was over. He had felt the inner tug of command, said good-by to the women and returned to his smaller compound within its own barrier dome.

Then came the invisible aura of strain in the air, the shimmering illusion of heat that was not heat that was prelude to his teleportation...if that were the word. It was neither pleasant nor unpleasant; it *was,* that was all.

He called it the training hall, not because it looked like a training hall but because that was its function. It didn't actually look like anything save some half-nourished dream a surrealist might have discarded as too nightmarish for belief.

As in all of this strange universe, excepting the dome-cages in which the captives were held, the training hall followed no rules of three-dimensional space. One wall looked normal for perhaps a third of its length, then it simply wasn't for a bit. It came back farther on at an impossible angle. Yet, walking along it, touching it, it felt perfectly smooth and continuously straight.

The opposite wall resembled a diagonal cross-section of an asymmetrical dumbbell—which was the closest Tennant could come to it in words. And it, too, felt straight. The floor looked like crystal smashed by some cosmic impact, yet it had reason. He *knew* this even though no reason was apparent to his three-dimensional vision. The ceiling, where he could see it, was beyond description.

The captor Tennant called *Opal* came in through a far corner of the ceiling. He—if it was a he—was not large, although this, Tennant knew, meant nothing; Opal might extend thousands of yards in some unseen direction. He had no regular shape and much of him was iridescent and shot with constantly changing colors. Hence the name Opal.

Communication was telepathic. Tennant could have yodeled or yelled or sung *Mississippi Mud* and Opal would have shown no reaction. Yet Tennant suspected that the captors could hear somewhere along the auditory scale, just as perhaps they could smell, although not in any human sense.

You will approach without use of your appendages.

The command was as clear as if it had been spoken aloud. Tennant took a deep breath. He thought of the space beside Opal. It took about three seconds and he was there, having spanned a distance of some ninety feet. He was getting good at it.

Dog does trick, he thought.

HE WENT through the entire routine at Opal's bidding. When at last he was allowed to relax, he wondered, not for the first time, if he weren't mastering some of the alleged Guru arts. At once he felt probing investigation. Opal, like the rest of the captors, was as curious as a cat—or a human being.

Tennant sat against a wall, drenched with sweat. There would be endless repetition before his workout was done. On Earth, dogs were said to be intellectually two-dimensional creatures. He wondered if they felt this helpless futility when their masters taught them to heel, to point, to retrieve.

Some days later, the training routine was broken. He felt a sudden stir of near-sick excitement as he received the thought:

Now you are ready. We are going through at last.

Opal was nervous, so much so that he revealed more than he intended. Or perhaps that was his intent; Tennant could never be sure. They were going through to Tennant's own dimension. He wondered briefly just what his role was to be.

He had little time to speculate before Opal seemed to envelop him. There was the blurring wrench of forced teleportation and they were in another room, a room which ended in a huge irregular passage that might have been the interior of a giant concertina—or an old-fashioned Kodak.

He stood before a kidney-shaped object over whose jagged surface colors played constantly. From Opal's thoughts it appeared to be some sort of ultra-dimensional television set, but to Tennant it was as incomprehensible as an oil painting to an animal.

Opal was annoyed that Tennant could make nothing of it. Then came the thought:

What cover must your body have not to be conspicuous?

Tennant wondered, cynically, what would happen if he were to demand a costume of mediaeval motley, complete with Pied Piper's flute? He received quick reproof that made his head ring as from a blow.

He asked Opal where and when they were going, was informed that he would soon emerge on Earth where he had left it. That told him everything but the date and season. Opal, like the rest of the captors, seemed to have no understanding of time in a human sense.

Waiting, Tennant tried not to think of his wife, of the fact that he hadn't seen her in—was it more than a year and a half on Earth? He could have controlled his heartbeat with one of his new powers, but that might have made Opal suspicious. He should be somewhat excited. He allowed himself to be, though he obscured the reasons. He was going to see his wife again...and maybe he could trick his way into not returning.

**

THE maid who opened the door for him was new, although her eyes were old. But she recognized him and stood aside to let him enter. There must, he thought, still be pictures of him around. He wondered how Agatha could afford a servant.

"Is Mrs. Tennant in?" he asked.

She shook her head and fright made twin stoplights of the rouge on her cheeks as she shut the door behind him. He went into the living room, directly to the long silver cigarette box on the coffee table. It was proof of homecoming to fill his lungs with smoke he could *smell*. He took another drag, saw the maid still in the doorway, staring.

"There's no need for fright," he told her. "I believe I still own this house." Then, "When do you expect Mrs. Tennant?"

"She just called. She's on her way home from the club."

Still looking frightened, she departed for the rear of the house. Tennant stared after her puzzledly until the kitchen door swung shut behind her. The club? What club?

He shrugged, returned to the feeling of comfort that came from being back here, about to see Agatha again, hold her close in no more than a few minutes. And stay, his mind began to add eagerly, but he pushed the thought down where Opal could not detect it.

He took another deep, lung-filling drag on his cigarette, looked around the room that was so important a part of his life. The three women back there would be in a ghastly spot. He felt like a heel for wanting to leave them there, then knew that he would try somehow to get them out. Not, of course, anything that would endanger his remaining with Agatha; the only way his captors would get him back would be as a taxidermist's specimen.

He realized, shocked and scared, that his thoughts of escape had slipped past his mental censor, and he waited apprehensively for Opal to strike. Nothing happened and he warily relaxed. Opal wasn't tapping his thoughts. Because he felt sure of his captive...or because he couldn't on Earth?

It was like being let out of a cage. Tennant grinned at the bookcase; the ebony-and-ivory elephants that Agatha had never liked were gone, but he'd get them back or another pair. The credenza had been replaced by a huge and ugly television console. That, he resolved, would go down in the cellar rumpus room, where its bleached modernity wouldn't clash with the casual antiquity of the living room.

Agatha would complain, naturally, but his being back would make up for any amount of furniture shifting. He imagined her standing close to him, her lovely face lifted to be kissed, and his heart lurched like an adolescent's. This hunger was real, not implanted. Everything would be real...his love for her, the food he ate, the things he touched, his house, his life...

Your wife and a man are approaching the house.

The thought message from Opal crumbled his illusion of freedom. He sank down in a chair, trying to refuse to listen to the rest of the command:

You are to bring the man through the gateway with you. We want another live male.

TENNANT shook his head, stiff and defiant in his chair. The punishment, when it came, was more humiliating than a slap across a dog's snout. Opal had been too interested in the next lab specimen to bother about his thoughts—that was why he had been free to think of escape.

Tennant closed his eyes, willed himself to the front window. Now that he had mastered teleportation, it was incredible how much easier it was in his own world. He had covered the two miles from the gateway to the house in a mere seven jumps, the distance to the window in an instant. But there was no pleasure in it, only a confirmation of his captor's power over him.

He was not free of them. He understood all too well what they wanted him to do; he was to play the Judas goat...or rather the Judas ram, leading another victim to the fourth-dimensional pen.

Grim, he watched the swoop of headlights in the driveway and returned to the coffee table, lit a fresh cigarette.

The front door was flung open and his diaphragm tightened at the remembered sound of Agatha's throaty laugh...and tightened further when it was followed by a deeper rumbling laugh. Sudden fear made the cigarette shake in his fingers.

"...Don't be such a stuffed shirt, darling." Agatha's mocking sweetness rang alarm-gongs in Tennant's memory. "Charley wasn't making a grab for *me*. He'd had one too many and only wanted a little fun. Really, darling, you seem to think that a girl..."

Her voice faded out as she saw Tennant standing there. She was wearing a white strapless gown, had a blue-red-and-gold Mandarin jacket slung hussar-fashion over her left shoulder. She looked even sleeker, better groomed, more assured than his memory of her.

"I'm no stuffed-shirt and you know it." Cass' tone was peevish. "But your idea of fun, Agatha, is pretty damn..."

It was his turn to freeze. Unbelieving, Tennant studied his successor. Cass Gordon—the *man,* the ex-halfback whose bulk was beginning to get out of hand, but whose inherent aggressive grace had not yet deserted him. The *man,* that was all—unless one threw in the little black mustache and the smooth salesman's manner.

"You know, Cass," Tennant said quietly, "I never, for a moment dreamed it would be you."

"*Roger!*" Agatha found her voice. "You're *alive!*"

"Roger," repeated Tennant viciously. He felt sick with disgust. Maybe he should have expected a triangle, but somehow he hadn't. And here it was, with all of them going through their paces like a trio of tent-show actors. He said, "For God's sake, sit down."

Agatha did so hesitantly. Her huge dark eyes, invariably clear and limpid no matter how much she had drunk, flickered toward him furtively. She said defensively, "I had detectives looking for you for six months. Where have you been, Rog? Smashing up the car like that and—disappearing! I've been out of my mind."

"Sorry," said Tennant. "I've had my troubles, too." Agatha was scared stiff—of him. Probably with reason. He looked again at Cass Gordon and found that he suddenly didn't care. She couldn't say it was loneliness. Women have waited longer than eighteen months. He would have if his captors had let him.

"Where in hell *have* you been, Rog?" Gordon's tone was almost parental. "I don't suppose it's news to you, but there was a lot of suspicion directed your way while that crazy killer was operating around here. Agatha and I managed to clear you."

"Decent of you," said Tennant. He got up; crossed to the cabinet that served as a bar. It was fully equipped—with more expensive liquor, he noticed, than he had ever been able to afford. He poured a drink of brandy, waited for the others to fill their glasses.

AGATHA looked at him over the rim of hers. "Tell us, Rog. We have a right to know. I do, anyway."

"One question first," he said. "What about those killings? Have there been any lately?"

"Not for over a year," Cass told him. "They never did get the devil who skinned those bodies and removed the heads."

So, Tennant thought, they hadn't used the gateway. Not since they had brought the four of them through, not since they had begun to train him for his Judas ram duties.

Agatha was asking him if he had been abroad.

"In a way," he replied unemotionally. "Sorry if I've worried you, Agatha, but my life has been rather—indefinite, since I—left."

He was standing no more than four inches from this woman he had desired desperately for six years, and he no longer wanted her. He was acutely conscious of her perfume. It wrapped them both like an exotic blanket, and it repelled him. He studied the firm clear flesh of her cheek and chin, the arch of nostril, the carmine fullness of lower lip, the swell of bosom above low-cut gown. And he no longer wanted any of it or of her. Cass Gordon—

It didn't have to be anybody at all. For it to be Cass Gordon was revolting.

"Rog," she said and her voice trembled, "what are we going to do? What do you *want* to do?"

Take her back? He smiled ironically; she wouldn't know what that meant. It would serve her right, but maybe there was another way.

"I don't know about you," he said, "but I suspect we're in the same boat. I also have other interests."

"You louse!" said Cass Gordon, arching rib cage and nostrils. "If you try to make trouble for Agatha, I can promise…"

"*What* can you promise?" demanded Tennant. When Gordon's onset subsided in mumbles, he added, "Actually, I don't think I'm capable of making more than a fraction of the trouble for either of you that you both are qualified to make for yourselves."

He lit a cigarette, inhaled. "Relax. I'm not planning revenge. After this evening, I plan to vanish for good. Of course, Agatha, that offers you a minor nuisance. You will have to wait six years to marry Cass—seven years if the maid who let me in tonight talks. That's the law, isn't it, Cass? You probably had it all figured out."

"You bastard," said Cass. "You dirty bastard! You know what a wait like that could do to us."

"Tristan and Isolde," said Tennant, grinning almost happily. "Well, I've had my little say. Now I'm off again. Cass, would you give me a lift? I have a conveyance of sorts a couple of miles down the road."

HE NEEDED no telepathic powers to read the thoughts around him then. He heard Agatha's quick intake of breath, saw the split-second look she exchanged with Cass. He turned away, knowing that she was imploring her lover to do something, *anything*, as long as it was safe.

Deliberately, Tennant poured himself a second drink. This might be easier and pleasanter than he had expected. They deserved some of the suffering he had had and there was a chance that they might get it.

Tennant knew now why he was the only male human the captors had been able to take alive. Apparently, thanks to the rain-slick road, he had run the sedan into a tree at the foot of the hill beyond the river. He had been sitting there, unconscious, ripe fruit on their doorstep. They had simply picked him up.

Otherwise, apparently, men were next to impossible for them to capture. All they could do was kill them and bring back their heads and hides as trophies. With women it was different—perhaps the captors' weapons, whatever they were, worked more efficiently on females. A difference in body chemistry or psychology, perhaps.

More than once, during his long training with Opal, Tennant had sent questing thoughts toward his captor, asking why they didn't simply set up the gateway in some town or city and take as many humans as they wanted.

Surprisingly there had been a definite fear reaction. As nearly as he could understand, it had been like asking an African pygmy, armed with a blowgun, to set up shop in the midst of a herd of wild elephants. It simply wasn't feasible—and furthermore he derived an impression of the tenacity as well as the immovability of the gateway itself.

They could be hurt, even killed by humans in a three-dimensional world. How? Tennant did not know. Perhaps as a man can cut a finger or even throat on the edge of a near-two-dimensional piece of paper. It took valor for them to hunt men in the world of men. In that fact lay a key to their character—if such utterly alien creatures could be said to have character.

CASS GORDON was smiling at him, saying something about one for the road. Tennant accepted only because it was luxury to drink liquor that smelled and tasted as liquor should. He raised his glass to Agatha, said, "I may turn up again, but it's unlikely, so have yourself a time, honey."

"Oh, Rog!" said Agatha and her eyes were fraudulently wet. Tennant felt pure contempt. She knew that Cass intended to try to kill him—and she couldn't play it straight. She had to ham it up with false emotion, even though she had silently pleaded with her lover to do something, anything.

He put down his empty glass. The thought that he had spent eighteen months yearning for this she-Smithfield like a half-damp puppy made him almost physically ill.

"You'll make out," he told her with savage sincerity. In her way, in accord with her desires, Agatha would. At bottom she was, he realized, as primitive, as realistic, as the three who waited beyond the gateway. An ex-waitress, an ex-forewoman, an ex-model of mediocre success—and Agatha. He tried to visualize his wife as a member of his involuntary harem and realized that she would adapt as readily as the other women. But he didn't want her.

He turned away and said, "Ready, Cass?"

"Right with you," the ex-halfback replied, hurrying toward the hall. Tennant considered, took another drink for his own road. The signals had been given, the game was being readied. He had no wish to upset the planning. He had some plans also, and theirs gave his enough moral justification to satisfy his usually troublesome conscience.

Agatha put her arms around his neck. She was warm and soft and moist of lip and playing her part with obvious enjoyment of its bathos. She murmured, "I'm so sorry, Rog, darling—"

"Cut!" he said almost in a snarl and wrenched free. He brought out a handkerchief—he had remembered to have one created, praise Allah—and rubbed lipstick from his face. He tossed the handkerchief to Agatha.

"You might have this analyzed," he told her lightly. "It could be interesting. The handkerchief, not the lipstick."

"I'm glad you're going!" she blazed, although her voice was low. "I'm *glad* you're going. I hope you *never* come back."

"That," he told her, "makes exactly two of us. Have fun."

He went out into the hall, where Cass was waiting, wearing what was intended to be a smile. They went out to the car together—it was a big convertible—and Cass got behind the wheel. He said, "Where to, old man?"

"The Upham Road," said Tennant, feeling nothing at all.

CASS got the car under way and Tennant sensed them coming through. They warned him that his chauffeur was carrying a weapon concealed in an inside pocket.

As if I didn't know! Tennant snapped back at them.

Cass tried to drive him past the spot beyond the bridge where the gateway lay hidden in its armor of invisibility. He evidently planned to go miles from the house before doing whatever he had decided to do.

Tennant thought he knew. It would involve riding the back roads like this one for fifteen or twenty miles, perhaps farther. He suspected that the quarry pond in South Upham was his intended destination. There would be plenty of loose rock handy with which to weigh down his body before dumping it into the water.

If it were recovered, Cass and Agatha could alibi one another. In view of his earlier disappearance, this would be simple. Of course there was the maid, but Cass had enough money and smooth talk to manage that angle. They could undoubtedly get away with killing him.

"Stop," said Tennant, just across the bridge.

"What for?" Cass countered and Tennant knew it was time to act. He wrenched the key from the ignition switch, tossed it out of the car. Cass braked, demanded, "What in hell did you do *that* for?"

"I get out here," Tennant said. "You didn't stop."

"Okay, if that's the way you want it." Cass' heavy right hand, the little black hairs on its back clearly visible in the dashboard light, moved toward his inside pocket.

Tennant teleported to the side of the road, became a half-visible shade against the darkness of the trees. He felt Opal's excitement surge through his brain, knew that from then on his timing would have to be split-second perfect.

It seemed to him as if all the inchoate thoughts, all the vague theories, all the half-formed plans of more than a year had crystallized. For the first time since his capture, he not only knew what he wanted to do—but saw the hint glimmer of a chance of doing it successfully.

He was going to try to lead Cass to the gateway, maneuver him inside—and then escape. They wouldn't get Tennant; the power of teleportation they themselves had given him would keep him from being captured again. It would work. He was sure of it. They'd have their male specimen and he'd be free...not to go back to Agatha, because he wouldn't, but to help the three women to get back, too.

CASS was plunging after him now, pistol in hand, shouting. Tennant could have him killed now, have him flayed and decapitated as other male victims had been. Opal might even give him the hide as a reward after it was treated. Some Oriental potentate, Tennant reflected, might relish having his wife's lover as a rug on his living room floor. Tennant preferred the less operatic revenge of leaving Cass and Agatha alive to suffer.

He teleported farther into the trees, closer to the gateway, plotting carefully his next moves. Cass was crashing along, cursing in frustration.

"Stand still, damn you! You shift around like a ghost!"

Tennant realized with sudden terror that Cass might give up, unable to solve his prey's abrupt appearances and disappearances. He needed encouragement to keep him going.

Jeeringly, Tennant paused, simultaneously thumbed his nose and stuck out his tongue at Cass. The scornful childishness of the gesture enraged Cass more than the worst verbal insult could have. He yelled his anger and fired at Tennant. There was no way to miss, but Tennant was five yards farther on before the explosion ended.

"Calm down," he advised quietly. "Getting mad always spoils your aim."

That naturally made Cass even angrier. He fired viciously twice more before Tennant reached the gateway, both times without a chance of hitting his elusive target.

Opal, Tennant discovered, was almost as frantic as Cass. He was deep inside the passage, jittering visibly in his excitement, in his anticipation of the most important bag his species had yet made on Earth. And there was something else in his thoughts...

Anxiety. Fear. The gateway was vulnerable to third-dimensional weapons. Where the concertina-like passage came into contact with Earth, there was a belt, perhaps a foot in width, which was spanned by some sort of force-webbing. Opal was afraid that a bullet might strike the webbing and destroy the gateway.

Cass was getting closer. It would be so easy...keep teleporting, bewilder him, let him make a grab...and then skip a hundred yards away just as the gateway shut. He would be outside, Cass inside.

And the three women? Leave them with Cass? Leave the gateway open for more live or mounted specimens?

Tennant concentrated on the zone of strain at the point of dimensional contact, he was there directly in front of it. Cass, cursing, lunged clear of the underbrush outside, saw Tennant there. Tennant was crouching low, not moving, staring mockingly at him. He lifted the automatic and fired.

TENNANT teleported by inches instead of yards, and so blood oozed from a graze on his left ear when he rejoined a shaken Opal in the world that knew no night. For a long time—how long, of course, he could not know—they stood and watched the gateway burn to globular ash in a dark brown fire that radiated searing cold.

Opal was in trouble. An aura of anger, of grief, of accusation, surrounded him. Others of them came and for a while Tennant was forgotten. Then, abruptly, he was back in his own compound, walking toward the house.

In place of his country Napoleonic roll-bed, which he had visualized for manufacture with special care, Dana had substituted an immense modern sleeping device that looked like a low hassock with a ten-foot diameter. She was on her knees, her back toward the door, fiddling with a radio.

She heard him enter, said without turning, "It won't work. Just a little while ago it stopped."

"I think we're cut off now, perhaps for good," he told her. He sat down on the edge of the absurd bed and began to take off the clothes they had given him for the hunt. He was too tired to protest against the massacre of his bedroom decor. He was not even sure he wanted to protest. For all its anachronism, the big round bed was comfortable.

She watched him, her hands on her thighs, and there was worry written on her broad forehead. "You know something, Rog."

"I don't *know* anything," he replied. "I only think and have theories." Unexpectedly he found himself telling her all about it, about himself, where he had been, what he had done.

She listened quietly, saying nothing, letting him go on. His head was in her lap and he talked up to her while she ran gentle fingers through his hair. When he had finished, she smiled down at him thoughtfully, affectionately, then said, "You know, you're a funny kind of man, Roger."

"Funny?"

She cuffed him gently. "You know what I mean. So now we're really cut off in this place—you and me and little Tom and Olga and Eudalia and the twins. What are we going to do, Roger?"

He shrugged. He was very tired. "Whatever they'll let us do," he said through a yawn. "Maybe we can make this a two-way study. They are almost human, you know. Almost."

He pulled her down and kissed her and felt unexpected contentment decant through his veins. He knew now that things had worked out the right way, the only way. He added aloud, "I think we'll find ways to keep ourselves amused."

"You really enjoy playing the heel, don't you, Rog?" Her lips moved against his as she spoke. "You had a chance to get out of here. You could have changed places with Cass. Maybe you could have destroyed the gateway and stayed on the other side and still saved other victims. But no, you had to come back to—us. I think I'm going to be in love with you for that."

He sat up on one elbow and looked down at her half angrily. "Are you trying to make a goddam hero out of me?" he asked.

THE END

Finders Keepers

By MILTON LESSER

*Amhurst wanted to get married. But then an invisible ingénue moved in on his
wedding day...*

EDDIE AMHURST WATCHED the scissors get up from the
dresser and march across the room. If they had marched on the
floor it would have been bad enough—but not this bad. They
marched across the air of the bedroom, one thin metal leg after the
other, to where Eddie was sitting on the edge of the bed in his
underwear.

They went *snip, snip*—once, twice, rapidly. Then they marched
again across the air of the room and plunked down on the dresser.

In his right hand Eddie held a silky piece of black cloth. In his
left hand he held a similar item. On the floor at his feet were two
other pieces of black cloth. If you glued the sections together
you'd have a pair of black silk socks, size twelve. They were so
new that you could still see where the paper telling the brand name
and the size clung to one of them.

But they weren't much good as socks anymore. In his hands
Eddie held what could have been a pair of black-silk spats except
that no one wore black-silk spats. On the floor at his feet were two
black silk fingerless gloves.

"Hey, George!" Eddie called. "George, come here quick."

George ran in from the bathroom, shaving-soap still on one
side of his face. He looked at Eddie and the two pieces of black
silk in Eddie's hands. He said, "What the hell did you do that for?"

"Me? I didn't do anything."

"Anyone can see that you went to the dresser, got the scissors,
cut your socks in half, then put the scissors back on the dresser.
What I want to know is why. *Why?*"

"I didn't," Eddie said lamely then he told George how the
scissors had got up, marched across the room, and cut his socks.

"Yeah," said George. "Right away. Take it easy, kid. I know you're about to be married. I know you're nervous. But relax. Just take it easy—calm down."

"Hah!" said Eddie. *"Hah!"*

"What's so funny?"

"I can prove to you that I didn't get up, take the scissors and cut my socks. I can prove it, that's what."

George told him to go ahead.

"I just took a shower, right?"

"Right."

"I always powder my feet after a shower, right?"

"Howinhell should I know?"

Eddie sat back on the bed and stuck his feet out. "Look."

There was white powder all over the bottoms of his feet, a lot more of it in between his toes.

"Okay," George said. "I see it. What does that prove?"

"You go ahead and find the powder on the rug. If I walked from here to the dresser and back there'd be powder all over the rug where I walked. Find it."

George looked but the rug was solid blue without any white marks on it. "So you crawled on your hands and knees, so you walked on your hands. Just don't tell me the scissors did that themselves. They couldn't."

"I didn't say they did it by themselves. *Something made them do it.* Something doesn't want me to get married, George. Take last night. Someone put pineapple in my fruit cup. You know I'm allergic to pineapple. It makes me itch all over for two days but luckily I found it. When I came back from the florist the bridge was out. I could have been killed if I hadn't noticed it."

George shook his head. "The bridge was *not* out. I went back and looked for myself later. You went the long way for nothing because the bridge is standing as it always stood. Did you hear anything over the radio about the bridge being out?"

"No-o-o..."

"There wasn't even any rain. Eddie-boy, you're just nervous. You're imagining things. Judy will have a nervous wreck on her hands if you keep this up. Look—you just sit here and wait for me while I run downtown and get you another pair of black socks."

"Uh-unh. It's Sunday and the stores are closed."

"Okay, I'll let you wear mine. I'm only the best man and I'll wear navy blue and no one will know the difference." George sat on the edge of the bed next to Eddie and took off his shoes and socks. He gave the socks—just a half-size too big—to Eddie, then padded across the room to the chest of drawers to find a pair of navy socks for himself.

The scissors got up off the dresser again while George's back was turned and Eddie wanted to yell, only no sound came out. He just sat there watching while the scissors cut this new pair of black socks neatly in half. Then George began to turn around and the scissors dropped quickly at Eddie's feet.

George held up a pair of navy socks. "I got 'em..." he began. "Eddie, what the hell did you do *that* again for?"

"Honest..."

"Never mind. We'll both wear navy." Plainly he thought his cousin Judy was marrying a lunatic.

The thing that surprised Eddie most was the fact nothing happened during the first part of the ceremony. It was an outdoor wedding and he stood with George at the makeshift altar in the garden while Judy came down the aisle with her entourage.

Judy was lovely in her getup, all right, only Eddie could have done without all the pomp and ceremony. And lately there had been something about Judy—little meannesses, some annoying petulances—which had left Eddie on the irritable side.

It was her mother as much as anything, a fat overbearing dominating windbag...Eddie-boy, stop talking to yourself that way about your future mother-in-law...

Why should you? Go ahead, keep thinking like that if it's what you feel. Assert yourself.

"Who said that?"

"Said what?" George wanted to know. "I didn't hear anyone. And be quiet, Eddie—people are looking at you."

You don't have to be quiet unless you really want to. Don't let them rope you into anything, Eddie—it still isn't too late.

Eddie looked in vain for the source of the voice but everyone around him seemed so utterly unperturbed that he could only conclude that he was hearing things. Could this have been the voice of his conscience, telling him to get out while the getting was good?

Conscience, smonscience. No such thing, Eddie. It's me.

"Well, who are *you?*"

George said, *"Will* you shut up, Eddie? Everyone's staring."

After that it wasn't easy. Judy joined him at the altar but he listened to the ceremony with only one ear. With the other he tried to pay attention to the voice which he alone heard. Since it continued and since he was the only one who heard it, he concluded quite logically that he was going off his rocker. Then maybe he *was* being roped into something—because if the prospect of marriage to Judy made him feel this way, then maybe he'd better call the whole thing off before it was too late.

Or had the strange voice put that idea into his head? Come to think of it, here was a nice pleasant female voice. It didn't rasp like Mrs. Wilkins' voice and it didn't hold the slight suggestion of a whine dormant in her daughter Judy's.

"Do you, Edward, take this girl Judy, to be your lawfully wedded wife?"

Silence, except for a few sobs and whimpers in the sea of faces around them.

"Do you, Edward..."

Don't do it, Eddie. Do it and that'll be the end for you. You'd regret it something awful.

"You think so, Miss, ah—"

I'll tell you my name after you refuse. You'll find out a lot of things after.

George wailed in Eddie's ear, "For gosh sakes, boy—you're holding up the works! And quit that mumbling to yourself. Just say yes."

"Hmmm," said Eddie, cogitating.

"...And do you, Judy, take this man Edward—"

Apparently his *hmmm* had been taken as an affirmative if nervous response.

You're right, Eddie—that's just what happened. Only don't let them go on. In a moment it will be too late, and you'll be stuck.

"You think so, eh?"

"Shut *up!*" George hissed in his ear.

"...To have and to hold through sickness and in health, till—"

The wind came up so suddenly, and with it the clouds, one moment they stood in a bright sunshiny garden, the next it was dark and somber and overhead lightning flashed and thunder rolled sullenly.

The rain came down in thick sheets from what had been a moment before a wonderfully clear blue sky. Even George's composure received a serious dent. "It just can't happen that fast!" he cried.

Judy sobbed, "My gown. Oh, my precious gown!"

"I said, do you, Judy..."

Don't let him go on, Eddie. The rain will add to the confusion. Tell him you never said yes—you never did, you know.

"That's true. I didn't."

"Didn't what?" George demanded as several men ran out to them with umbrellas.

"I never said yes," Eddie told him, but the thunder all but drowned him out. "I never said yes!" he fairly screamed.

Since everyone had heard him that time, the ceremony had to begin anew. "Do you, Edward..."

Better, better that you don't, Eddie.

"Will you *please* be quiet and let me make up my own mind?"

"Eddie!" This was George.

"...to have and to hold, through..."

Judy was trying vainly to pull the entire length of her gown under the umbrella and the fact that she couldn't made her pout. Her makeup was running in the rain too—and quite suddenly she looked rather unpretty. Definitely positively irrevocably unpretty—a younger thinner somewhat more attractive image of her mother. A thoroughly revolting thought.

"Uh-unh," said Eddie.

You tell 'em, Eddie-boy.

"Uh-unh."

George whispered, "What does that mean? Say yes so everyone can hear you, especially with this thunder."

"That doesn't mean yes," Eddie explained patiently. But then, because the thunder roared still louder, he shouted, "In fact, it means the opposite of yes."

You tell 'em, Eddie.

"It means that this is all a mistake. I will not marry Judy. The answer to the question is no, *no*, NO!"

No one did anything. They all just stood there, looking at him, and Judy even forgot to see how the rain was ruining her gown. Eddie became embarrassed—they all just stared. Presently he kissed Judy's cheek politely, said he was sorry, turned on his heel and strode down the muddy aisle.

Everyone looked but no one tried to stop him.

The voice said, *You told 'em, Eddie. You sure told 'em!*

He took a hot shower and it made him feel much better. When he finished and got into a pair of dungarees and a tee shirt and lit a cigarette, the bell rang. It was George.

"I ought to punch your nose, Eddie Amhurst."

Don't let him talk that way, Eddie. Until now the voice had been silent since the ruined ceremony.

"Don't talk to me that way. Just because she was your cousin and just because you introduced us on a blind date—"

Splat! Something hit Eddie's nose, just as had been predicted and he sat down on the floor.

He hit *you! Get up and knock the stuffing out of him, Eddie.*

Eddie's nose bled easily. It was bleeding now. He stood up and George hit him again and then his nose was bleeding more than ever.

This time Eddie sat there and did not try to get up. He knew there were about nine quarts of blood in his body and he must have lost at least a quart by now.

George readjusted his high hat. He took a step towards the door but never reached it. A big redwood bookend took off from an end table and thudded against the side of his head. His high hat fell off and he sat down next to Eddie, muttering something about hitting him from behind.

The voice said, *I couldn't bear to let you take a beating. If you can't defend yourself, then I've got to do it for you.*

For the first time a concrete thought on all this came to Eddie—perhaps it was a girl, just an ordinary girl, only she was invisible. He had seen a movie once and while the invisible man in it had remained invisible, if you put some clothing on him you could see his shape.

Eddie ran around the room with George's high hat, trying to find an invisible head. But after a time he felt silly. The hat kept falling to the floor every time he tried to put it on something.

The voice giggled. *You're wasting your time, Eddie. I'm not invisible, not in the way you mean. Now that you didn't marry that Judy-thing, you have no ties. Right?*

"Umm."

No parents?

"Nope."

No close relatives of any type?

"A bunch of third cousins in Chicago I think."

They don't matter. Any close friends?

Eddie looked down at the floor, where George was trying to get up. "I used to have one," he said.

But not now—not any longer. Good! Then you can come with me, Eddie. I had to make sure of that first. You ready?

"Where are we going?"

Just have some patience and you'll see for yourself.

"Maybe I won't like it."

"He's talking to himself again," George said. "Am I glad my cousin didn't marry *him!* Lucky Judy."

Ready, Eddie? Hah! A poet and don't know it!

"Umm."

Eddie began to feel dizzy but he reasoned that was because George had punched him in the nose not once but twice. Soon the floor came up to meet him because he no longer could keep his balance and then, as he sat there, everything began to grow hazy, foggy, unreal. Soon the room was only a shadow of a room and he could not even tell that the rug was blue. Less than a shadow, it seemed to dissolve in water—in very hot water, because it dissolved quickly.

This Eddie did not know—but he dissolved with it...

***

"Edam Hurst! Wake up!"

Eddie sat up groggily. He was on a big comfortable couch and the voice came out of a loudspeaker on the wall. There were the couch and the loudspeaker, a closed door and Eddie—and outside of that the room, a small one, was empty.

"You got it wrong," Eddie said. "Just a matter of pronouncing. Not Edam Hurst. Ed Amhurst. Get the difference?"

"Subtle," the voice said. "It doesn't matter. There isn't another Edam Hurst or Ed Amhurst here. No confusion."

"Well, where's the other voice? The woman."

"Early cultural trait," the voice mused. "High sex-identification. Eeb did nothing to assert her femininity, yet he knew the voice for a woman's. Interesting, extremely interesting."

"Of course she's a woman."

"The timbre isn't that much different for you to know it as a certainty ever. High sex-identification in your time, young man. If I simply heard Eeb's voice I'd never know her sex—not just from her voice. "

"Well, she *is* a woman."

"Certainly, certainly—and a mighty troublesome one. First time something like this has happened in nearly a thousand years. What do you think we ought to do?"

"How the heck should I know? I don't even know what happened."

"True, true. I'd forgotten you're no telepath. I wonder if telepathy came in when high sex-identification began to wane. Umm, no—hardly possible. Eeb is obviously a throwback and she has both. Intriguing."

The door opened and a woman entered the room. She was dressed in shorts and some sort of negligible halter. She walked across the room to the loudspeaker and Eddie, who had, armed with tape measure, once judged a local beauty contest, was sure she was the most beautiful woman he had ever seen.

She said, "I'd better shut that thing off before Rajuz lulls you to sleep with all his scientific talk." She flicked a switch on the loudspeaker. "Of course he can still speak through telepathy but your mind won't get the impulses without that loudspeaker, Eddie. See? I can hear him now but you can't."

Eddie had to take her word for it because he couldn't hear a thing. He hardly cared. Of paramount importance was this fact—here was *the* voice. Not any voice but the one that had brought him here, wherever *here* was.

Eddie tried to be patient. "You're Eeb," he said. "That much I know. But where the hell are we?"

"You mean, in space?"

"Uh-huh."

"We're exactly where your room was. We haven't moved an inch."

"So where's my room? Where is it then?"

"It isn't. It *was*. Fifty thousand years ago it was, Eddie. Not now. Now it's gone, with the building, with the city, with your whole civilization. We've left your time and entered mine."

"Yeah," said Eddie. His voice sounded lame.

"You don't believe me."

"Nope, sorry—I don't." In truth Eddie was glad he hadn't married Judy but as for the rest of this, well—he was from Missouri.

"It's simple. I'm a professor of history and my period of study was yours, the second millennium of the Christian Era."

"Do you—ah—teach history in that outfit?" He pointed to the enticing lines of her halter and shorts.

"Certainly. It's comfortable. Anyway we use no guesswork in history. We use a time-scanner. That, of course, makes history the most accurate of all the sciences. It's mental travel through time—not physical unless you will it.

"Elementary stuff, Eddie. Just as they learned teleportation through space ten thousand years ago, so they learned you can do the same thing through time. Mental effort, applied properly, can move physical objects. It was always latent in human beings through some unknown ancestor—they just had to learn how to control the power."

Eddie was still skeptical. "So you studied history by actually going back there?"

"Something like that. Then I found you, Edam Hurst."

"Ed Amhurst."

"What's the difference? I found you and once I did, purely by chance, of course—that was the end of history. No more studying. They tell me I'm a throwback—less psi quotient, more sex identification than anyone here. Maybe that explains it.

"Anyway I had to bring you back. People constantly teleport trophies through time—but not in a thousand years has anyone brought back a human being. I saw that you had no ties and I brought you. Unfortunately there's a law against it, I think."

Eddie asked her why.

"It can cause a lot of trouble. You can change history by bringing someone where he doesn't belong. But I had to. I'm a throwback. I couldn't be satisfied…"

Slowly, almost imperceptibly, she had been walking closer and closer to Eddie, ever since she had turned off the loudspeaker. Now, abruptly, she was standing next to him—and then she was sitting on his lap. She snuggled in close and then she began to kiss him and Eddie knew at once that kissing had come a long way in fifty thousand years, even if the psi quotient was greater and sex identification had diminished.

Three minutes later Eeb got up and Eddie knew quite suddenly that while he had always known love at first sight to be ridiculous and impossible, love at first kiss was a very different matter.

"Damn that Rajuz! He's the Dean, and he wants us in his office. So it goes, Eddie—if it's not one thing it's another. We have no choice, of course. We'll have to go."

They left the room and stood on a moving sidewalk with a lot of other people and this first five-minute glimpse of the place was enough to convince him that he had indeed been teleported through time. A lot of what he saw, could not even register in his brain simply because he had no standards for comparison. But he did notice almost at the outset that everything seemed simplified— possibly because telepathy and teleportation were the reigning king and queen.

"You've seen enough of the city for now," Eeb told him. "All these people are out walking for the exercise. Let's take the shorter way to Rajuz's office."

One moment they stood there on the moving sidewalk, the next they were in the presence of Rajuz.

Rajuz sat at what must have been a desk, a spherical desk, but he did not look much like a dean. He could have been a technician or even a truck-driver.

Eeb explained, "The trend has been away from differentiation since the sex-identification patterns were decreased. But I'm fed up with it. They all look the same, like that. You know something, Eddie? I like you better."

Rajuz tuned in another of the loudspeakers on his desk, and Eeb explained that it was necessary because the psi quotient varied in everyone.

"Eeb Lym, Edam Hurst, you have committed a misdemeanor."

"Not him," Eeb said. "It was all my fault."

"Motivation is above suspicion here, you know that. It is the law—if someone does something it is because he wants to. Edam Hurst is as guilty as you are."

He scowled at them for a time and then continued. "Frankly, I don't know what to do. This is the first crime of this nature in a thousand years and while it's merely a misdemeanor it will have to go punished."

"Yes," Eeb agreed. "I guess so. You name it and we'll oblige."

"You won't like it."

"Name it anyway."

"The punishment simply is this—you are to take Edam Hurst back where he belongs."

"Oh, no! Not after I found him—"

"That is the punishment. Throwback or no you must learn that sex identification is decidedly secondary to psi quotient. When can you take him?"

"Well, I—"

"Don't I have anything to say about this?" Eddie demanded.

"A feeble bit at best. Just sit still and listen, young man."

"—I suppose I can take him this afternoon if the scanner room is vacant."

"It will be vacant, we'll see to that. I'm glad you're being sensible about this whole unhappy affair, Eeb Lym."

"What are you so cheerful about?" Eddie said.

They stood in the scanner room and the girl was humming a little tune. "Don't worry, Edam Hurst. Relax, Eddie. I'm cheerful because I know what I'm doing, that's why. Just bear with me."

He had no choice. But now that suddenly, devastatingly, he felt about Eeb the way she felt about him, he did not want to lose her. It was as simple as that.

"Time is huge," Eeb told him. "You didn't think that once I found you I'd let you go? Oh no, I found you and you're mine— that's all there is to it. Even Jeeva, Lord of the City, couldn't do a thing about it. Nossir. Time is big and while I said..."

She flicked a switch and kicked nonchalantly at a pedal with her foot. "That ought to do it. Just don't be frightened, Eddie. The important thing—"

"The important thing," he finished for her, "is that we want to be together, right?"

"Right," she said, kissed him soundly and turned a little knob on the wall. "*Now* we're ready."

As before Eddie became dizzy and soon he was sitting on the floor watching the room spin and fade, spin and fade.

By the time it dissolved, Eddie was whirling away into a giddy limbo.

He stood up and heard the wild nature sounds all around them. The bulk of the time-machine was big at his side in a green wooded glen. Eeb came dancing up to him with an armful of fruit. "Here, it's delicious. Taste it—"

She held out her hand and he took a bite, then looked up sharply. With a whirring sound, the machine faded, disappeared.

"I sent it back," the girl said. "I wanted to make it permanent, just you and I. Time is big and they'll never find us. Besides, they'll think this is punishment enough. We're exiled back here."

"Well, where is *here?*"

"Oh, I'm not exactly sure. Right around the time the human species emerged. It should be a wonderful life, Eddie—"

Eddie began to sing a popular song. Popular? It had been popular—when? This all was very confusing.

"Edam Hurst, you have positively the worst singing voice I've ever heard."

He smiled and told her to be quiet, kissing her to put more force behind the command. Then, hand in hand, Edam and Eeb walked through their glen.

THE END

The names of those congenital skeptics who insist that time-travel is impossible, even in theory, are Legion. Nor is their stand difficult to comprehend. They say that no man or woman has yet trawled backward to meet a younger him or herself face to face. They say this is immutable paradox. And by way of clincher they add a query as to why, if time-travel is to come, has it never happened? Why haven't we recorded instances of visitations from the future?

However, those in favor of time-travel have answers ready and waiting. These optimists (?) use the parallel universe theory to meet the first question. Such return, they claim, would immediately cause a forking of the Earthways, leaving our version of the world untrodden by time-traveling feet. As to the clincher, they counter-question with a how do we know we haven't had such visitors? Time-travel, when it comes, will come in a far-distant future. At such a distance the mere six thousand years of recorded human history is a mere flyspeck on the annals of Earth. So why should this tiny dot in the continuum have been favored?

The Rag and Bone Men

By ALGIS BUDRYS

Unfortunate castaway! Marooned far from home—with nothing to share his loneliness but humans!

THE other one—Charpantier, he called himself—he and I were going back up the hill to the Foundation, carrying our bags, when I happened to remark I didn't think the Veld was sane anymore. (I call myself Maurer.)

Charpantier said nothing for a moment. We kept walking, up the gravel path between the unimaginatively clipped hedges. But he was frowning a little, and after a while he said in an absent way: "Now, how would one determine that?" He looked straight into my eyes, which is something that has always upset me, and challenged: "I don't think one could."

I felt the shock of inadequacy. Words come out of me—perfectly accurate words, I know; but I never know how and sometimes when asked I forget.

Now I must be very lucid. I must be his kind of man, I thought, and picked my way among my words. "These things he's had us get," I said, putting the burlap bag down and stopping so as to hold Charpantier in one place.

"He wants to build something unEarthly," Charpantier said, annoyed because I was playing his kind of trick on him, and so baldly. "What standards do you propose to judge by?"

But I was right and he was wrong. Now it remained to make him see how. "Yes. He wants to build something unEarthly. Out of Earthly parts. He wants to take six radio tubes for an Earthly radio, three pieces of Earthly Lucite exactly ¼ Earthly inch thick, a roll of Earthly 16-gauge wire, a General Electric heat lamp, and all these other things—the polystyrene foam blocks, the polyurethane plastic sheeting, the polyvinyl insulating tape; what have you in your bag, Charpantier? Out of all this, he wants to make a Veldish thing."

"He's spent years learning about Earthly things," Charpantier pointed out. "For years, we've brought him books. Men. Everything he needs. Now he's learned what the Earthly equivalents of Veldish materials are, and he's ready to make his new transporter." Charpantier had a dark face—dark hair, dark beard, dark eyes. When his dark brows drew together it was easy to see that his best expression was dark scorn.

"I THINK he's desperate," I said. "I think he's learned all he can. He's learned what the nearest Earthly equivalents to Veldish things are. And he's learned that all Earth can give him nothing closer. I don't see how he could do better. Even he. You cannot make apples of cabbages. But he wants to get home—you know he wants so much to leave here and get home—and now he's desperate, and is going to try making a new transporter out of materials nothing like those in the one that broke and marooned him here."

"And it won't function?" Charpantier asked. "There is that risk. But why shouldn't he try? What's insane in that?"

"I fear it might work. I fear it might work in ways a transporter should not." And I shivered, for if I say something I feel it, and I do not feel anything I don't believe is right. I have been wrong, but not often...or perhaps I forget.

Charpantier smiled. "How should a Veld transporter work?"

"That's not the point!" I cried at Charpantier's obstinacy in being Charpantier. "I don't have to know. The Veld has to know, and be insane enough to try something different. Look—" I said, searching, being my own kind of man, now, and letting the words come straight from the images in my head. "Assume a man. Assume a man stranded on an island, for years. Assume he has ways of realizing his heart's desire, if only he can find the things to work with. But it's a small island. And while it's a good island how can it give a marooned man not only comfort but heart's desire? He searches. He perhaps sends messengers, if he himself cannot penetrate the jungle; such messengers as he can command. And, in the end, after years, he knows he cannot have exactly what he wants. But he can have something very near it. So, in the end, he takes a rag, and a bone, and a hank of hair—"

"And makes a woman?" Charpantier laughed. "If he fails, what of it?"

"But if he succeeds, Charpantier! If he *succeeds!*" Couldn't he see? "What sort of woman?"

Charpantier looked at me for a moment, but I hadn't made him see. He saw only me, and I had taken up his time without delivering value. So he chastised me.

"The Veld made me and you. Are you dissatisfied?"

He had that trick, Charpantier. If you tried to give him a problem he couldn't solve, he gave you a greater problem of your own, to add to the one you already carried.

I picked up my bag and followed him up the hill to the Foundation, where the Veld timelessly waited.

It was dusk, and as I walked I turned my eyes up to the stars. One eye was larger than the other, and a different color. My nose sat askew on my lumpen face. Though Charpantier was a hunchback, and lacked a finger, still he was a handsome hunchback. But I, whom the Veld had made second, with Charpantier's example, was merely whole. And from my eyes, tears.

WE entered the Foundation. It had been erected around the Veld, when he first came and there were men who could question.

Now the building was neat and kept up, but all its many rooms were empty, and all its many machines were still. Charpantier had his cottage on the West—a very learned man had used it, while working with the Veld—and I had mine on the East, where a military commander had kept his family.

The Veld lived in the heart of the Foundation, in the odd-shaped room whose walls traced the configuration he had been forced to assume when his broken transporter had interrupted his journey between—where?—and the home he pined for. Men came from the town below the hill to care for the building, but Charpantier or I had to go fetch them. They no longer questioned. They distressed us with their constant need for commanding, and so every time they were finished with their work we commanded them homeward. No Earthly creature lived on the hill.

The Veld was kindly, but an end comes to kindness. The time came when the questioning of men would have led them, if answered, irrevocably into Veldish ways.

It was perhaps a kindness, too, that the Veld did what he did to questioning creatures. But however it may have been, now there were only men to be commanded. Charpantier commanded in the West, and I in the East, and the Veld, though he permitted us to question all men, and each other, commanded us.

Charpantier and I did not often speak to each other while in the Foundation. We were too near the Veld, and insufficiently full of ourselves. But as we rode down the elevator, with its noise of metal sliding all alone in the world, Charpantier looked at me. And I knew what he looked.

I have thought to myself that Charpantier says of everything: "Why is this thing not perfect?" while I say to myself: "Where is the perfection in this thing?" Surely my thought is as potent as his. But you see his advantage over me, for he was forever safe from what I might look at him, but I, I was not safe.

We reached the chamber of the Veld. We opened the door and displayed our accumulation to his perceptions.

"My-being reflects you," the Veld told us from his perception, and seeing that he was become beautiful, I knew we had done well. "Now will I make, and take my way, and you in your sorrow stay to see the world restored."

This was as he had promised the world, and us, before he put an end to questioning. Though only we remembered. But I wondered—I did not question; I wondered—as I imagined his making of the new transporter, taking my imagined thing from what I knew of how he had made us; I wondered whether the world was safe.

I thought of the chamber beside this one, where we had been born. I had often been there, only to look. There is the tank—the Rochester, Minnesota, Biophysical Equipment Co. tank. And there is the Velikaya Socialisticheskaya Rossiya coagulator, and the IBM 704, and the Braun, Boveri heater. There stand the cabinets, with their Torsen, Held Artztmetal refrigeration units. And the cabinets stand full of flasks and ampules, and there is the autoclave full of

Becton-Dickinson Yale syringes, and dangling from the wall are the Waldos the Veld used to manipulate all these things.

And of all these Earthly things, the Veld made men not entirely Earthly, for the Veld is a Veld.

Now soon, the new transporter would take the Veld away—in ways I wondered were perilous—and it would be Charpantier and I who stayed to see the world restored.

Charpantier and I, who called ourselves, but had no names.

He commanded us to go and we went, I East, Charpantier West. I saw Charpantier hurry down his side of the hill, handsome and hasty under the stars. I walked—for me, to run is to risk—and I trembled, for me to feel is to know, and the Veld was desperate. He slept at night, secure from questions even though he slept, for his power once exercised was irrevocable so long as he existed. But tonight he did not sleep; he made.

I thought of my assumed man, on his assumed island, red-eyed and tremulous of hand, bent over his pot, stirring, stirring, unable to wait for morning. I thought of the light from his fire, shining on the dumb eyes of his faithful messengers waiting at the edge of his clearing. The messengers are dismissed from service, yet not quite sure they are dismissed. And I thought of this Earth, and the Veld's old promise to us that tomorrow it would wake knuckling its eyes, and need a loving voice to say there was an end to nightmares.

I would speak and Charpantier would speak, but what would we say? And in what voice, born of the Veld's touch on the Waldos? And would there be more than speaking to do?

I did not think there was much I could do but speak. Charpantier lacks a finger, but I...I have hands, but I lack them.

Oh, but the stars were cold! The Moon in this season was a day Moon, and now below the horizon. Stars, stars and galaxies, but beyond them, where the Veldish beings lived, nothing I could see, and below the stars, too, here where I reached the brow of the hill and clumsily opened my wings, here, too, nothing, as I lurched into the night and in great strain beat toward the places of men.

I HAD a favorite place; the place I had chosen to begin to speak from. It was small, as men measure things—a few lights in the darkness, here the sheen of a lake, there the tiered wooliness of trees—a town in which I had disposed those men who must first unbind themselves from the years of no questioning. For unlike the Veld and his transporter—and even the Veld needed a transporter—Charpantier and I could not be everywhere.

It was my thought to reassure these men first, and have them go out and reassure others, as older brothers will soothe the younger in the night. I knew from an old argument that Charpantier planned the same. But, of course, they would not be the same sort of men for Charpantier as for me.

Still, they were all men. Once they had all rubbed the sleep from their eyes they would tell each other what they saw, and in the end and all men would have agreed on the shape of the world, so it would not matter what imperfections Charpantier pointed out, or what implicit glories I perceived.

If the Veld's hand did not tremble as he stirred his pot.

And yet it had—it had; Charpantier had said more than he thought, when he thought to stop up my mouth with myself.

I faced away from the Foundation, now mile on mile behind me. But my eyes turned inward, and in me my mind hovered over the Veld. I had no actual distant eye—no way of seeing beyond the curve of the world or through the haze of the air; no ear to listen to a sound so far away it cannot urge the molecules of air my pinions grope at. But often it is well enough to think, for any thought seems accurate enough to act on, and in time thoughts grow so practiced that they might well be eyes. And so I saw the Veld, though I did not see him, and I saw him falter.

In me, the Veld suddenly told: "I have made, and I go. Forgive me for your sorrow." And I forgave him, as I had forgiven him long ago. For his duty was to men, not to ourselves who were part of that duty. And Charpantier, I knew, had nothing to forgive, for he was glad of his sorrow.

The wind numbed my eyes. I wept.

Under the cold stars, my crude cheeks glistened. I hovered over the town, where some men slept and some men worked, because some machines run during the day and some run at night, and I listened for anything else the Veld might have to tell, for he was my irrevocable commander as long as he existed on this Earth. I also listened with the ear of habituated thought.

And I heard. In my mind's eye, I saw the Veld use the Earthly transporter, but it was not with my mind's ear alone that I heard what I heard.

The pot erupts. The stranded man claws back in agony so great he cannot even scream, arms, legs and face smoldering, and jounces on the ground, to lie, to moan, to be a long mindless time dying. And at the clearing's edge the little messengers have no one to say what could be done to soothe him.

What now? Where to go, what to do, how to repair?

Oh, Veld, Veld, long-living Veld, what truly eternal sorrow!

I sank down through the air, bereft and graceless. What could I do for the Veld? All that remained to me was what I could say to men. But I knew as I landed among them that the Veld's promise could not be kept, since the Veld was still here.

I cried out to the men: "Awake! Arise!" They stumbled out of their houses, but when I said to the first of them: "Question me!" he obediently answered: "How?"

I GO back to where the Foundation was, now and then. I bring doctors with me, after each time it seems to me I have found a way to tell them what to seek. The Veld lies where his chamber was, before the stone decayed, and tells me nothing.

If he truly reflects me, as he is now, then I don't know if I can bear to wait for the day when I can dash myself down from the outraged air and surrender myself to the sea-speckled rocks. The doctors say that if only someone would tell them what questions to ask about the Veld, and if only someone would give them the answers to the questions, they might be able to do something.

Charpantier is there sometimes, and mocks me. "You're getting crazier every day Maurer," he says. "Suppose you restore the Veld? Then what? Does he make another transporter?" He shakes his head. "Poor Maurer. What're you doing to these people you bring here? What do you want from them? Something the Veld himself couldn't accomplish?"

I try. I try to tell them how to question, and I command them to question. And I hope the Veld dies. But though Charpantier and I—even Charpantier and I—are growing a little older, the Veld is only moribund, and no more dead than he was before the days when thirty generations of men battled to keep the southernmost edge of the creeping ice from burying the Veld beyond the reach of hope.

For I hope—though I can see a sprig of silver, here and there, in Charpantier's darkness now. The Veld must be accessible to my hope, though I must command millions of men.

And I think Charpantier hopes, too, because so long as he can see me failing he knows I am imperfect, but he wishes perfection for me. I know he brings no doctors only because he has not yet found a way for a man to respond to the command, "Be perfect!"

Each time the hope dies, I tell my men: "Go home, now. Rest." And they go home. But I? I blunder about, thinking that perhaps if I could kill the Veld, that would be an end to it. But nothing can kill the Veld, unless it be something the Veld knows of. So first we must heal the Veld. And healed he will once again seek his heart's desire, hopelessly. As do I. As do I.

THE END

One Leg Is Enough

By KRIS NEVILLE

The planets wanted men, and Al Lyons wanted those planets. But how could he be of any use up there as only half a man?

A FIRE-FLASH from Richardson Field illuminated his room. After a moment he heard the hissing roar of the rocket as it hurtled skyward.

That was the fifth one this month.

He lay between the crisp, cool sheets and stared out through the window. They're probably shooting for Venus again, he thought.

He felt his self-imposed isolation acutely. At night it was the worst; that was why he had demanded that they take the television set out of his room: for fear that, in a moment of midnight weakness, he would turn it on to try to find out what was happening. During the day, it was easier; whenever Doctor or Nurse tried to volunteer information, he could cut them short with a half-animal snarl. But at night, when he was alone...

One of the most important things in the world was that he go on *not* caring; that gave him a solid rock to cling to. He repeated over and over to himself, "I don't care what they're doing."

But the fifth already this month!

No. He didn't give a damn about it; he was too proud to give a damn; he would lay here and die without giving a damn.

Every night he promised himself that he would ask Nurse to transfer him to the other wing, first thing in the morning, where he wouldn't even be able to *see* the rocket fire. But every morning he always found a reason to postpone the request for one more day. Deep inside he knew that he did not want to transfer rooms. Each fire-flash sent him wallowing in a wave of self-pity, and it was like a drug.

Nurse had said something about that the other day.

He could remember her words quite clearly, just as she had spoken them. Of late, he had discovered that his memory was very good.

"You don't want to get well, Al," she had said. "You lay here and feel sorry for yourself, and you don't want to get well. That's your trouble."

Well, he told himself, suppose I don't want to get well. If I don't want to get well, that's my own business.

He turned his face into the pillow. Not to me, he shrieked mentally.

Not to me! Such things are bound to happen when men and machinery mix; but always to the other guy. Not to me.

For six months he had lain between the white sheets of the hospital bed, studying the ceiling during the day and tossing restlessly at night, waiting with a wild mixture of emotions, bitterness, hatred, jealousy, pity, contempt, for a rocket flash to light his room and announce that another ship had headed outward.

And more and more as he lay there, he found escape from the oppression of his room in memory...

"HOW'S THE patient today?" Doctor asked.

"Still alive, I guess."

Doctor made professional motions with his hands. "Sleep well last night?"

"So-so."

"Noticed the leg lately?"

(Remembering that question, Al winced. The leg wasn't there anymore, but for the first month after they had amputated, he had been kept awake most of the time because he could feel a cramp in it.)

"No," he said sullenly.

Quit thinking about it, he told himself. Think of something pleasant...

HE CAME out of Hanger 5 and started toward the Rec hall.

"Hey, Al!"

"Yeah?"

"Old Man wants to see you."

"What's he want?"

"Didn't say."

"Well, thanks... Thanks, Jerry. Guess I better go see."

Al heard his feet clip-clop hollowly. It was nice to walk, to feel the free and easy sway as the legs moved like pistons.

"Al Lyons," he told the Space corporal at the reception desk.

"Lyons, eh?" The corporal eyed him. "Go on in."

The Old Man was a Space Service captain. He was a big, friendly man who realized that the civilian maintenance crews really *were* civilians. The men in 314 all swore by him.

"Oh? Come in, young fellow."

"I'm Al Lyons, sir. You wanted to see me?"

"Yes. Indeed I did. Glad you could come right over. Take a chair."

Al sat down.

"I believe you submitted an application last year for Space School."

"Yes, yes, sir," Al gulped.

The Old Man smiled. "Well, I got the report on it this morning."

Al Lyons could feel the sweat break out on the palms of his hands. "Yes, sir?"

The Old Man stood up and came around the desk. He extended his hand.

"Let me be the first to congratulate you."

"You mean...you mean...I made it?" There was disbelief in his voice.

The Old Man was pumping his hand. "First quintile. Leave Richardson Field Monday for Seaton."

Al Lyons tried to think of something to say. He told himself that he was a grown man, now. "Well, I'll be damned," he said.

But that was what he was trying to forget; everything connected with the Space Service. He tossed restlessly in his bed.

His mind, too, refused to be still...

WHEN HE stepped off the night train (which had made a special stop) at the railroad siding and passenger depot, the air of the desert almost took his breath away. The stars, overhead, were pinpricks of brilliance set against an inconceivably vast loneliness.

He could see, by sallow moonglow, the double spur lines stretch away across the desert to Richardson Field, New Mexico. No cars stood now on the lines. It was the weekend. The depot itself, an Army unit, was lifeless.

He had wired, according to instructions, and he had expected someone to meet him. Now, being away from home for the first time, he felt small and isolated.

For five or ten minutes he walked around the depot. After that, he sat down on the rough boards of the cargo platform to wait.

He swung his legs.

After half an hour alone with the stars and the flat, white sands, he saw the lights of a car creeping toward him along a darker ribbon that was the asphalt road. The twin headlights grew larger and larger until finally the car, a new jeep, rattled up to the depot.

The driver cut the engine.

"You the man for 314?"

"Yes. Yes, sir," Al Lyons called.

"Grab your gear, kid, and let's go."

Al Lyons picked up his two suitcases and walked over to the jeep.

"Toss 'em in back."

He did and then climbed into the car.

The driver started the engine, shifted, sent the jeep leaping backwards, spun it around in a tight circle, and headed toward the distant lights.

After a while, the driver said, "Been waiting long?"

"Not very."

"Sorry. These don't go as fast as I thought. Should have been here twenty minutes ago."

"That's okay."

There was silence again. Then:

"What's your name, kid?"

"Al Lyons."

"Al, eh? Where from?"

"Ohio."

The driver grunted.

"What's your name?" Al Lyons asked.

"Willie. Willie Cord."

Al Lyons nodded. "What do you do out here, Willie?"

"Pilot."

"Jets?"

"Space."

"Space?" Al Lyons gasped. "You mean a *space* pilot came all the way over here just to pick me up?"

WILLIE CORD studied the road ahead. "Might as well. We're blasting in another couple of hours. Didn't have anything else to do to kill time."

Al Lyons said, "Oh." He, too, studied the road. "Been in long?"

"Eight years at it almost from the first."

"Then you must have known Richardson?"

"...Yeah. Used to get drunk with him... Crazy guy... Wild..."

Al Lyons decided that wasn't any way to talk about a hero.

"Told him, Rick, quit. Quit while you're winning. You got to the Rock. Let someone else try Venus."

Willie Cord clamped his jaw.

"Nope. Said he was lucky." Willie Cord smiled grimly. "He was wrong."

"What do you think—happened?"

Willie Cord shrugged. "Cracked up landing. Any of a million things. Can't tell..."

Al Lyons kept silent for a mile. Then he asked:

"What do you think of Seaton?"

Willie Cord considered this a grind...

"You go four years. Okay. You get out. An engineer. If you're lucky, a pilot's job, like mine. Otherwise: Lug you up to Mars...or the Rock. You dig ditches, or set on your fanny, or map terrain. Or look for uranium. All comes to the same thing...

"I hauled up the first graduates last years. Eager kids, all excited. Dumped 'em on Mars. What the hell. Nothing to do. All there is is Marsport: a dome a quarter mile across: fifty men. A year at a stretch. Living like dogs. Sit around, play cards, cuss, talk about dames."

"But to be on *Mars,*" Al Lyons protested. "That must be something. Exciting, just to be there."

"Better than the Rock, maybe, but exciting, no... On the Rock you really work. Putting up the damn rocket base for the Army or the damn telescope for the astronomers. Army don't need the base and the astronomers don't need the 'scope. But you bust a gut for them, just the same... On Mars, better, in a way. Don't do nothing but set, most of the time. Exciting, hell no. To be on Mars...kid dreams...as the Congress will tell you: they cut our appropriations one more time, and *we* won't be there."

"But someday there'll be a giant dome, miles and miles across, and people can live under it almost as comfortably as they live here..."

"Not in our times, kid. No reason. Costs too much."

Al Lyons looked away from the road, up at the stars.

"You're wrong, Willie."

"No, kid. I'm right." He mused for a moment. "Take last trip. What did I bring back? Samples. That's all: five hundred pounds of rock. And not even a damn smell of pitchblende. Ain't no uranium on the whole damn planet. If there were, the Space Service couldn't squeeze out the money to mine it. We'd just keep it out there for a rainy day with a big 'hands off' sign on it. Hell, the boys have quit lookin'..."

Al Lyons shook his head vigorously. "It *can't* be like that. There's something out there. I don't know what. Maybe not adventure or excitement, but something like that. It's like the sea is to some people. You may cuss her and cuss her, but you keep going back, if only just for the sake of going."

Willie Cord smiled. "I know, kid."

AL LYONS stared at the ceiling.

A man with one leg can't get into the Space Service. *A man with one leg can't ever get into the Space Service.*

And those things rolling down his cheeks weren't tears; weren't really tears. He was twenty-one, and people twenty-one don't cry.

Maybe it wasn't the thing itself; maybe it was just wanting it so bad.

When he was eleven years old, Richardson made the first trip to the Rock. But even before that, he had dreamed about going to space. When he was a little child. First he had wanted to be an explorer; go to Africa or some distant place. Later, as soon as he could really understand, the longing had transferred from Africa to the Moon, and after that, to the planets themselves, as they came within the horizon of possibility.

He had taken a job in civilian maintenance at Richardson Field as soon as he had graduated from high school, just so he could be near the rockets. He had studied hard, after working hours, denying himself many of the pleasures of youth, and last year he had taken the Seaton tests—

He had been seventeen when Richardson tried for Venus; eighteen when Comsky first landed on Mars...

Max Comsky had been born and raised in his hometown. Once, Al Lyons had actually met him. At the time, Al had been sixteen.

MAX COMSKY was a big man; sharp, bold eyes.

"The Rock, kid? Wonderful life... Wonderful. Work, sure. But excitement, too."

Al Lyons listened open-mouthed.

"Never know what's gonna happen. Last month, ship before mine, Old Nancy they called her, busted her shielding halfway in. Crew landed her, believe it or not. Half dead, all six of them, but they set her down; pretty a job as you ever hope to see, too. Every man on board radioactive, but they got her down... Silly... Anything happen to me like that, and I'd turn the ship sunward and let her rip, hell for breakfast..."

(Max Comsky's last ship never returned, Al Lyons remembered: Lost out of Mars.)

Max was the type who loved to tell his stories of adventure in a big, booming voice, a voice you could hear all over the room. He took an animal delight in it. But, Al Lyons suspected, he was not averse to lowering his voice, on moonlight nights, in female company, to speak softly of the stars and of the strange longing...

"There was once," Max had told him, "when I went into the jet room. Operator was space sick. Out like a light. Mass needle almost to the red. Couple more minutes and we'd have gone with a bang. I slammed in the dampening rods. That threw off the pilot, who had been counting on more power. Lost our cut back drive and we slipped way inside Earth, on our way to Venus sure as God made little green apples. I had to run the room for an hour and a half. Rough! Pilot would yell through the intercom, 'Give me nine point lateral,' and I'd yell back, 'How?' and then he'd have to explain it all to me. Didn't know anything about the damn jets room...

"That's why they're starting Seaton: so they can get somebody on those rockets who can blast with a little better than their luck and a prayer."

He had told wonderful and exciting tales, for a boy of sixteen to listen to.

"On the Rock. Out looking. Curious... No air. You feel like you can jump a thousand feet, and the stars look like little, steady-burning electric bulbs... It was quiet, and kinda lonely. I was on the rim of Crater 9 about a mile from the dome. All at once, I had a hell of a time breathing. Suit was leaking... I switched on the emergency tank of air, and I started to run, and I mean *really* run. Every time I'd jump, I'd *float* down, and that seemed to take an eternity... Scared? Boy! I thought sure if I ever got out of that one I'd had enough..."

AL LYONS thought about running across the surface of the Moon. Just to think of it hurt so badly that he wanted to be sick at his stomach.

"God damn," he said. Saying that didn't help very much...

Morning began to break. He wondered if he could get some sleep. His mind began to fuzz up with fatigue...

The way it had happened. That was so unfair.

His last day of work, just before the weekend. Monday he would have gone to Seaton...

"HEY, AL, hand me that lug wrench, willya?"
Al Lyons reached out for it.

"My God! Look out!"

He tried to twist out of the way. Then he could feel the weight crash down on his leg. He could hear the excited babble of voices...

"GOD DAMN, God damn," he said to himself. "I've got to get some sleep."

Sunrise.

He slept.

At eight, Nurse came.

At ten, Doctor came.

At ten twenty-five—

"Al, there's a visitor to see you."

"Don't want to see him."

"He's coming in, Al."

Al Lyons turned over in the bed. He faced the wall. After a while he heard the voice.

"Hi, kid."

"Go 'way," he choked.

"Nope."

He heard Willie Cord draw up the chair. It squeaked under his weight.

"How's it going, kid?"

No answer.

"Just got in from Mars. Somebody told me about a kid over here. Said name of Al Lyons. I remembered: kid I lugged out here in a jeep. Come over to see if I could do something."

"Please let me alone."

"Said the kid wouldn't get well, down at the desk. Because he didn't *want* to get well."

"So what?"

"Damn childish."

"I don't care."

Willie Cord hesitated a moment.

"Thought you might like to hear something."

"No."

"Fine," Willie Cord grunted. "You're going to hear it sooner or later. Might as well hear it now. I pulled some wires for you, kid."

For a moment, Al Lyons felt his heart pound—but then, sick realization came to him. No amount of wire pulling could get a man with an artificial leg in Space Service.

"Remember I told you how there wasn't nothing on Mars? No reason to go there?

"Well, I was wrong."

Willie Cord stopped to let that soak in.

"Remember I told you about hauling back some rock?"

Al Lyons was holding his breath now.

"Well, damn stuff was gold ore... Rush is on..."

"Friend of mine formed a company. Bert Drexal. You may have heard of him."

Al Lyons had. If Bert Drexal was in on it, it was big time.

"Mars Mines, Inc. They're putting up a big dome. Plenty big. And it'll get bigger. Civilian stuff, kid. And in a year, maybe two— three years at the most—they'll be needin' clerks, hydroponics men, all sorts of men: civilians. One-legged ones, even, if they're willin' to work. Bert said you'd get a job, sure as hell, if you can qualify and if you're outta that bed. First opening they can use you."

Al Lyons was afraid to turn over; afraid Willie would see how bright his eyes were glistening.

"Gosh—" he said.

"Sound okay to you, kid?"

"Yes...yes," he answered. "I think I'd like something like that."

THE END

She Who Laughs

By PETER PHILLIPS

It's really a very simple story—if you refuse to believe in ghosts and know that time is circular!

I'D been waiting two hundred years for this guy. He stood there in the graveled driveway with the estate agent, looking over the frontage of the mansion.

The sun was hot. The agent took off his hat, mopped his balding head. I wondered whether I could spit that far from the upstairs window where I was watching them. I decided I probably could, but I wouldn't.

The agent said, in a thick brogue I can't reproduce in its glottal richness: "If it's se-clusion you're wantin', Mr. Mullen, you'd not better this foine upstandin' place this soide of Ballygore. There's room to stretch your legs and fill your lungs with air that shweeps down from the mountains, over covert and shweet pasture for your own special delectation and delight."

My lips were moving with his. I'd heard it before. I knew the sucker would take the place. And I knew the agent, back in Thaughbeen, having dropped most of his beautiful stage brogue, would soon be saying: "He's paying in dollars, too, boys. And then, in the season, I'll sell them to the English tourists. This is an occasion to celebrate. Porter all round, on me."

Mullen, casual as all hell, standing there with the agent, pretended to be considering.

I whisked down the baluster rail, stood just behind the door as they came in.

"Nice hall," Mullen said unenthusiastically. He was wearing a drape suit. He didn't need drapes to bulk him out. Those shoulders had spearheaded the forward line three seasons at college, if my information was correct.

Indignant, the agent said: "Nice? It's talking like an Englishman you are, instead of a citizen o' the greatest country in the world." ("Bar Ireland," he added under his breath.) "Lookit the size of ut—the staircase, the paneling, the great wide windows and that landin' there where the mighty O'Rourke stood and with the Sword of Kings defied the brayin' cowards o' Cromwell till he was struck a traitor blow from behind, and, like a great girthed tree smitten in its prime, fell among the cur-dogs and carried a full half-dozen of them to death with him. Here at this very spot!"

The agent flung out a dramatic hand. I'd crept up behind them during the spiel. I never tire of hearing it.

Mullen stepped back. I dodged.

"Fool place to make a stand anyway," he muttered, looking at the balcony between the two staircases.

"Arragh! The O'Rourke could foight as well with the two hands as the one. A sword in each, there he stood, facin' them both ways—"

"Sure, sure. Now how many bedrooms did you say?"

I followed them around. Mullen wasn't interested in bedrooms, only in the cellar. But I was waiting for the final spiel, dictated by what the agent retained of a conscience.

"There's jist one small matter," he said, standing in the hall again after they'd looked the place over. "You may have been hearin' lies about this place in Thaughbeen, maybe from those loafers around Golighan's bar, and though I wouldn't be askin' yez to disregard ut entoirely—"

"The haunt, you mean?" said Mullen. I grinned to myself. "I heard about it during the war when I was stationed just across the border. That's when I became interested in the place. I looked it over, saw the power plant. There's quite a head of water in that stream. The memory of that stayed in the back of my mind until the other day, when I was in London with my wife, seeing some friends. Then I remembered this place. I have some work to do. I want electrical power and privacy. So I hopped the jet liner to Dublin and came up here—"

"And you'll take it, sorr? Ghost an' all?"

If Mullen paid extra for a ghost, I thought, he'd be thoroughly had. But he said firmly:

"I'm not buying your ghost. In another minute you'll be saying it's an asset to the place. It's a hundred years since my folk left this country, but we haven't gone soft. What's your price for this tumbledown she-been?"

"The final price," said the agent, taking a deep, careful breath, "for a year's tenancy, in advance, in dollars, is—how much did you offer?"

"I didn't. But you can tell your client I'll pay a thousand."

"Don't be shamin' me," said the agent, as I blew a cool breath down his neck. "It's meself that owns the place as you well know, if you know as much as you do."

He drew up his coat collar. "Now let's be discussin' the details elsewhere."

I FOLLOWED them down the drive, into the shay. I could get away from the place now for a while.

It was late afternoon. The green border hills in the distance were drawing up mist from the shadowed bog as their green darkened in the slanting sun; and the new-cut hay in the nearer fields brought relished delight.

Two hundred years I'd waited for this jaunt. I enjoyed every second of it, even the acrid stink from Pethal's ill-cared-for hogs as we passed the holding. The hoppity-clop of the pony's hoofs on the dust-blown road was music.

Over the green-lichened bridge by the trout stream trotted the pony. I promised myself to do some fishing there soon. I'd use a quiet worm and snooze in the sun. Fly-fishing was too strenuous in this moist heat.

And I'd look over my shoulder now and again at the long pile of Thaughbeen House and laugh. The laugh would be on me. That always makes it funnier, in Ireland.

Down from the bridge, and the road broadened into the village of Thaughbeen.

The agent introduced Mullen to Golighan. "Stationed in the Six Counties durin' the war," he said, "and mindful of the beauties of the country, and wishin' to do a little book-work or such, decided to take over the place for a year or maybe more. And you'll be wastin' your time, Michael, me boy, tellin' him about the haunt to take the bread out of me very mouth, for Mister Mullen knows all about it."

"Sit down and rest the onaisy tongue of yez," said Golighan, trying to outdo the agent's brogue. "Y'don't think he'd be taken in onyway by yer gabblin', wid a name loike Mullen. What'll you drink?"

Mullen ordered Jamieson's Irish whisky. The agent took thick Dublin stout.

I watched Mullen roll the smoky-peat flavor around his tongue. Two hundred years since I'd had the sweet, rare tang of it tickling my gullet...

I licked invisible lips in anticipation.

They stayed through the evening, with the real talk beginning when the lads drifted in.

There was Sean Healey, Tom O'Reilly—both, if I remembered right, working a pittance on Lord Freightowel's estate. Seamas Mulvaney, smallholder—how many times had I seen him, as a barefoot gossoon, nicking plums from the kitchen garden at Thaughbeen House, looking often at the silent, window-eyed place with his own green, feary eyes, and me at an upstairs window holding in my breath not to give one of the ghostly groans I'd practiced so long and send him in a tear-breeches scramble down the tree.

Then there was gutsy Bran Bailey who'd actually come inside one night, stood in the hall and with all his big little heart bawled: "The hell an' back wid banshees! I don't believe in 'em!"

I'd been so pleased with his common sense that I forgot myself and called out the truth: "Good for you, kid. I'm no banshee. I'm no kind of goddam ghost. There's no such things."

But poor Bran was running so fast, I doubted he'd heard me.

Anyway, here he was in Golighan's, grown big and broad, and putting in his two cents' worth about the goings-on at Thaughbeen House.

"It was during the war," Bran said, "and, being so near the border, we had a jeepful of your fellers running in here every night to stoke up on Mister Golighan's brew. And one night we tell them about the House, and about how poor daft Johnnie Maur goes up there now and again to play chess with the ghost, as he said. Poor Johnnie, gone eleven months now—"

Johnnie was dead? I'd missed him.

Every time I heard that Johnnie was dead, it shocked me.

He'd stumble into the House, liquored up to the fringe of his red hair, white face vacant and mild, shouting in the empty echoing hall:

"It's a game of chess I'm offerin' yez, for, banshees or not, ye're the only dacent player this soide of Dublin who can tax me wandhering wits!"

I hope Johnnie's found another "decent player," wherever he's gone.

Bran Bailey was talking on in Golighan's bar, with Mullen leaning forward and taking it all in.

"So one night," says Bran, "the whole near-dozen of 'em starts off up there, with this great roarin' sergeant straddlin' the front and shoutin': 'Look out, ghost, here we come, eight little Yankee boys full of rum!'

"And the jeep goin' so slow with them aboard," says Bran, "and the rain makin' a bog of the road, we follow after these fellers to see what the Thaughbeen House ghost does with 'em.

"And they get halfway up the drive to the house, and the jeep stops, and there's the driver thumpin' and pullin' everything and callin' on all the saints, until the sergeant unstraddles himself and pulls up the front coverin'.

"Then he jist stands there, rain sweatin' off his great red face and him suddenly as sober as a hangin' judge on a Monday, and he says: 'Put it back! Put it back quick before I believe my eyes, and I swear I'll never touch another drop again!' And we come up and look over his shoulder.

"And there's nothing there under the hood. Nothing at all, at all."

I hadn't meant to swipe the whole motor at first. The teleport exhausted me for days. But I got annoyed when I'd yanked off three plug-leads and that damned jeep kept banging away on one cylinder.

"And never a sight of the motor since," concluded Bran Bailey.

Said Mullen: "Yes. I heard of it. I was captain of their unit. We had to have the jeep towed away."

"So you're not troublin' yourself about the creature at all?" asked Sean Healey.

"Why should I? It's never harmed anybody, far as I can see."

Thanks for them kind words, pal.

Mullen decided to stay at Golighan's until a few essentials had been carried up to the House. Meantime, he wired his wife to join him.

FOUR days later, he took up residence. He came early. But early. The energy of that man! I was still resting when I heard, him poking around in the cellars, tracing through the wiring from the turbo-house.

I slipped down from where I go when I take a rest—don't ask me where that is; it's a state, not a place—and gummed down after him. He was lifting a tarpaulin in a corner of one of the smaller cellars; it used to be a cold-larder.

He looked at the jeep motor and made funny disbelieving noises.

"So," I said, "it wasn't the potheen. I figure you owe the sergeant and the other Company D boys one big-handed apology—plus the dough you docked 'em to pay for it."

He came around so fast, he tripped and planted the tight part of his pants on one of the hobbly bits of the jeep motor.

"What—where are you?"

"Not in heaven or in hell, but just as elusive as the Pimpernel. As to what I am, you're going to tell me, I hope. That's what I've been waiting for—a long, long time. Meanwhile, Mr. Mullen," I said, "you're soiling those nicely creased pants of yours."

He upped off the engine, dusted his pants automatically. Something the Army did for him, gave him a pride in his clothes.

"Do you mind," he said, his brain beginning to work, "showing yourself? I hate like hell accepting sartorial advice from a voice without a body."

"That takes energy," I said, "like compressing these air molecules to make sound waves. But it takes a lot of energy and a lot of material and right now I don't feel like dressing up to give you something to look at or talk at. However, I don't mind giving you a slight idea. Scrape some dust off those shelves, toss it up under that bulb, and stand back."

"I am nuts," he enunciated carefully.

"Sure. But do it. And mind your coat cuffs."

As the cloud of tiny particles drifted down, I slipped in and charged them so they hung around the vortices of my antiparticles.

"Almighty catfish!" Mullen gulped. "A naked ghost!"

"I'm no ghost, and I don't have to be this shape, either," I said, adjusting the network. "Is this any better? Dogs are always naked."

He backed off, slapping at the air. "For God's sake, be human if you can't be natural! I mean—"

"Listen," I said, peeved, "that was a prize mastiff I once saw. I can always do a mountain lion or a grizzly. Get me a roll of cheesecloth, or even a bedsheet at a pinch, and I'll really show you something."

"I've seen enough," he said, digging knuckles in his eyes and shaking his head as if something was loose inside. "Go away."

"Maybe you're right. I've got more important things to do with my energy than fool around to amuse you."

"*Amuse* me?" He made a noise like an emptying bathtub. "I'd laugh easier in a morgue. Get back where you came from and make the worms laugh."

"I'm not," I repeated patiently, "a ghost, a ghoulie, a banshee, or anything of the whatsoever kind. I've never met up with one and I don't expect to. Like young Bran Bailey, I don't believe in 'em. Neither do you, fortunately. But explanations can wait. Has any of the stuff turned up yet?"

That got him. "What stuff?"

"Couple of tubes from Marshall's of London, specification alloy plates from Birmingham, that dingus you borrowed from the Sorbonne."

"Your intelligence service must be good."

"You'd be surprised."

"Then you tell me where it is."

"I was just making conversation," I said. "It's on the way to Thaughbeen station now. Johnny McGuire will be carting it over around lunchtime. And your wife, who is wondering what in hell you're up to anyway, has reluctantly left her bright friends in London and is on her way to ask why you took over this moth-eaten old shack without consulting her first, especially since it's her money you're fooling around with."

Mullen's lower jaw was nearly resting on his collar by this time.

"Incidentally," I asked, "how is the darling girl? Has she enjoyed the European tour so far?"

"Leave her out of this," he managed to say. But his tone was defensive.

"Poor Mullen," I sighed. "She's still keeping the reins on you, huh? I pity you, feller. I know just how it is. I'm under the Iron High Heel myself. You'll have to meet my wife sometime."

"This is too much! Two of you? Too damned much! A double haunt!" Mullen frowned. Then he began to laugh at his own sudden thoughts. "How do you make out, mister?"

I considered explaining to him, but decided he'd never understand. "Wife" was the simplest way I could describe "her"— the only way in earthly language.

"Your mind needs deodorizing," was all I said.

"So does this whole situation. Hey, if these forecasts of yours turn out right, how about giving me the winners at Ballymuchray this afternoon?"

Mullen was recovering pretty quickly, it seemed.

I said: "I don't play the horses. If you've finished down here, you might as well get up to the kitchen and make yourself some coffee. No need to check that wiring any more. I've already done it. You've got a lazy morning ahead."

"The morning," he said, "hasn't yet started. I'm not awake yet."

"So now I'm part of a dream, am I? Get upstairs before I bat you with a clod of hard air."

He muttered his way up to the kitchen, plunked an open pot on the stove, which he'd already lighted. Blue smoke puffed intermittently between the bars, filling the place with pungent haze.

Mullen looked up at the ceiling, addressed it politely: "I suppose, Mr. Fixit, you can tell me what's wrong with this thing?"

"Naturally. Get hold of the poker and belt that flue pipe about halfway up. The plate's jammed and doesn't operate from the outside. Shank broke off way back."

He belted. The fire roared up suddenly.

"Thanks," be said. "Could I interest you in a cup of coffee?"

"Very funny," I grunted sourly.

WHILE he sipped his brew, I slipped out to tell my "wife" how things were shaping up. My wife was born to lay the eggs and—crow as well. I'd suffered two hundred years of hell from her tongue. Blamed me for everything. She even beefed about my innocent games of chess with Johnnie Maur.

And I remember when the Marchmont family was in occupation of Thaughbeen House, she'd scare half the life out of little Lilian Marchmont just because I happened to remark casually on her good looks. That gives you a picture of my wife—a possessive shrew, to keep it in human terms, which really don't apply very well.

She started in on me now, so I grabbed up the chessboard and pieces from the attic and skipped down from the Tenth Plane, where she was lying up and waiting for me to do most of the work.

When I got back to the kitchen, Mullen was tapping at the walls and ceiling with a broomstick.

"No secret panels or hidden amplifiers," I said. "It's all genuine physical phenomena."

He looked round and breathed heavily. "Now I've seen everything."

I dumped the chessboard and pieces on the kitchen table.

"No," he said. "No! I'm not going to confirm myself in my own madness. Take 'em away."

I started setting out the pieces.

He watched with a kind of horrible deadpan fascination. In a faraway voice he said: "Queen on her own color."

"That's better," I told him. "Pull up a chair."

He went to the kitchen window, looked at the soft sunlight glancing through the apple trees. He looked for quite a while. Then he shrugged, grabbed a chair and came back to the table.

"Anywhere but Ireland," he observed, "I'd have run halfway to Thaughbeen by now."

Twice during the game, which stretched out over three hours, he tried to make talk, but I dodged the questions. Once he made a grab in the air over my QKt as I was making a move.

"Can you," I asked politely, "feel a magnetic field? Or an air current, if your hand is moving with it? Or put a half nelson on a frame of reference? Or poke a De Sitter anti-particle in the eye?"

He gave up.

Finally, as we heard the clattering roar of McGuire's cartage van down the road, he said: "This is the damnedest game, in more than one sense. Check. Hold it until I'm back in this room."

I heard them dumping the stuff into the hall; and a female voice ordering the carter around; and the bland, blarneying voice of McGuire somehow soaring above the authoritative female voice and quelling it.

When Mullen came back into the kitchen, he looked determined. He closed the door carefully behind him.

"McGuire," he said, "is a breath of fresh air. Sanity returns. I've just realized what I've been doing all morning. I have a hell of a lot of work on hand and I can't get on with it until this is straightened out. And I'm not going to have my wife scared. Now just what are you, and what's your racket?"

"Patience, pal," I said. "Finish the game, then I'll talk. I fixed you some fresh coffee." Voices were raised again in the hall. "Incidentally, I don't think your wife scares easy. She's busy for a while anyway. Your move."

He gulped coffee, watched me interpose on his check and threaten his own king simultaneously. He was compelled to exchange pieces, which made it a draw.

"You've been playing for that," he accused.

I sighed. "Not deliberately. If we played a dozen, games, they'd end up on a draw. Or a stalemate. One or the other."

"I don't get it. Quit the crosstalk. What are you?"

HE sat more easily in his chair. He frowned at the coffee. I hoped I hadn't laced it too much. He'd get the idea soon enough anyway.

"You've got a couple of books in your bag," I said. "One is a pretty detailed family history of this place, written and published at his own expense—because no one else would be interested—by Mister Patrick O'Rourke, Gentleman, at the turn of the century.

"There are only passing deprecatory references to me in that. He never took kindly to the idea of a family banshee, or banshees. The other was written twenty years ago by an earnest and sober investigator from the English Psychical Research Society. It's my biography. My wife, being what you'd call plumb lazy, never made an appearance for him. I've often regretted that the Society never got around to following up his report. I'd have shown 'em plenty."

"Then you *are* a haunt," Mullen said. "A plain, ornery haunt! But how do you tick? How do you move things around?"

"A disembodied psyche—" I began.

That got him. He snapped up straight and mouthed for breath. Coffee slopped over the table. It didn't matter. He'd drunk enough for my purpose.

"A disembodied psyche," I repeated firmly, "which is a focus of consciousness freed from hindering matter, and thus from the bonds of inertia and entropy, not to mention sex, can be a pretty powerful thing. It doesn't upset any energy balance because it utilizes extant potentials."

His eyes were growing rounder. He tried to get up, then slumped back.

"You soon master the mechanics of perception for yourself," I said. "It's largely a matter of that curious mental force called imagination. And you learn how to induce illusion in others. But it takes about ten years before you find a way to store enough free energy from cosmic sources in your own field-web of antiparticles to move solid objects around."

He had trouble with his voice. "Ten years? Ten year from *when?*"

"From pretty damn soon," I said sweetly.

"Then you're—you're—" He gulped. His eyes were glazing.

"That's right," I said. "Sleep tight, brother."

I was testing the last circuit when he came around. He opened his eyes and moaned a little.

"Don't worry about the slight hangover," I said. "I'll be taking it over in a moment."

He looked around at the setup. Only his head could move. The rest of him was tied pretty firmly in the stasis area.

"Pretty neat, huh?" I said. "It would have taken you months. Years, maybe. It probably did—once. That's something I've never figured out. It took me four hours flat, even with the know-how. I had two hundred years to work it out."

Mullen muttered: "It's a dream."

"Check. That's how the thing started, if it ever did start. With Dunne's theories of precognition and post-cognition in dreams—a freed psyche moving backward and forward in time. Or, as in this case, staying put and letting time flow by. No mass, so no trouble with entropy or inertia. All the paradoxes of time travel smoothed out."

He'd gone bug-eyed again. I could almost see his brain wriggling.

"What happens when I—when you—when this body dies?"

"You answered that question when you devised the math," I said. "Does the past die? No. It's co-existent. Effective immortality."

"But death—"

"Is pretty final," I agreed. "Dust to dust, et cetera. And since we don't believe in an afterlife, that makes it a tough problem. But you've got a couple of centuries to figure that one out, too!"

"You mean you have figured it?"

"I didn't. You didn't. We didn't. We never will because we never have."

"How many times has this happened?"

"Once," I said patiently. "This is the first time. It always is."

"But with memory of this conversation, I can change the pattern! I can—"

Then he got the idea. His mouth dropped open. Slack-jawed dope...

"That's it," I said. I felt sorry for him, as usual. "You've already tried everything. You can't even leave the place until this turns up." I prodded his stomach. "It's the only body our psychic matrix will fit into, and there's a psychic compulsion to stay right here until it arrives. You can't lick time. You never could."

I STOOD by the switch. The tubes began to heat up.

"No!" he yelled. "Hold it! About my wife—"

"Our wife," I corrected him, looking around cautiously. This time I might get away with it. Maybe the pattern wouldn't always be the same. It was worth trying anyway. "You'll find her on the Tenth Plane when you figure out how to get there."

I gave him the wave-off sign.

"I've got a date with a bottle of Jamieson's Irish whisky and a fishing rod. By the way, when you meet up with old Johnnie Maur again, give him my love. He won't understand. He never does. Look out for his rook game in the endplay. So long, sucker," I said. "Good haunting."

I WAS reaching for the switch, when—

"Hold it or I'll blast you!"

I sighed resignedly and looked at the cellar steps. A body slumped inelegantly into view, dangling like a puppet from invisible strings.

The voice came from above its head.

How I hate that voice!

"Dear, sweet Bernie," cooed my wife dangerously. "Trying it again? Don't you ever learn? If you touch that switch before my say-so, I'll fry that body of yours as soon as spit in your eye."

Mullen choked: "That's Betty!"

"Uh-huh," I murmured. "And that's Betty's body. She wants it back. I always try to leave her behind, but I guess I never succeed. I'd like to try living with a wife I haven't lived with for two hundred years. But she's spent months soaking up energy on the Tenth Plane, and if I don't play ball, she'll burn my body before I get it."

"How right, darling," said Betty. Arsenic and molasses in that voice. "Now tie this down in the stasis field."

I looked at the limp, blonde head and laughed. "I suppose you whanged her with the skillet again?"

"That's my headache," the voice snapped.

"Right! That's why I'm laughing, sweetheart."

I laid Betty's unconscious head near Mullen's—that is, near my shoulder. She stirred a little and moaned. I passed ropes over her and through the ringbolt of the time lock and stood back admiring the scene.

"Don't we look sweet?" I said.

"Beautiful," said Betty. "Now pull that switch."

I went to the handle.

"No—" pleaded Mullen.

"Yes," ordered Betty.

I pulled.

For a milli-second, a soft, impossible wind soughed through intergalactic nothingness. A condition of no-life. Binary stars flamed into view. Incorporate with a star, become corporeal, or cease. An incredible longing, fulfilled at its conception. Homing to this star—No! Get out! Occupied! Incorporate or cease!

THE time lock snapped open, and ropes loosened round my body.

Body.

Beautiful word.

Even with a headache like this.

Headache!

I gave a little scream and sat up.

Mullen—I mean me—I mean Betty—stood there grinning like an ape.

"Beat you to it, heel," she—he said.

I'd been wrong about the psychic matrix.

That damned woman had always wanted to wear the trousers. Now she was wearing them, the ones that should have been mine.

A little thing like the sex of the body I inhabit shouldn't really matter, of course. Sex doesn't actually apply to me, as such. But...

Anybody know where I can get some nylons?

THE END

If you've enjoyed this book, you will not want to miss these terrific titles...

ARMCHAIR SCI-FI & HORROR DOUBLE NOVELS, $12.95 each

D-51   **A GOD NAMED SMITH** by Henry Slesar
         WORLDS OF THE IMPERIUM by Keith Laumer

D-52   **CRAIG'S BOOK** by Don Wilcox
         EDGE OF THE KNIFE by H. Beam Piper

D-53   **THE SHINING CITY** by Rena M. Vale
         THE RED PLANET by Russ Winterbotham

D-54   **THE MAN WHO LIVED TWICE** by Rog Phillips
         VALLEY OF THE CROEN by Lee Tarbell

D-55   **OPERATION DISASTER** by Milton Lesser
         LAND OF THE DAMNED by Berkeley Livingston

D-56   **CAPTIVE OF THE CENTAURIANESS** by Poul Anderson
         A PRINCESS OF MARS by Edgar Rice Burroughs

D-57   **THE NON-STATISTICAL MAN** by Raymond F. Jones
         MISSION FROM MARS by Rick Conroy

D-58   **INTRUDERS FROM THE STARS** by Ross Rocklynne
         FLIGHT OF THE STARLING by Chester S. Geier

D-59   **COSMIC SABOTEUR** by Frank M. Robinson
         LOOK TO THE STARS by Willard Hawkins

D-60   **THE MOON IS HELL!** by John W. Campbell, Jr.
         THE GREEN WORLD by Hal Clement

ARMCHAIR SCIENCE FICTION CLASSICS, $12.95 each

C-16   **THE SHAVER MYSTERY, Book Three**
         by Richard S. Shaver

C-17   **GIRLS FROM PLANET 5**
         by Richard Wilson

C-18   **THE FOURTH "R"**
         by George O. Smith

ARMCHAIR SCIENCE FICTION & HORROR GEMS SERIES, $12.95 each

G-5   **SCIENCE FICTION GEMS, Vol. Three**
         C. M. Kornbluth and others

G-6   **HORROR GEMS, Vol. Three**
         August Derleth and others

If you've enjoyed this book, you will not want to miss these terrific titles…

ARMCHAIR SCI-FI & HORROR DOUBLE NOVELS, $12.95 each

D-11 **PERIL OF THE STARMEN** by Kris Neville
THE STRANGE INVASION by Murray Leinster

D-12 **THE STAR LORD** by Boyd Ellanby
CAPTIVES OF THE FLAME by Samuel R. Delaney

D-13 **MEN OF THE MORNING STAR** by Edmund Hamilton
PLANET FOR PLUNDER by Hal Clement and Sam Merwin, Jr.

D-14 **ICE CITY OF THE GORGON** by Chester S. Geier and Richard Shaver
WHEN THE WORLD TOTTERED by Lester Del Rey

D-15 **WORLDS WITHOUT END** by Clifford D. Simak
THE LAVENDER VINE OF DEATH by Don Wilcox

D-16 **SHADOW ON THE MOON** by Joe Gibson
ARMAGEDDON EARTH by Geoff St. Reynard

D-17 **THE GIRL WHO LOVED DEATH** by Paul W. Fairman
SLAVE PLANET by Laurence M. Janifer

D-18 **SECOND CHANCE** by J. F. Bone
MISSION TO A DISTANT STAR by Frank Belknap Long

D-19 **THE SYNDIC** by C. M. Kornbluth
FLIGHT TO FOREVER by Poul Anderson

D-20 **SOMEWHERE I'LL FIND YOU** by Milton Lesser
THE TIME ARMADA by Fox B. Holden

ARMCHAIR SCIENCE FICTION CLASSICS, $12.95 each

C-4 **CORPUS EARTHLING**
by Louis Charbonneau

C-5 **THE TIME DISSOLVER**
by Jerry Sohl

C-6 **WEST OF THE SUN**
by Edgar Pangborn

ARMCHAIR SCIENCE FICTION & HORROR GEMS SERIES, $12.95 each

G-1 **SCIENCE FICTION GEMS, Vol. One**
Isaac Asimov and others

G-2 **HORROR GEMS, Vol. One**
Carl Jacobi and others